I0552429

The Guardians of Eden

Book Three

"A lion chased me up a tree, and I greatly enjoyed the view from the top." - Confucius

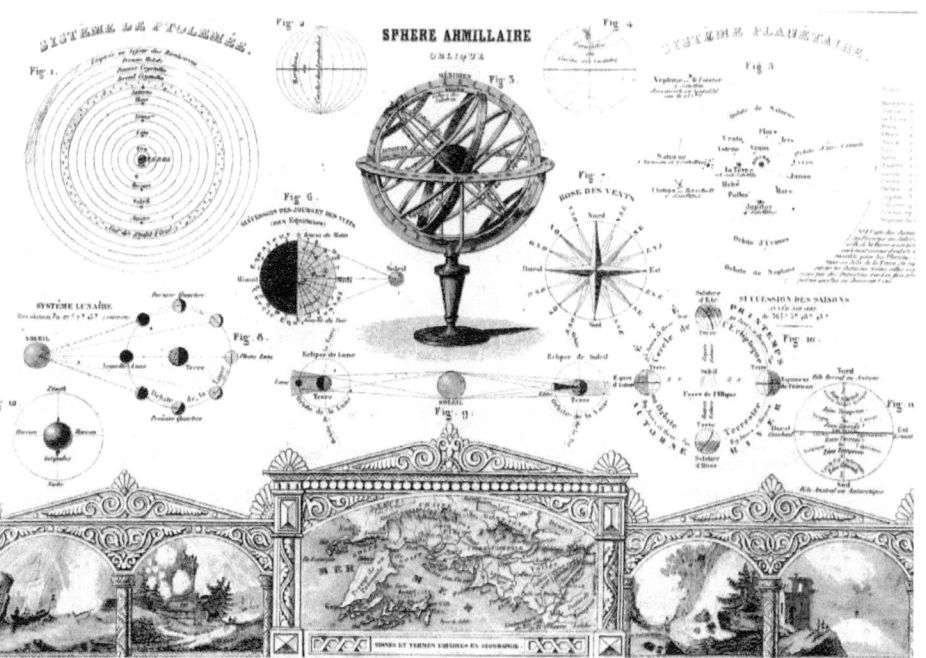

CHAPTER 1

Altair returned to his usual spot at the edge of the shoreline as specks of gold rippled across the water. His watchful eyes, drained of hope with each passing day, remained focused on the waves as he hunted for any glimmer of Deneb. Familiar footsteps approached from behind as he answered the question before it was spoken, "Nothing yet."

Stan put a comforting arm around his shoulder as he joined him for what had become their daily routine. Before he could say his usual words of inspiration, Altair interrupted.

"You know, I had the oddest dream last night. I was here in this very place, but it was a different time period. Waves battered the shoreline as I followed a man who I believe was King Arthur, over a bridge and through a fog covered forest. We reached a lake, and there I watched him lean in towards the water, as if he had seen something or someone there. For being such a powerful knight, he sure didn't keep the best balance," Altair laughed. "He fell into the water, and when he emerged, a woman wearing an elegant white lace gown was by his side."

"You don't say?" Stan smiled for the first time in weeks.

"It was the oddest dream, and the weirdest part of all, was that the woman who came from the water looked just like Deneb."

"Well, Altair, while you were 'away' some very interesting things transpired. Vega and Deneb found a way to travel back to the time of King Arthur, and when they returned, Deneb was wearing a dress very similar to what you just described. She mentioned something about disappearing into the water, and when King Arthur and his sword fell into the lake, she somehow became whole again."

A flicker of hope emerged in his eyes as he turned his head. "Do you think that the sword can somehow bring her back?"

"It's worth a try." Stan's sympathetic eyes suddenly looked a tad more hopeful.

"We try tonight. I don't want anyone to see what we're doing."

"Tonight then."

The full moon peeked through the quickly passing clouds as Altair darted down the rocky path leading to the shoreline, hoping that tonight's memory would replace the one that kept replaying in his mind. The air felt electric, as if a storm were coming. Stan cautiously hurried down the path behind him and called out, "Don't wait for me! There's a nasty storm headed this way!"

Altair looked up, wondering what stars the clouds had concealed as he made his way out into the darkness of the sea. As the water reached his waist, he pulled the sword from his long black coat and watched as the moonlight danced upon the crystal, pulling his thoughts towards the memories of its keeper. A drop of rain splashed onto the blade, shifting his attention to the ominous clouds moving in.

Stan squinted as sheets of rain overtook his vision, and thunder shook the pebbly beach. His eyes quickly scanned the water, only to see the shadowy outline of Altair and his mighty sword disappear into the depths. Several minutes passed as he anxiously paced the water's edge wondering if this idea of his was another mistake. Just as Stan stepped out into the water to call Altair's name, he emerged, trudging through the waves with his woolen coat floating out behind him like a cape. He gripped the sword tightly in his hands as if he were about to battle another beast, while catching his breath. Stan yelled through the rain, "What happened down there! Did you see her?"

Water spilled down his determined yet invigorated face as he replied, "I heard her! She's alive!"

"Oh thank God! Well -- where is she?" Stan frantically searched the water.

"I said I heard her, I didn't see her. She said she was trapped in a maze of some kind! I tried to ask her where, but I was running out of air. All she said was to follow the crown, and I'd find her there."

"Come on! Let's get out of this storm!" Stan's voice battled the unrelenting rain. "I need to show you something!"

CHAPTER 2

Three sharp knocks came at the door as Altair quickly attempted to dry off. He twisted the handle with one hand, and continued wringing out his clothing with the other.

"Sorry to interrupt," Stan said as he pushed his way into the room. "After you said the word 'crown' I remembered a book of mine," he said as he fumbled through the worn pages, stopping on the page titled, "The Crown of the Sky, Corona Borealis."

"What is that? A constellation?"

"Yes, a constellation that belongs to the Ursa Major family!" he said expecting Altair to know what that meant.

"Right. You don't know what that means. The Ursa Major family includes the constellations Draco, Coma Berenices, Lynx, and Bootes -- to name a few!"

"So a family of villains?"

"You could put it that way. The thing that has me worried is the wording that Deneb used. You said she was trapped somewhere, right?"

"She said she was in some sort of maze, but she didn't know where she was or how to get out."

Stan flipped to the next page, "The constellation Corona Borealis derives its name from the Latin word 'crown.' In mythology it represents the crown of Ariadne, who helped Theseus slay a beast that was hidden away in the Labyrinth of Crete." He placed his finger in the book and continued to tell his own version of the story. "As I remember, there once was an Athenian hero named Theseus, and he was challenged to kill a powerful creature that was hidden away in a labyrinth. A young woman had fallen for Theseus and gave him a spindle of golden yarn to carry with him. That way, he could follow the yarn back out of the maze and return to her. The labyrinth itself was built by a master blacksmith named Daedalus, who created winding tunnels and turns that seemed to have neither a beginning nor an end. Daedalus constructed the maze so exquisitely that it is said that he himself could barely escape it."

"Why would someone build a maze like that?"

"Well, he was hired to do so by a powerful king who wanted to hide away a powerful creature."

"So you think that somehow Deneb has been taken to this Labyrinth?"

"I know it sounds crazy, but that's the only maze I know of that is affiliated with a crown. Now, the physical place where this labyrinth resides is on the island of Crete. However, there are no visible remnants there today, only speculations regarding where it might be found. I say we take a trip to Crete and see what we can find," Stan said while flipping to the next page in the book, with the heading *Corona Australis, the Southern Crown.*

"I think you may know what I am about to say," he smiled at Altair as he scanned over the words on the page, 'The Southern Crown is part of the constellation family belonging to Cygnus, Aquila, and Lyra.'

In a moment of synchronicity, they responded, "We need Vega."

CHAPTER 3

The phone rang for the fourth time as Vega picked it up and effortlessly dropped it back upon the receiver while yelling over the music, "I don't want to talk to you people!" She strutted back to the bathroom, where her roommate Eva sat idly waiting with champagne in hand and mud mask tightly molding onto her face.

"Who was that? Another news channel?" she asked while sneaking a slice of cucumber in her mouth.

"I've stopped asking," Vega smiled while turning up the obscurely perfect 1970's song. She shifted her attention to the ridiculous ambiance of their homemade spa day and hoisted her plastic champagne flute into the air as she attempted to sing the mismatched words, "He sailed down the Nile, he ate a crocodile, King Tut." Synchronous giggles echoed through the bathroom as both girls sipped their champagne.

"Hold still while I put this on you," Eva dabbed her fingers in the bowl of muddy slop.

"This looks disgusting." Vega twisted her face, fighting her friend's tattoo covered hands as she attempted to apply the soothing, yet appalling mask.

"Trust me, this stuff is all organic and will work wonders for your skin. Not like you need it, but it's nice to have some company while I do it," she laughed, while eyeing the traces of wrinkles on her own face.

"How long do we have to leave this on?" Vega paced the bathroom; sitting on the counter, then jumping down, then hopping back onto the counter once more.

"The point is to relax," her friend reminded her while smoothing the last bit of mud onto her face. The phone rang once again causing her to slam her drink down, and march back into the other room.

"Look! Whatever news channel you are from, please stop calling me! I have nothing to tell you people!"

Before the phone could fall from her fingers, a familiar voice called out from the other end, "Wait! Vega! It's me, Stan!"

She fumbled the dropping phone and scrambled to press it back to her ear.

"Stan?" her heavy breaths filled the empty air, normally filled with vulgarities or some quick jab at the caller on the other end.

"Yes, it's me. Hi, how are you?" he asked, already knowing the answer.

"Been better," he could feel her smirk through the phone.

"I figured as much. Look, I know this is the last thing that you want to talk about since Deneb's accident, but I need your help."

"Help with what?"

"It's Deneb, she is alive."

"How? Where? I need to see her!"

"Well, that's what we need your help with. Altair and I haven't *exactly* found her yet."

"What in the world do you mean by that? How do you know she's alive then?"

Altair reached for the phone and jumped in, "Vega. It's me Altair."

The tone in her voice changed to sympathetic agreement as she replied, "Hey Altair, just tell me where I need to be and I'll be there. I... I feel so bad for, well, you know."

He stopped her before she could wallow in her guilt once more, "It's okay Vega. Meet us in Athens and we'll fill you in on everything."

"Athens? Why in the world do we want to go there?"

"Because that is where we'll catch the ferry to Crete."

She hung up the phone and walked silently back into the bathroom toward her friend who had waited all week, through repeated days of twelve-hour bartending shifts, for this moment of pampering.

"Who was that?" she removed a cucumber from one eye, squinting like a mud-masked pirate at the only girl who had ever earned her trust.

"That was Stan." She leaned against the counter trying to collect her thoughts.

"Well, what did he say?"

"They think they found Deneb. I need to go to Greece."

"What do you mean they think they found her? Either they did or they didn't. I don't know how I feel about you leaving here, I mean, if anything would ever happen to you I don't know what I'd do."

She removed the cucumber from her other eye, nervously chomping on the soothing fruit, as she realized how equally gross it was at the same time.

"It's a long story, but it's one that I know I need to be a part of. I don't think that Altair can do this alone. He'll need me, if there's even a shot at bringing her back."

8

"Well, we can't have you going to Greece with bad skin," she smiled while reapplying the mask to her face.

"True." Vega walked to the couch and placed fresh cucumbers over her eyes, relaxing for the first time in months. As she laid back, thoughts of the coming days twisted through her mind, creasing the mud as it set to her face.

"So… I'll take you to the airport okay? And, I think it would be good if you left a list of the places you'll be, so I can check in with you, okay?"

Vega laughed at the thought of an itinerary. "With this group it's like following a treasure map where the dotted lines constantly change."

"Okay then. Oh, stay right there!" she yelled to the clearly comfortable girl with her feet kicked up. Vega, sensing the shadow looming over her, pulled the cucumbers from her eyes once more.

"Okay, so…. this may not mean anything to you now, but I found this many, many years ago when I visited Cairo with my parents. I want you to have it, and just know that any time you feel alone, or like you just need a connection back to a safe place, you can reach for this." She opened her secretive fist, sliding a simple figurine into Vega's hands.

She studied the small golden phoenix, looking somewhat like a shiny origami toy, and smiled. "Thanks Eva. You found this in Cairo? It doesn't look like it would belong there."

"A lot of things end up in places where they do not belong," she winked.

"What's so important about it?" Vega examined the simple figurine.

9

"I don't really know, but it reminds me of you... you know; someone who ends up in places that they don't really belong," she laughed.

"I promise. I will try to call you from wherever we are, and this will stay with me for my entire journey."

"Okay, enough of the sentimental stuff. What do you say we watch a movie?" she grabbed the remote and flopped down on the couch next to her, stopping on Thelma and Louise.

"You always know what's best," Vega nudged as they settled into the couch.

The sun outlined two familiar silhouettes as Vega stood, suitcase in hand, waiting at the port for the ferry to come in. She placed her hand to her forehead, creating a perfectly shaded view of Altair's face. She joyfully dropped her suitcase and ran to meet them, nearly knocking him over with her bear of a hug.

"I'm so happy to see you! You know...I didn't know if I'd ever see you again, you know after the tunnels and then you didn't come to the funeral, and then you were just kind of gone, and then you finally snapped out of that spell and then this whole thing happened with Deneb..."

"Vega!" Stan interrupted her excessive rambling.

Altair appreciatively smiled, "It's been a hard couple of months. I still haven't been back to my house; it just doesn't feel like I can go home without her."

Vega choked back an unexpected tear as she hugged him once more. "So, where have you been? In England this whole time with Stan?"

He nodded. "And you moved back to New York with your roommate?"

She smiled, "She's helped me to get through so much. I didn't realize how important having a good friend was until I lost Deneb. Don't worry Altair... we are going to get her back. Right Stan?"

"What?" he replied, while keeping his watchful gaze on the approaching ferry.

"We were just saying how you have a plan to bring back Deneb, right?" her voice raised in unintended excitement as the massive ship pulled into port.

"Of course I do. Come on now, we have a lot to discuss."

As they boarded the ferry, Vega darted to take the window seat, and then shied away, feeling Altair right behind her.

"You go ahead," she smiled, with an extended hand.

"Alright," he nodded appreciatively as he moved to take his seat.

As the ship pulled away from land, they fell into a whispered conversation, informing Vega of their research and why they felt the need to visit Crete in the first place.

"Well, wait one minute. If you heard her say she is in a maze and she is a part of the water, then shouldn't we be looking in the water for her? Maybe there is some labyrinth somewhere in the ocean, or tunnels of water somewhere that we don't even know about?"

"Well, I guess I hadn't thought about the labyrinth being in the water. See, long ago there were gold coins found with an ancient symbol engraved upon them, which looked a lot like a labyrinth. Archeological scholars have suggested that the coins resemble the great labyrinth of Knossos, implying that both the palace and the treasure are there."

11

"Do you have a picture of the coin? I want to see this symbol," Vega leaned in towards yet another book that Stan had brought with him.

"That symbol!" She slapped her hand over her mouth as flashbacks of dreams carried through her mind.

"I've seen it in dreams," she whispered through the cracks of her fingers.

"What kind of dreams Vega?"

"I dreamt I was catching my breath next to a rocky shoreline, as if I had just completed a really intense dive. While sitting there on the rocks, a giant oyster shell washed up next to me. I looked inside of the shell and saw a strange symbol that looked like a square shaped maze, just like what is on that coin. In the dream, I knew that somehow, the design made the shell incredibly special, and so I looked up the hillside to see where I was. Just above me was an ancient palace shaped exactly like the maze-shaped symbol within the shell."

"Well, Vega, some have argued that the coins of Knossos were designed to replicate the palace they came from. The word Labyrinth dates back to a pre-Greek word 'labrys', meaning double-edged axe, which is a symbol of royal power. Within the remnants of the palace of Knossos, traces of a maze like structure remain, as well as a hallway dedicated to the symbol of the double axe. I believe the symbol is somehow connected with entering the maze."

Her eyes glazed over as she slipped deep into her memories; ignoring every word Stan said past 'axe.' Her faint 'out of time' smile grew, as she recalled the face of the only man she had ever known to carry an axe; the only man she had ever loved.

"Vega?"

12

"Huh?" She nearly toppled her drink as she snapped back to reality.

"So you think the symbol in my dream is significant then? The maze somehow equals the double axe, which is a royal symbol or something?" She raised an eyebrow.

"I'm not entirely sure, but I want to explore Crete and see what we can find. Back to your point about the water, perhaps what we are looking for is not on land. Remind me to research sacred wells, and arrange a few dives for us while we are there."

"I hate to interrupt you guys, but if we are going to the depths of the sea, I'm sorry to say I've never gone diving before," Altair bashfully admitted.

"Altair, I'll be with you the entire time. We don't need any special training to go to these places, right?" Vega asked.

"Well, come to think about it, I think we might need a certain level of certification for some of the dives. We'll figure it out when we get to the island," Stan inclusively smiled.

The boat came to a stop as the eager passengers grabbed their luggage and made their way toward the exits. Vega, devoid of manners, somehow managed to weave herself to the front of the line and disappeared down the stairs. Stan's somewhat annoyed voice wafted through the breeze, falling upon deaf ears, as he slowly made his way down the stairs toward the abnormally calm girl. Her constantly anxious demeanor had completely disappeared and majestically morphed into calmness.

"This place is like paradise," she whispered to herself as a gust of sea salt graced her face.

The backdrop of Stan's voice served as a guide to her daydream, "Welcome to Heraklion."

13

Altair meandered off the ferry, noticing the oddly calm look on Vega's face. "What did I miss?"

"Nothing much, actually you're just in time. That shuttle heading our way will be taking us to the hotels." He nodded at the arriving bus as he picked up his bag.

They filed onto the simple bus, packed with happy vacationers and laid back locals, and took their seats. As they made their way through the busy port, their minds drifted to different places. Altair's face remained solemnly hopeful as he stared out to the ocean; silently hoping that maybe he would catch some glimpse of her out there. Vega's eyes locked on the front window of the bus, trying to gage how soon they would be there, while Stan's fiery glare honed in on Vega's anxiously tapping foot as he recalled other moments when she had acted in a similar manner. As the bus rolled to a stop, Vega swooped up her bag and quickly called out behind her, "See you guys out there!"

Passengers pleasantly plucked their bag from the bus, except for one.

"Hey," Stan placed a comforting hand on Altair's shoulder as he moped toward his bag, "Besides the obvious, is something the matter? You seem completely different since we got here."

"I don't know, I just keep looking out to sea, and it just looks so intimidating. I'm not a diver like you and Vega, and as much as I want to save Deneb, I'm nervous that I won't be able to." He sullenly dragged his suitcase down the stairs of the shuttle as Stan scrambled behind.

"Don't worry Altair. We're going to find her," he reassured as he spun him by the shoulders toward the majestic island hotel that rose up in front of them, expecting a reaction similar to Vega, who was already twirling around the lobby in excitement.

14

His lackluster face remained unmoved. "This place is beautiful. I just can't enjoy myself without her right now."

Stan gave him a fatherly pat on the back as they entered the lavish resort and made their way to reception.

"Checking in?" a composed, elderly man asked from behind the counter.

"Well, yes, but we don't exactly have reservations. We're hoping you can make room for us," Stan grinned.

Moments passed, filled with slow typing, and inquisitive staring before the man responded, "You're in luck! We have two rooms remaining."

Vega paused mid-pour of the complimentary fresh mint lemonade, and interjected, "Two rooms? We need three."

"Sorry miss. Unfortunately, the only rooms I have available are these two, and the only reason the honeymoon bungalow is open is due to a cancelation. I will tell you what; I will give you the honeymoon bungalow at the same rate as the other room. Would that be alright?"

Vega and Altair shot frightful glances at one another as they responded in unison, "Honeymoon bungalow?"

The old man chuckled as he nodded, "Well, that's the best I can do."

Stan interjected before their discomfort could get the best of them. "That will be great. Thank you for being so accommodating."

As they sheepishly grabbed their room keys, Stan chimed in once more, "Hey guys, so I was thinking we could grab dinner tonight and talk about what we are doing tomorrow. I want to get plans set for our dive and exploration of Crete. What do you say we meet down here at the restaurant in about an hour?"

15

Vega and Altair agreeably nodded before wheeling their bags down the long hall, leading outside.

"This place is a freaking maze," Vega laughed as they turned down another perfectly landscaped walkway while Altair checked the map once more.

"Doesn't look like it's too much further," he glanced down, then up, at the final cobblestone walkway leading to their beachside bungalow. Simultaneously, their pace slowed as they took in the breathtakingly romantic setting. Vega stood beneath the wooden archway, perfectly draped in fragrant, lacey vines and flowers. Altair slowly moved beside her, silently looking just past the glow of their private pool, to the ocean. Their hearts both settled in the same lonely place, as they soaked in the torturously romantic surroundings.

"What a place," Vega huffed while rolling her worn, patch-covered suitcase over the bamboo deck towards their room. She slid the heavy glass doors open, sending the whimsical white curtains into a romantic twirl behind her, as she zipped through the living room to the bedroom. Sadness swarmed her eyes as she looked upon the chaos of silky red rose petals, delightfully spread across the crisp white linens of the bed. Altair silently entered the room behind her, carefully approaching the unexpectedly heartbroken girl.

"Vega?" He placed a careful hand on her shoulder.

"Geeze!" she whipped around nearly punching him.

"Are you... are you okay?" he asked, already knowing the answer.

"Sorry, it's just that this ... this... display of rose petals here on the bed is the last thing I want to see after losing the only man I ever loved."

He laughed under his breath. "I hear ya."

She exhaled while admiring the view from the bedroom. "But I guess we could be in worse places."

"Couldn't agree more," he smiled while heading back to the living room.

"Hey, so, I'm going to get in the shower and clean up for dinner," Vega called while digging in her suitcase for an almost equally sized bag full of soaps, shampoos, perfumes and makeup.

"Take your time," he said as he relaxed into the oversized cushions of the couch.

A soft breeze blew through the room as Altair's eyes struggled to stay open. The sound of peaceful waves danced upon the shore and pushed him further into slumber. A voice echoed in the distance like a lullaby as he followed a soaring eagle deep into the forest of his dreams. Ancient pillars of trees surrounded him as he looked up toward an eagle, perched atop a hilly underground fortress. He entered the dark cave-like structure and looked up in wonderment at the enchanting painting that spread across the ceiling. His inquisitive eyes moved to the words written beneath the artwork, which seemed to circle around the ceiling above him. Before he could ask aloud where he was, a powerful voice responded, "you are in the citadel, and once those words are spoken, she will be free."

Before he could memorize the words, he was transported to another scene, looking down on a ceiling made of glass and metal. The eagle flew to his side as he asked, "Where am I now?"

Once more, the voice replied. "You are at the Louvre. There is a portal from here to the citadel. Eighteen degree turns will open the door between these places."

17

"Hey, you ready?" Vega shook his arm as he frantically awoke.

"Whoa! Sorry! Didn't mean to scare you," she laughed in amusement. "We have to meet Stan in about ten minutes, so I thought I should wake you."

He calmly ran his fingers through his hair in an attempt to hide his disheveled demeanor. "No problem. I can be ready in just a moment."

Vega triumphantly giggled to herself as she walked barefoot out to the pool, her long dress blowing in the breeze behind her.

"Something funny?" he squinted a judgmental eye as she dipped a toe in the water.

"I've just never seen you so startled before. I mean, even when we were in the tunnels of Egypt you never seemed frazzled or scared, and here I come, waking you from a dream and look at you," she laughed again.

"Well, I guess I had my guard down... I was sleeping you know."

An uncomfortable silence loomed while she waited for more details.

"Fine," he bashfully smiled. "I was having a dream and you interrupted me."

"Must have been one heck of a dream," she said while hoisting her dress up and stepping down to the first step. "Wow, this water is surprisingly perfect. I mean, how do they manage to make everything here so freaking perfect... even the water!" she said with a pleasant, yet frustrated tone.

A small grin graced his stoic face, "It is pretty perfect here, isn't it?"

"Okay... well, we'd better get down to the perfect restaurant and meet Stan for our perfect dinner!" she laughed.

Their unamused faces remained grim as they entered the fairytale setting of enchanted, moonlit dining. Soft white lights wrapped around the tops of the trees, casting angelic shadows of light over each table. The air felt like silk, laced with aromatic scents of freshly baked bread, rosemary and sea salt. Stan's excited face gleamed by candlelight as he waved them over to the table.

"How beautiful is this?" He said as his eyes scanned the twinkling restaurant.

They nodded in unison as they took their seats across from one another, each looking out to their own blank portion of the sea.

"So, I've researched quite a bit since we've arrived, and I think we should spend our first day on the land, exploring the remnants of the 'proposed labyrinth of Crete.' What do you guys think?"

Vega remained unusually quiet as Altair pulled his eyes from the hypnotic waves, "Land sounds best to me. After all, we still need to figure out how I'm going to join you out there."

"Right. So, let's start with the places we know we can go, and then... " Stan stopped mid-sentence, and cast an annoyed glance at the loud, celebrating table next to them.

He struggled to keep focus as the table of loud, laughing men thoroughly drowned out his thoughts, which returned Vega's attention to the present moment.

Her distant eyes honed in on the loudest one of all, nearly spitting his beer as his raucous laughter disrupted the peaceful energy of perfection around them.

Altair watched her eyes light up in silent amusement, while Stan bustled through his frustration. "Anyway, there is a place here that is thought to be the Labyrinth of Crete, and I think tomorrow, we should explore it and see what we can find. There may be things there that speak to us individually, and it is worth a look, at the very least."

"I'm up for that." Altair raised his glass with a humble smile. Vega mindlessly raised hers in an automatic response, as her eyes remained glued on the dark haired man at the next table.

"Vega?" Stan's muted voice repeated until at last she turned her head. "Are you okay?"

"Fine," she quickly replied while reaching in her purse for lip-gloss.

A menacing laugh slipped from Altair's lips as he shook his head.

As the waiter slid their drinks in front of them, Altair hurriedly spoke before he could leave. "Can we order now?"

Vega's eyes lit up brighter with each obnoxious laugh erupting from the man who had stolen her attention, as the waiter stared at the mesmerized girl, awaiting her order.

"Mmm hmm," Stan coughed.

"Right! So, I will have the... um... I'll have the smoked pork."

A relieved huff came from the waiter as he collected their menus and scurried away.

"Sheesh. What is wrong with that guy? I mean, sorry for taking a few minutes to order. I just lost the love of my life -- AND my best friend, so sorry if I seem distracted!" Vega's outburst hushed all of the nearby tables as alarmed gazes enhanced the silence, which now settled over the patio.

She shook her head in embarrassment. "Sorry everyone," she recanted, loud enough for those within earshot to hear as she scanned the faces of those she may have offended. She paused for fragments of a second, unintentionally locking eyes with the handsome man from the adjacent table.

"Vega, it's okay. You have been through so much, as has Altair. Now -- let's move on to what we're going to do while we're here. We've already determined that tomorrow we'll be exploring the proposed remnants of the Labyrinth of Crete, but we'll also need to figure out where we plan to dive and how exactly, to get Altair down there."

Stan's words faded to a mere whisper as Vega silently looked the man over, wondering what kind of work had placed him in the same location as her. His demeanor was careless, in a sense of celebratory youth but his face seemed threatened with scars and battles with the sun. She moved her eyes up to his hair and watched as he ran his fingers through the dark locks that laughter continued to toss in his face. His eyes seemed deep, and as blue as the ocean... She snapped back to the conversation.

"Right, so we need to figure out how to get Altair down there. We just need to get him clearance or whatever is needed, right?" Vega said, before sipping her drink.

She felt the roving eyes of the nearby table as a voice interrupted, "Don't mean to eavesdrop, but are you guys diving here?"

21

Shocked at the massive size of the towering man who sat beside her newfound crush, she replied, "Yes, well, we hope to. Why? Are you guys divers or something?"

They quickly looked at one another with concealed smiles, as the center of Vega's attention replied, "You could say that, yes."

"I don't see what's so funny about that," Altair murmured loud enough that Vega could hear.

"Right, what's so funny about that?" Vega echoed his whisper.

"We're a group of treasure hunters, and most of what we seek is out there. Some people call us divers, some people call us worse," he laughed in amusement before sipping his beer.

"Well ... what are you guys doing here?" Vega asked in a more serious tone.

He leaned towards her table with a sly whisper, "If I told ya, I'd have to kill ya." His giant of a friend pounded the table in laughter, rattling everything atop the nearby tables.

Silence loomed as he interrupted with a laugh. "Just kidding, but we don't really like to tell folks what we're after. It just attracts unwanted attention."

Stan interrupted, "Well, I don't mean to impose, but would you mind if we dove with you all? Vega and I are certified, but he isn't," as he glanced at Altair, "so we're looking for some assistance to get him down there with us tomorrow."

"Vega? That's a unique name," the dashing man quickly winked, which sent her mind into a whirlwind. 'Had he just winked at her? Or perhaps he was blinking, or had something in his eye. She could be all wrong, but then again...'

"Vega?" Stan interrupted. "He just said that he could dive with us if we need help getting Altair down there, but they are diving tomorrow."

"Well, I thought we were going to some cave tomorrow ... where the labyrinth was thought to be?"

Unanimous laughter came from the table of treasure hunters, as the skinny, somewhat creepy, dark haired man replied while lighting a cigarette, "You'll waste your time going over there. That cave is off limits to the public, and it hasn't been safe to set foot in since the 1940's. Besides, you won't find anything down there except bats and old wartime ammo."

"Well then .... Where do you suggest we look?" Vega snapped at the intimidatingly dark man.

"I suggest, if you are looking for the Labyrinth of Crete, to look in Knossos, where the remnants of the palace stand today." He paused before looking directly at Vega. "There are plenty of easy dives all around this island if you guys want to just do those."

The words 'easy dives' echoed annoyingly in her ears while she silently composed a response. The waiter dropped the checks onto their table, as she blurted out, "We're not here for easy dives. We'll join you."

As the most handsome of the three stood from the table, the romantic lights that she hated upon arrival, cast a flattering glow across his ruggedly handsome face. His eyes fastened on hers, as he slid a piece of paper on the table, forcing her to look down at the scribbled room number. As he turned to walk away, Stan quickly extended his hand across the table in an attempt to take the receipt, only to be met with Vega's iron fist.

"I'll hold on to this." Her love-struck eyes remained firm, as she tightened her grip on the paper.

23

Altair chuckled to himself as he shook his head, choking back the long list of one-liners he wanted to throw her way.

"Well, guys, now that we are alone… " Stan shot a parental glare at Vega, "I want to discuss our plans for tomorrow. I say we explore the palace at Knossos, and then if we're all up for it, we can do a dive around there."

Stan looked around the table for feedback, as conflict displayed itself across Altair's face.

"Something the matter?"

"You know what might be a better idea? Why don't you and Vega do a dive tomorrow, and I will explore the palace of Knossos alone. That way you will not feel limited by me. I want you guys to be able to do as much as you can out there and if I'm diving with you, I feel like I will just hold you back."

"That might not be a bad idea Altair," Vega answered, completely devoid of empathy.

"It's a plan then," he said, as he placed his napkin neatly upon the table.

"Alright kids. Get some good sleep and we'll meet down here in the morning, say around nine." Stan stood from the table and motioned to the exit with an extended hand.

"Sounds good." Vega whisked her dress around her, basking in the effect of the whimsical lighting, hardly noticing her sulking roommate.

She slid the heavy glass doors open once more, sending the freshly placed whirlwind of rose petals spinning around the room.

"More rose petals! What's with this place?" Vega yanked the top cover off the bed, scattering the last remaining petals to the floor.

24

A condescending laugh came from the adjoining room, "Oh! And look! They brought us newlyweds a bottle of champagne -- and chocolate covered strawberries!"

Vega paused before answering, noticing the pain in his voice. "Open it up!"

"What?" he called from the living room.

"I said open it up! It was meant to be a gift for whoever was staying in this room, and that is us now! We have been through an awful lot. I say we open it up and celebrate."

Disgust settled in the lines of his smile as he eyed the bottle. "What's there to celebrate?"

Vega skipped across the room and snatched the bottle from his hands. "How about being alive? That's something to celebrate!"

"I thought you weren't supposed to drink before a dive?"

"I can have just a little," she popped open the bottle, while catching the foaming bubbles in her mouth. She smiled as she wiped her lips on her forearm. "Come on, let's sit outside."

"He grabbed two glasses and followed behind her as she confidently led the way out onto their private balcony overlooking the ocean.

"Cheers," she said while holding her glass up to the full moon overhead.

"Cheers."

She paused, while holding her glass. "I want you to say at least one thing you are happy about... please," she demanded, with an exaggerated stare.

"Okay. Cheers to being on this beautiful island, with this tasty champagne," he forcefully smiled.

25

Vega took a small sip. "And cheers to this beautiful pool that I am about to get into! Stay right here! I'm going to go change!"

Altair stopped mid-sip as she came back out, hoping she hadn't noticed his gaping stare; which she hadn't. As she slipped into the silky water of the glowing pool, Altair averted his gaze, taking another sip of the champagne. Her contagious smile spread across her face as she snatched her glass off the deck.

"Hey! You should get in here!" She said while joyfully twirling through the water.

"Maybe you're right," he smiled.

He paused upon returning to the pool, admiring the simplistic joy on her face as she floated on her back, looking up to the shooting stars above. Her fiery red hair swirled weightlessly around her, as if she were some kind of mythological sea creature. His shadow slowly moved across her body, as she splashed to her feet.

"How long have you been standing there?" she said with a startled laugh.

"Not long," he said as he again refilled his glass.

As he dipped down into the warm, welcoming water, Vega swam to the edge of the pool, and put her elbows up onto the deck. Her eyes remained focused on the faint outline of the distant waves as Altair swam up beside her.

Before sadness could creep back into their minds, Vega snatched her glass from the side of the pool, insisting on another 'cheers.'

"Cheers!" ... she began, falling short of words as another shooting star crossed the sky.

26

"Cheers... to finding our soulmates," he painfully said as he looked out to the sea.

As she thrust her glass towards the sky, her heart grew heavy with thoughts of Lan.

"Oh Vega, I'm sorry. I... I don't know what happened while I was gone, but I know you lost someone very special."

Making a timely escape from her tears, she disappeared beneath the water, only to reemerge looking surprisingly refreshed.

"You're right! Cheers to finding our soulmates!" she confidently hoisted her champagne towards the stars, stirring waves as she twirled through the water once more. "You know what? We have a lot to talk about!"

"We do - huh?" he laughed as he sipped the bubbles before they could spill into the pool.

"We do." She took a more serious tone as she swam beside him. "A lot happened while you were 'away.' I know this is going to sound crazy to you, but Deneb and I were able to travel through time using two different mediums. I used my song, which is something I will have to explain to you another time, and she used the crystal and some ancient tool that you've probably never heard of -- called a Vajra."

He set his glass down upon the ledge of the pool, "I know what a Vajra is Vega. You forget -- I'm a blacksmith and I make all of my own tools. Though I've not made that one, I've researched just about every tool ever invented."

"That's right. Well, anyway, we found this tool and she was able to use it in conjunction with her crystal to open a doorway through time. I was also able to do the same exact thing using my song."

27

"What are you getting at?" His eyes returned to the darkness of the shoreline where he trusted the waves were cresting.

"I'm saying that you need to catch up. You need to realize what your life purpose is, because Deneb and I already have. It's like you've been asleep this entire time, and are a little late to the party." Her smile faded.

"You think that somehow I can do the same? Travel through time?"

Vega floated on her back once more, reflecting the night sky upon her body as if she were but a reflection of the universe.

 "I don't know what your power is. That's your job to figure it out."

He floated beside her, joining her gaze on the starry scene above.

"I'll be on the same level as you guys in no time, trust me."

Silent moments passed as he wondered if her ears had been submerged underwater the entire time.

She triumphantly smiled, "Trust me Altair, we're going to get her back, but I need you to be on the same level as me. I need you to dig down deep into that soul of yours and discover who, or what, you are destined to be."

She decisively exited the pool and walked over to the stack of freshly folded towels, wrapping one around her head like a turban.

"One more thing... I have Deneb's dream journal if you want to use it to record what you receive. I'm going to go out on a limb and say you've been dreaming of places you've never been?" She laughed as she shoved a chocolate covered strawberry into her mouth.

He nodded as he staggered towards the steps, "Why don't we get changed and I'll tell you about a dream I had."

She smiled as she tossed a strawberry his way. "That's what I'm talking about!"

CHAPTER 4

"Good morning!" Vega pounced into the room and yanked the curtains open, arousing a groan of discomfort from the couch.

"What time is it?" he peeled his head from the pillow, shielding his eyes from the morning with his hand.

"It's seven, sorry, too early?" she smiled while walking into the kitchen to pour the coffee.

"This should help." She moved the steaming cup into his line of eyesight, evoking a smile. "Maybe the free champagne wasn't as good of an idea as we thought," she laughed while pulling the curtains closed a tad.

"Thanks." He eyed the chipper girl with jealousy as she leaned her head outside in excitement. "Man! I am excited for today!"

"Right, today... " He sat up and took a sip of his coffee.

"So, I'm going to dive today with Stan and hopefully those guys," she smirked. "What are you going to do?"

"Well, I think there is a bus that goes over to the palace, so I will probably go there. I also want to see if there is a citadel somewhere on this island."

"Sit-a-what?" she laughed.

"I had a dream last night about a laborer carrying two buckets of water towards this fortress, and it was called the citadel. I've dreamt about this place twice now, and in one of the dreams I was inside of this fortress looking up at a golden painting that covered the ceiling."

"Interesting.... so what do you think this place has to do with Deneb?"

"Well that's the thing. There were words written across the ceiling that only I could see, and a voice said, 'once you speak the words, she will be free.'"

"No way! We need to find this place!"

"Well there is more. Before I had a chance to read the writing on the wall I was transported to the Louvre."

"That's weird. Why would you go from the citadel to the Louvre?"

"At the end of my dream the voice spoke again, and said that there was a portal that could be created between the two; something about using 18 degree turns to open the door."

"Wow! Well, I cannot wait to hear what you find today! Have more of that coffee, you're going to need it."

Vega shot an alarmed glance at the clock. "Oh man! I am late! I have to go meet Stan! I'll see you back here tonight for dinner okay?" She grabbed her bag while shoving a muffin in her mouth, and waving goodbye with her free hand.

"See you later," he said as loud as his headache permitted. He slowly made his way from the couch to the shower, and back again to the couch to drink more coffee. He slid open the glass doors and stepped onto the balcony to gather his thoughts, as he slowly returned to normalcy. The wind felt like silk on his skin, as the fresh morning sun sparkled upon the waves below, filling his mind with thoughts of Deneb.

"Don't worry, I'm going to figure this out," he said with a determined stare.

31

The sun's rays danced upon the water like a vibrating sheet of light, and for a second he imagined she was speaking to him, saying, "I know you will."

He slid on his sunglasses and made his way outdoors, through the maze of fragrant hallways to the lobby, where the same delightful old man greeted him with a humble smile.

"Enjoying your stay sir?" he queried.

"Actually yes, I am," he paused before stepping outside. "Tell me, do you know of any citadels on this island?"

The old man shuffled over to his stack of island pamphlets and pulled out one titled, 'The Abandoned Island of Spinalonga.'

"You might find what you are looking for here," he kindly smiled.

"Thank you," he said, as he turned to ask another question. "If you were going to choose between exploring the palace of Knossos and this citadel, where would you go?"

He raised his brow and responded, "Depends what you are looking for."

"That's a loaded question." Altair smiled, wishing he had more time to share tales with the old man.

His thoughts battled one another. His heart was with her; trapped somewhere within a labyrinth, so maybe he should go to the palace of Knossos where the labyrinth is said to be. Conflicted, he was pulled in another direction; perhaps he should follow his intuition and go where the dreams were leading him...but was this even the right citadel?

"Well, I'd say, follow your heart and see where that takes you," the old man graciously interrupted his clearly conflicted silence.

"Right, follow my heart," he smiled.

"Young man?" the elderly gentleman called from behind, "If you do decide you'd like to see the palace, there is a shuttle coming in a few minutes to take hotel guests on a complimentary tour," he smiled like a grandfather giving helpful advice.

"Perfect! Thank you so much!" he ran out the door to the approaching shuttle and jumped in line with the other vacationers. His excitement drained as he took his seat among the sea of happy couples, off to tour remnants of a royal palace together. His eyes shamefully glared at each clasped hand and playful caress, as he quickly directed his gaze to the folded map he had nearly forgotten was in his hand. With a relieved exhale, he opened the pamphlet and became absorbed in the tales of the palace, both historical and mythological.

"Knossos (pronounced Kuh-nuh-SOS) is the ancient Minoan palace and surrounding city on the island of Crete. The settlement was established well before 2000 BCE and was destroyed, most likely by fire, c. 1700 BCE. Knossos has been identified with Plato's mythical Atlantis, and is also famously known for the myth of Theseus and the Minotaur."

His excited eyes peeled to the next page as he continued,

"According to the myths surrounding the early city, King Minos hired the Athenian architect, mathematician, and inventor Daedalus to design his palace, and so cleverly was it constructed that no one who entered could find their way back out without a guide. In other versions of this same story, it was not the palace itself, which was designed in this way, but the labyrinth within the palace, which was built to confine great secrets, heroes, and beasts.

"I better write some of this down," he whispered to himself while reaching into his bag. The familiar canvas of Deneb's journal, worn with desert sand, slid across his hands like a memory not even his calloused fingertips could conceal from him. He flipped past the ghostly handwriting and scoured for a blank page as he began to write, "Labyrinth designed so intricately no one could escape, contained great heroes and beasts."

"Ladies and gentlemen, we are approaching the great palace of Knossos. Feel free to take a complimentary pamphlet as you exit the bus and don't forget -- we will have lovely "Snake Goddess" souvenirs available for sale upon departure," the driver systematically announced to the bus full of happy guests.

Altair cringed at the thought of a snake goddess, capturing the gaze of the driver.

"Something the matter son?" the man questioned his look of disgust.

"I've not had the best of encounters with snakes in my life, and if there is a snake goddess, I would like to steer clear of her," he laughed.

"Pardon me asking, but are you here alone?" he looked behind him for any stragglers on the bus.

"For now," he smiled with a glimmer of hope.

"Well, today is your lucky day. See, I have been giving private tours of this palace for years, but stopped when my knees started giving me some trouble. Nowadays I just drive the bus, but today I'd like to get out and join you, if that's alright with you?"

"I'd like the company," he nodded.

The old man reached for an ornately carved wooden cane, hiding next to his bus seat. His hands shook in excitement as he wrapped his weathered hands around the emerald eyes of the lion proudly posted at the top. With an adventurous push, he heaved himself upright and shuffled down the stairs.

As they slowly made their way to the palace, the old man systematically recited the familiar lines he had shared with countless groups before.

"Five Thousand years ago the great Minoan civilization lived on the island of Crete, and as you enter the remnants of the palace you will see what remains of this once flourishing society. Beautiful frescos, exquisite carvings, and of course the sound of their own unique language remains sealed inside the palace walls, leaving only questions behind."

They walked up the wide precisely carved stairs to one of the many outdoor areas, where crumbled walls resembling remnants of rooms sparked a unified vision of what the palace once had looked like. The old man smiled, delighting in the racing thoughts that had Altair's eyes darting from place to place, around the masonry. He extended his palm out ahead of him, motioning toward even more awe-inspiring places.

The sun beat down overhead as they twisted and turned through the remains of the palace, stopping every so often to turn and look out at the island beneath them.

"Even without any walls I feel as if I could get lost in here. Some of these hallways and rooms look as if they just wind and wind around one another forever, with no real outlet." Altair squinted an eye as he peered back at the remnants of the room they had just passed.

"This palace was built by a seasoned mathematician and master architect, and according to legend, Daedalus built it in such a way that it truly was a work of art. His name after

35

all means 'cunningly wrought,' so it does seem fitting that such a man would construct such a place."

"I've heard his name before. Can you tell me more about him?" Altair questioned while eyeing the massive crimson pillars just ahead in the distance.

"Of course," the old man continued, as they walked across a wooden bridge and into another section of the palace.

"Daedalus is most famously remembered for creating the Labyrinth of Crete, which he was tasked to design by King Minos. It was said that he was far beyond his years in wisdom and skill, and surpassed all of the King's men when it came to challenges of art, design, and masonry. Homer's language… you know, Homer the author of the Iliad?" he paused to make sure Altair was following.

"Yes, I'm aware of who he is," Altair chuckled at the old man's question.

"Right, so he often used the word 'Daidala,' which means finely crafted objects, when referring to objects of fine worth, including armor, bowls, jewelry, and swords which were made by Hephaestus, the god of blacksmithing, but secretly looked after by the goddess of the sea."

His eyes lit up with confused excitement, "Goddess of the sea?"

"Yes, there are tales of Hephaestus falling in love with a goddess of the sea, though little is known about her."

"And just who was Hephaestus?" he asked.

"Ah right, so … he is the god of fire, metalworking, stone masonry, and creations of art and sculpture; not to mention he is the brother of the god of fire, Apollo. It has been told that he held within his power the ability to surge life into objects of silver, metal, and gold, and that he made the lions and wolves that guarded the palace of Alkinoos come to life when invaders came near," he laughed in amusement. "Some say that he taught this practice to Daedalus, and when he built the labyrinth of Crete the walls were actually alive, and moved to his accord.

Hephaestus was known in tales to be much like Athena in the sense that he had a soft spot for helping mortals, particularly artists. Several legends suggest that Daedalus was a descendant of Hephaestus, others just say that he took a liking to him and helped him construct some of the most legendary pieces of armory, masonry, and jewelry there ever was."

Altair smiled, "I think I'd like that guy. I'm a blacksmith myself."

"I knew I liked you!" The old man laughed as they neared the towering pillars of crimson just ahead. As the awe and wonderment consumed Altair, the old man spoke again, "I've been coming to this palace for nearly three decades and every time I'm here I always think the same thing."

Altair turned his eyes away from the remnants of the royal scenery. "What's that?"

"There are many paintings, and statues that were found here and they all feature a woman with serpents in her hands. People have obviously labelled her as the Serpent Goddess, but there is a part of me that thinks that the serpent represented something more than just snakes. Think about the waves of the sea, and waves of energy, what do they resemble?"

Altair attempted to rattle an answer from his somewhat foggy mind as the old man answered for him, "the waves of energy strongly resemble the serpent shapes coming from the woman's hands -- conductors."

"You think there was once a woman who was worshiped here, and somehow she held within her possession some sort of great conductor?"

He nodded in agreement, as they walked towards the edge of the precipice. "Not just one conductor, two."

Everything faded around him as his mind vanished back into previous conversations with Vega. He recalled her words 'she had a Vajra and her crystal, which allowed her to travel through time.' His mind raced towards the crystal, resting safely within his sword. Spinning up new thoughts to challenge him, was Deneb lost without it?

"The symbol of two snakes twisting together can be seen in many common symbols today, can you think of one?" he stared with hopeful wide eyes.

"DNA?" Altair guessed.

An appeased exhale began his next sentence. "The symbol you are about to see here, in the Hall of the Double Axes, is also affiliated with the Serpent Goddess. So, where others may see two simple axes, I personally see something altogether different. The symbol of the labyrinth dates back to a word meaning 'axe' and it is said that this royal symbol was indeed the key to something spectacular, something bigger."

"Creation itself?" Altair whispered to himself, not needing any validation to his question.

"Precisely," the old man proudly replied as they continued towards the Hall of Double Axes.

As they entered the quiet, ancient hallway, devoid of elaborate frescos or towering pillars, Altair carefully paced, looking for the symbol.

The tour guide interrupted his gazing, "You know some folks say that the Serpent Goddess was so powerful she

38

could actually use the energy beaming forth from her hands to bring another serpent back to life. You know... the symbol of DNA and all."

"Wait - what?" Altair jerked his head away from the faint etchings in the wall toward the subdued, yet excited man.

"Yes, well, I don't expect you to know about these things, so forgive me, but she is said in legends to have the ability to use two surges of energy to revive other serpents. I just thought you'd find that interesting."

Disgust and fear raced through is eyes as he envisioned a wave of life coming over the chalky dust of Hydra stained upon the beach where he left her.

"Well, things that are dead just don't come back into existence," Altair reassured himself, while realizing that the woman he loved had done just that.

The old man's green eyes sparkled in the sunlight, "Humans. Humans don't just come back. This... this is something different. The true battle of good and evil, darkness and light."

Confusion angered him, as he faced the man, "The only other serpents I've heard of are associated with darkness. So, why would one good thing bring back one bad thing? This just isn't logical at all!"

"There is a balance my child, good balances evil. It always has. Now, would you like to continue?"

Fear loomed around him as he continued through the sacred site, questioning for the first time if Deneb had been here before him, somehow.

Altair watched the humble old man carefully walk through the archways he had walked through hundreds of times before, and wondered if he had had conversations like this with every happy couple passing through the island, or if perhaps he was special. He had never thought of himself as special until this very moment.

"So, say this Serpent Goddess does exist, and possesses two incredible sources of energy, why would she use her powers to bring another serpent back to life, something that opposes her?"

"In life there are always sacrifices, perhaps she did it to save someone else? No one will ever know. I guess that is why people keep coming back to this island... so much mystery."

"What other mysteries could there be?" Altair laughed while scouring the walls for symbols of double axes..., which appeared more like a circle cut into equal triangular parts.

The old man rubbed the smooth head of the lion atop his cane as if petting his lifelong companion, "quite an interesting symbol isn't it?"

Altair's fingers traced over the faint outline of the double axe carved into the wall, as he pondered the ancient symbol. "This symbol," he laughed, "it looks more like a sliced pie than an axe, well at least to me. See this part here; it looks like there are traces of a circle around the triangles, and it just kind of looks like something other than a double axe."

"I agree, son. If we had more time together, I would share a book I have with you. Do me a favor, when you have time look up 'the wheel of time,' and you'll find a similar symbol."

"So, let me see if I've got this straight; the word labyrinth also equates to the double axe, and the double axe appears as the wheel of time. So, could it be possible that someone could be trapped in time?"

"Anything is possible, especially here where gods such as Apollo and Hephaestus once roamed."

"Interesting," he whispered to himself while pondering his dream that had mentioned eighteen degree turns to open doors of time, as the old man quickly checked his watch.

"Speaking of time, we had better get back; the tour will be ending soon."

As they slowly walked back towards the bus, sitting idly by the palace curb, Altair asked for one more tale, "Tell me, do you know any tales that involve the constellation Corona Borealis?"

The old man chuckled, "I really do wish we had more time together, you're a real treat! Alright, let me tell you a little bit about the Northern Crown. While classic myths will focus on the tale of the labyrinth and the golden crown that was tossed into the sky to celebrate the union of two lovers, another less known tale from Chinese lore affiliates the labyrinth with a place known as The Heavenly Market Enclosure."

The old man began gleefully rounding up his passengers. "One more stop for those who would like a souvenir," he jested towards the gift shop as Altair wandered inside.

"How was the palace? What did you all think?" excitement brimmed from him as he questioned the passing people.

Altair smiled at the sincere amount of love that the man held for the historical remnants, as he meandered towards a shelf lined with snake goddess figurines.

The familiar sound of the man's cane echoed off the tile behind him, as his fatherly hand wrapped around his shoulder, "find one you like?"

Altair laughed, "Don't think I could go wrong picking any one of these identical statues."

41

The old man nodded in agreement, "True."

As they headed back outside the old man offered one last token of advice. "If I were you I would seek to understand the secrets that the sea goddess holds, after all, tales of Melusine have been written upon scrolls through the ages."

"Melusine? That is the name of the sea goddess?" Altair questioned.

"It is the name I've come to know her by, yes. Tales of this beautiful creature have been passed down through whispers of mighty men for centuries and with each passing tale another man pauses, scared that she may hear their words and call them out to a watery death."

"So she is bad?"

"Not saying that!" he carefully selected his words. "Powerful. She is powerful." The old man winked as he opened the bus door for the approaching guests.

Before Altair could intervene another question, he addressed the approaching group with a cheerful smile, "Welcome back!"

Altair's heavy breath clouded the view of the passing scenery as he pressed his forehead to the window, glaring at the perfection of the aqua waves, which seemed to taunt him with their secrets. His mind twisted between scattered thoughts of Deneb and Vega, as he pictured both of them in uncertain waters.

The waves of pleasant laughter from the surrounding passengers pinched his nerves with each happy giggle, as he tore his eyes away from the window remembering treasures of his own. He dug within his bag, carefully pulling Deneb's journal from what seemed like sacred confines.

The worn leather of her simple journal slid under his rough fingertips, and for a moment, he thought of the first time he touched her hands, pulling her through the sweaty crowd at the party in Marseille. A reminiscent smile crept upon his face as he danced through is memories of her. The pages, all so sacred, contained the only thing he had left of her. He flipped slowly past scribbles and shapes haphazardly drawn upon the pages, seeking a plain sheet to jot his next entry. He smiled to himself, pressing his fingers to the next clean page, and just as he was about to write about his day, curiosity overtook him. He flipped back a page and began reading.

Dream:

An enchanting green chariot is traveling down the streets of Rome towards a lavish party. A beautiful fountain captivates all, and somehow I am at the party, but no one sees me. A mighty lion has been sent through time to comfort me. Above the lion is a beautiful circle of golden stars. Despite the oddities of a lion being at a party I am more concerned with why I cannot see the colosseum, I thought it was visible from everywhere in Rome.

Something looms here, a black and white snake, equally balanced of good and evil. It is sitting idly waiting for a lock of some sort to become opened so it can rule once more. I leave and speak with a royal man, who knows a lot about the gold hidden here. I look at his palace and see a sign that looks like "Di Villa?" I try to scream for Altair, to tell him where I am, and how to find the gold, but he cannot hear me. I point to the water, and tell him to find the gold, trade it, and free me.

Her words looped through his mind as he thought, 'When did she have this dream? Whose gold was he now seeking, and what would it be traded for?'

"Alright everyone, we are nearing our drop off point. I sure hope you all had as good of a time as I did today. Enjoy your visit here on the magical island of Crete."

Altair sat idly watching the happy passengers file off the bus, sneering at the normalcy of their vacations while a watchful glance caught his eye in the rear view mirror. He quickly resumed a transparent smile, as big as his emotions would permit, while grabbing his bag.

"Not so fast you," the old man said like a parent catching his child sneaking in at 2 am.

He paused, somewhat happy that his frustrations had been noticed.

The old man turned slowly, pulling his cane up beside him for balance to help him stand.

"You looked pretty upset by whatever you were reading back there. I want you to know that long ago, I also lost someone, and though she may not be with me in the way I was once used to, I know she is still there. The point is, don't ever give up," he said while wrapping his weathered palm around the sparkling emerald eyes of the wooden lion perched upon his cane.

"I won't."

CHAPTER 5

Altair excitedly walked up to the front desk, hoping to thank the old man for his recommendation to take the day's excursion, only to be disappointed by the vacant chair. He patiently waited, observing the neatly organized desk and perfectly placed lilies sitting on the counter, as a familiar voice came from behind.

"Altair!" Stan piped with abnormal excitement. "How was your day? Hungry? Let's go get something to eat and discuss over lunch shall we?"

45

Altair's suspicions were quickly outweighed by his hunger as he shifted his thoughts from what had Stan in such a rambling stupor, to that of a delicious Mediterranean lunch. Stan placed an appeased arm around his shoulders, guiding him away from the hotel lobby and out to the terrace.

"I thought we could try out this place just down the street. I read that they have an incredible menu and a fantastic view of the sea."

As they made their way down the old cobblestone sidewalks of the historical town that Stan would normally be giving history lessons on, Altair began to wonder what had Stan in such a hurry, and more importantly, where was Vega?

"Ah, here we are." Stan glanced up at the small wooden sign, hanging from an iron rod. The old archways gave way to a large open terrace bathed in golden sunlight as they made their way to a simple wooden table.

Altair's eyes traced over the vines winding around the room, sweeping over archways and down into beautiful old pots situated around the restaurant. "What a place," he smiled while turning his head to look at the soothing waves.

"I've heard great things about this place! I read that they make their own olive oil, and grow their own herbs and vegetables too. I love a good fresh meal," Stan smiled as he flipped open the menu.

Before Altair could ask about their day of diving, Stan began with questions of his own.

"So, what did you get into today? I'm curious to hear all about your adventures and sightseeing!"

The waiter placed a basket of freshly baked bread, paired with divinely fragrant olive oil, between them on the table, creating a pause before Altair's response. Stan wrinkled a nervous eyebrow and resumed his questioning, "Something the matter?"

"*Is* something the matter?" Altair returned the question, observing Stan's jittery demeanor.

A long exhale settled his tense shoulders as he hung his head, "I've never been good at keeping secrets."

"Is everything okay? What happened today Stan?"

He nervously grabbed a piece of the warm bread, and rested it on the plate of oil as he gathered his thoughts.

"Well, something happened with Vega today." He quickly continued before Altair could react. "Everything is fine, but she had a pretty jarring experience while diving today, and she would barely talk to me about it when she came back up. The only thing she wanted to talk about was finding that diver that we saw at the restaurant the other night, and something about needing to find gold and treasure for some kind of trade."

"A trade?" alarm flexed within his voice. "Wait, I thought you were diving with those guys today? Did that not happen?"

"No. Honestly, I think she was upset that he went on to do something without her, and just wasn't in her right mind from the moment we set foot in the water. She said that when she went to his room this morning he was already gone, and only a note remained stuck to his door. It said something like, "Big opportunity came up, let's meet another time."

"Ah that's too bad. She seemed so excited to spend time with him."

Stan leaned across the table with wide eyes. "Altair, in all of my years of diving I've never experienced anything like what happened today. I seemed to get her back into somewhat high spirits when I pointed out an old underwater cave, which was so exquisitely pristine and beautiful. Fish were floating around us in an electric swarm of orange and red and then, as odd as it sounds, I kind of lost her in the sea of fish. They matched her hair precisely and there were just so many of them. I grew nervous and swam closer, but at that point, she was already entering the mouth of the cave. Then, as if a vacuum were inside of it, she was sucked into the darkness with one mighty pull." He teared up, trying his best to contain the emotions that were shaking his voice.

". I....I.....there was nothing I could do, it just swallowed her. The cave was so murky; I could barely see a thing, but I could feel something unnatural there, like electricity within the water. Thank goodness I didn't swim any further, because if I would have swum just a few feet more I would have gone over what looked like a deep drop off into sheer darkness. I took one fearful glance towards it before high tailing it out of there. This pit -- it looked almost alive as it spiraled down into a black hole of powerful water... In all of my years of diving I have never seen anything like it."

"Well, how did you get her back?" Altair gripped the table in both anticipation and anger.

"I used the cave wall to guide me out, fearful that the black hole would suck me down too, and just as I was about to lose hope that I would ever again see Vega, there she was, floating just outside of the cave. It was as if it had sucked her in, decided it had seen enough of her, and spat her out to where she started. It was so bizarre, and terrifying. I... I...."

"It's okay," Altair wrapped a comforting hand around Stan's shaking forearm.

"She walked out of the water just fine, but kept talking about needing to find gold. I couldn't understand what she was talking about. I think she was delirious."

"Where is she now?" Altair nodded towards Stan's soaked bread still resting in the pool of olive oil.

He quickly pulled the dripping bread towards his mouth and replied between ill-mannered chews, "She's resting, back at the hotel."

A relieved exhale eased his clenched fist. "Good. Would you be okay with just ordering our food to go, and bringing it back to the hotel for her? I really want to make sure she's okay."

"Of course." Stan seemed more composed now that his secret had been shared.

The waiter collected their order of fish, dakos, and savory spiced pork and disappeared back to the kitchen.

"Do you think she'd want anything else?" Altair questioned his judgment behind the fleeting server.

"I'm sure she'll be just fine with our choices, if she's hungry at all."

Altair reflected on his day, switching the conversation for a moment. "Stan, while we wait for our food, I need to tell you about my day. I really wish you and Vega had been there with me, it was the oddest day I've ever...." He paused, retracting the remaining words of his sentence. "Well it was an odd day. I decided to take a bus to the palace of Knossos and I met an old man who used to be a tour guide at the palace, and he decided to walk with me. We walked for what seemed like hours through ruins of the palace, as he showed me remnants of beautifully painted frescoes and pottery. Contrary to the other vibrantly colored rooms, he led me into this hauntingly barren part of the palace called…"

"The hall of double axes?" Stan smiled at his anticipatory answer.

"Yes, the hall of double axes. There were these symbols that really struck me, and apparently the symbol of this double axe represents the labyrinth of Crete," Altair straightened his posture as he shared what he thought was a new idea.

"Yes, people have suggested that throughout the years, they also say that the grand architect of the labyrinth was affiliated with the God of blacksmithing, art, and magical creations." Stan leaned across the table and said in a whisper, "Some even say that his creations could come alive, and that is why no one could find their way out. Every time the seeker found what they thought was the exit, the walls would change."

"The old man told me a similar tale," he said while fidgeting with the ring around his finger.

As if Stan could read the thoughts of his daydream, he interrupted. "Legends say that Daedalus' powers came from a ring which allowed him to transform and awaken the lions standing at the palace gates, and transform any other object of steel, gold, or stone."

"Interesting." He smirked at the thought of awakening stone lions with just a twist of his ring.

"So, what else did you discover today?" Stan asked.

"Well, interestingly enough," Altair leaned in as the volume of his voice shrunk to the level of secrecy, "there was a snake goddess who was once worshiped on this island."

He paused for a moment, waiting for Stan to interject a factual tale, but then continued, given his attentive silence.

"This Goddess of the Sea is always depicted with two snakes in her hands. The old man suggested that these were never snakes, but rather currents of energy, or conductors of some sort..."

"My, oh my..." Stan whispered to himself as Altair continued.

"...which got me thinking of Deneb with the Vajra and the crystal."

"How do you know about the Vajra?" Stan questioned.

"Vega told me about it. Seems a lot happened while I was... away. She said that Deneb was able to use the crystal and the vajra to create enough energy to somehow project her through time, and open some kind of doorway."

"Yes, well, it would make sense that the snake goddess would be affiliated with energy," he exhaled at the magnitude of his spinning thoughts. "We have so much to talk about."

"Well, would it be possible that Deneb... you know, being part of the water and all, could be this Snake Goddess of the Sea?" he said in a barely audible whisper, as he watched for any judging eyes.

"As crazy as it sounds, it could be possible. It seems that with her tools, she was often able to bend time, and who knows, maybe she was once right here, long before this present time."

Stan observed the dismay spreading across Altair's face. "Something the matter?"

"Hearing you say that just reminded me of how far away she really is, and if she *is* somehow back in time, then she is even farther away than I thought."

Stan laughed, "Well, if you know Vega and Deneb like I do, you'll quickly realize that they are separated neither by time nor space. It is energy that connects them."

Relief slowly eased the muscles of his face allowing for another question, "So then... what do we know about this Goddess of the Sea?"

Stan gulped another thirst-quenching mouthful of water before responding, "The stories I've been told about the water creature called Melusine, originate from France and tell of a woman who was once human, but was turned into a two-tailed mermaid. Once she was spotted in France, she fled to the lost island of Avalon, where the Arthurian stories began. Stories link her with two magical rings, which have yet to be unearthed. These rings are not typical rings, just like the sword that was cast on Avalon was no ordinary sword," Stan gleamed in delight as he spoke of the golden tales of King Arthur.

"Why would this half fish, half woman...creature, possess two rings? If tales of her originate in France, then are the two rings from that area as well?" Altair absentmindedly twisted his ring around his finger as Stan continued.

"Well, no one knows how she came to possess the rings, but throughout history there are many tales about magical rings with powerful sigils. After all, the power of a ring does not come from its materials but rather the intention with which it is sealed. The ring itself represents the circle of creation, the beginning and the end, all in one continuous flow. Have you seen the symbol of the serpent eating its tail?" Stan stepped aside from his train of thought.

"I have," Altair simply replied, awaiting the continuation of the story of Melusine.

"The symbol is called ouroboros, and it originated in Ancient Egypt. It signifies eternal life; the cycle of rebirth and reincarnation. The snake is growing by feeding itself, while killing itself at the same time. As I see it, things do not perish, they simply become something else; a new incarnation of the same soul, a new cycle, time and time again, until they are free from the hunger… the karma. So, the image of the ring frequently symbolizes eternal love and eternal cycles, throughout history."

"Interesting. Sorry, can you go back to the inscriptions on those rings? You said the power of the ring rests within the seal on the ring… what does that mean exactly?" Altair stroked his dark beard, created by the lethargy of his mourning, which he had now grown to like.

"Right. Well, as with most powerful ceremonies that deal with creation, there is often a god or goddess being called upon, and some people have said that when certain totems were created in the name of something, (or someone) that their energy became infused within the object. So, there are many legends of magical rings created and sealed with the mark of someone or something. Some rings are said to provide passage into the realms of the guardians, and even allow entrance into the heavenly markets."

"Markets?" Altair wrinkled his brow.

"Sorry, markets are a part of Chinese astrology and star charts; they divided the sky up into different parts, resembling a wheel. You would know it here in the western world as the zodiac. Anyway, one part of the wheel is associated with the heavenly market enclosure, which can be found by looking at the different constellations. Now… one of the parts of this wheel is associated with Corona Borealis, or the crown constellation where we think Deneb is. According to myths, this exact market is associated with a prison of sorts."

"So you think that one of these magic rings can get us entrance into the market, or the labyrinth where Deneb is being kept?"

53

"I think this ring has something to do with opening the door to her. I just don't know how." Stan chuckled as he considered their conversation, "Do you know how crazy we sound?"

Altair bashfully dropped his head into his hands, as a small laugh escaped, "I think by acknowledging that it sounds crazy that makes us less crazy, right?"

"Sounds good to me," Stan smiled as the waiter placed their to-go bags on the table.

As the two of them headed back to the hotel Stan continued his story, "I think all of this is related, Altair. I don't know how yet, but I think that this sea goddess is the same as Deneb, and somehow, long ago, she had two magical rings and made sure that they were protected. If we could find the rings, or even one ring, we could gain entrance into the 'labyrinth' where she is trapped."

"So, I have a theory... I think that the labyrinth is not an actual maze, but a place in time that she is stuck in," Altair gauged his sanity for a moment.

"Well, if that is the case, then we need to find these rings, and see what doors they open." Stan stopped just outside of Vega and Altair's room. "How about you and Vega get some rest and if you're up for it, we can meet for dinner. Otherwise, I say we meet back up in the morning and decide on our plan."

Altair nodded in agreement.

"Knock, knock," Altair opened the door just a crack, poking a curious eye into the room.

"Vega? You here?"

"In here." A faint whisper piped from the darkness of her bedroom.

With food still in hand, he slowly walked toward the tornado of sheets she hid beneath.

"Hey! I heard you had quite the day today." He sat down on the bed, silently questioning the whirlwind of blankets tossed around her.

"What's that smell?" she whispered in disgust.

"Oh right, I brought you back a bunch of food. Well, some of it is for me, but most of it is for you. Fresh cheese, bread, pork, fish," before he could continue, she raised her voice as loud as her body permitted.

"Can you get it out of here? The smell is making me nauseous. Sorry."

"Sure," he quickly moved the food to the kitchen, before returning to see what answers he could pull from her.

"I know you had a hard day, but I need to know what happened down there. What's the matter? Are you sick?" Sadness and concern began to overtake his questions.

Her tired eyes peeked from the blankets, "Everything was fine. Stan and I were just exploring near this cave and then, I heard Deneb. I swear I heard her. I swam into the cave as fast as I could, and then it was as if I was sucked into the darkness of what I can only describe as a black hole. As I fell through it, I experienced intense visions. I saw a colorless garden, barren of life or joy. I could smell the decay of the flowers, which were grey and lacking color. Everywhere I looked, I saw cities turned to dust, and the world collapsing as an empire of darkness arose. I could feel the ground shake beneath me as billowing clouds of smoke began to fill the air, then the crackling sound of a crisp leather whip struck from behind, and as I turned and looked up and I saw… I saw…her."

Painful memories halted her words as Altair reached a comforting hand atop the blankets to where he thought her hand might be.

"Who? Who did you see?" he whispered, aware that the normal tone of his voice made her cringe.

"Hydra."

"Not possible. That just isn't possible Vega. We saw her die."

"It was her. And she was even more terrifying than before. She stood atop a tall dark tower, which looked like it was made of a familiar stone that I know I have seen somewhere before," Vega paused trying to recall where she had seen something of the same diamond hard composition.

"She stood guard atop a tower, surrounded by a slithering iron gate that was both protective, yet alive with her essence. I quietly approached, observing how she seemed to be a part of the castle, the gate, and the darkness itself. Clouds of smoke swirled around her, as the world around me reduced to ashes and darkness. As she sensed my presence, seven shadows slid from her hair, slithering down the side of the tower towards me. It was as if she could sense my fear. The more scared I grew, the closer they came.

Then, the weirdest thing happened, as if that was not weird enough, I saw Deneb. She was not herself though," tears choked the rest of the words from following.

"You saw here there? Altair asked with wide frightened eyes, before regaining his composure. "It's okay Vega, take your time. Tell me what you saw."

"It's hard for me to make sense of what I saw, but... a woman grabbed my hand and pulled me away from where I was, and then I felt like I was back in the ocean. The woman was still by my side, somehow bringing me back to the mouth of the cave where I had begun. Then, two bright flashes twirled around me like strands of Christmas lights. As the light slowed down, I caught a glimpse of what it really was, a tail, or... tails. I called out for whatever was there, trying to see what she was, trying for a moment to just say thank you for saving me, and then I looked at her face and it was Deneb, somehow the mermaid thing was her. I know that sounds crazy, but it was her. I tried to speak, but I couldn't. I heard the words, "find the gold," echo through the water and then as quickly as she had appeared, she was gone."

"We have so much to talk about Vega. I had quite a day too. Nothing like yours, but I learned about a creature similar to what you mentioned. The Goddess of the Sea is worshiped all over this island, and within her hands she holds two things that look like snakes, but we believe it is actually currents of energy. Stan and I think that Deneb was, or is, this same Goddess of the Sea. She is also said to have had in her possession two magical rings that allowed entrance into heavenly enclosures, or realms."

Vega painfully scooted herself up in bed, tearing the blankets away from her eyes, "Heavenly Market Enclosure you mean?"

"Right. Stan told me that this 'Heavenly Market Enclosure' is also associated with the Crown Constellation, or as we know it, the labyrinth. If the legends are correct, then maybe there is a way to enter using the rings."

"Well, while you were under Hydra's spell, Deneb and I actually travelled back to the time of an ancient Chinese dynasty and entered into the real Heavenly Market Enclosure. We didn't bother to look and see if people were

57

trapped there, but what we did find was a land of people worshiping Hydra. It was in that time period where I met Lan, and realized that he had traded my safety in exchange for his servitude to Hydra. He told me that at some point in time I was captured by her, and that he had offered his freedom to save me…changing from light to dark every 500 years. If it weren't for him, we would have never made it out of there…a giant tidal wave rose from the sea and nearly swallowed us all. It had to have been so painful for him to change like he did, both mentally and physically. Could you imagine? Trading all of that to save someone?"

"Seems that energetic trades have been a thing for centuries," Altair whispered, somewhat to himself.

"Remember the dream that you told us about, where you saw the symbol of the labyrinth inside of an oyster shell? I was thinking about that, and it does resemble the symbol on the gold coins that Stan showed us.

"Right!" Vega perked up a little at this reminder of her task. "When she told me to find the gold I immediately knew that it was for a trade. So… say we do find this gold that she spoke of; how do we even know if it is going to free her? Which raises the bigger question, who is she indebted to?"

Altair quickly reached for his bag and pulled out Deneb's journal, "Here," he hastily flipped through the pages until he reached her final entry. Realizing Vega's lack of energy, he summarized the last passage for her.

"Her very last entry detailed a dream that she had, which took place in Rome. She wrote about a well beneath a circle of stars, and it says some of the gold is buried there."

"Some of the gold?" Vega raised her eyebrows, already picturing the global treasure hunt ahead of them.

"Ever tossed money into a fountain before? It never stays there. Oh, and one more thing…" he cringed at the thought of speaking her name once more.

"The Goddess of the Sea holds within her grasp the powers associated with DNA, revival of life so to say." He paused before continuing the troubling sentence. "In particular, she is noted to have the ability to revive serpents. If you think about it, it makes sense given the symbol for DNA, and the uncanny similarity between the two waves of energy coming from the Sea Goddess' hands."

Vegas face crinkled in puzzlement. "The only serpents that I know of are Draco and Hydra, and I know she would never bring her back."

Altair shamefully said, "I think that she may have brought her back."

"What? There is no way! Deneb would never do that!"

"Well, we don't know what all was traded. Maybe she did it for a greater good."

"Greater good? So, you think that somehow Deneb traded her freedom for this prison, brought Hydra back into existence, and somehow still owes gold to someone? She must have traded something substantial for all three of those things!"

"That is quite the combination, I know, but that's what we are seeing now in the present time. Maybe she traded things throughout the course of history, and they all just added up."

As the concept of time invigorated her mind, a spark of hope flickered in her soul, contrasting her next sentence. "So you think that Hydra is back?"

"I said that - didn't I?" Altair cast an analytical eye at the suddenly excited girl, now sitting next to him on the bed.

59

"If she is back, then *he* is back." Her once love-sunk eyes brightened as she stood up from the bed.

"We don't know that Vega." Altair attempted to reel her back to reality as the determined girl dashed around the room throwing clothes into her bag.

"What are you doing?" Altair stood up as she yanked a shirt from beneath him.

"I'm packing for Rome, and you should do the same."

"Rome? Now? We can't leave; Deneb is here in the labyrinth!" He nervously twisted his ring around his finger.

"And we'll never get her out of there without the gold. We need to start with the clues, and the clues take us to Rome." She placed her hands on her hips, admiring the stellar job of quick packing. "Go tell Stan of our plans. In the meantime, I am going to find those treasure hunters. We are going to need some assistance."

Altair observed the suddenly galvanized girl while he carefully selected his words. "We need to be smart, not impulsive. We don't know if the gold is in Rome, and we certainly don't know a thing about these treasure hunters. I personally don't think it wise to share information about our journey with these strangers."

"We don't have to tell them why we're after it. We just need to convince them to help us. Maybe we offer them a split or a trade of some kind," she rambled, justifying her thoughts.

"Okay, but they are never to know about Deneb, or the reasons behind our interest in the treasure. Okay?" His wide serious eyes shook up her discomfort, and forced an agreeable answer.

"Of course." She locked eyes for a fraction of a forced moment, before anxiously wheeling her bag towards the door.

"I'll go find Stan. We'll leave after dinner."

"Sounds like a plan." Vega smiled as she pulled open the door.

CHAPTER 6

Golden light surrounded Vega's silhouette, creating a fiery glow around her, as if she were part of the sun that was setting in front of her. Her typical anxiety sank into the rhythm of the waves, as she stood looking out over the restaurant terrace.

"Hey!" Altair slid his fingers over the stone ledge of the balcony, cringing at the lack of calluses on his hands.

"Hey." She replied while keeping her eyes locked on the peaks of gold, rising and falling upon the waves.

"So, did you find your treasure hunter?" he smirked.

"I did." She turned to catch a glimpse of his menacing smile.

"What's with the weird smile?" she asked.

"Nothing." He silently pictured the emerging conflict in her heart.

"Okay, well then why are you acting so weird?"

He locked his answer between clenched teeth while shrugging.

"To return to your question, yes I found him. I told him that we are going to Rome and needed assistance in accessing a few places there. Honestly, I thought it would be harder to convince him but he agreed right away."

"Wait, so he just agreed to leave here and go to Rome with you? Just like that?"

"Yep," she triumphantly smiled.

"Well, that's good... I think."

"Hey you two," Stan cheerfully called from behind, interrupting the line of questions Altair had prepared for her.

His ceaseless, yet refreshing, smile welcomed them as he waved his hand for them to join him.

"I found a table for us; overlooking the water," he nodded towards the restaurant.

"Sounds great, I'm starving!" Vega took off ahead of them toward the patio of twinkling lights.

Stan sprung on the opportunity of solitary time with Altair while she raced on ahead, "I wasn't sure if Vega was delirious when she came up from the water; has her story changed from what I told you?"

"No, it hasn't, and interestingly enough, between her experience and mine we were able to weave our stories together to form some sort of crazy hypothesis," Altair raised an eyebrow awaiting Stan's questions.

"Well... go on," Stan urged.

"We believe that Deneb is locked in the labyrinth, which is also associated with the crown constellation and the Heavenly Market Enclosure. Remember when we spoke of the master blacksmith whose work was said to come to life? We think that somehow he made the rings, which open doors and allow entrance into the labyrinth."

"What about Vega's insistent talks of gold?" Stan kept his voice down as he asked.

"We believe that a trade will need to take place. Vega was right; there is a debt of gold that is owed."

"About time," Vega jokingly huffed from the podium while tapping her foot.

"Sorry about that Vega, seems we got carried away in conversation there for a bit. Shall we?" Stan motioned towards the simply adorned candlelit table.

"Thank you," Stan said with exaggerated politeness, while handing her a silver coin.

"What was that all about?" Vega wrinkled her face in judgement, which quickly disappeared when she saw the delightful pictures of food on the menu.

"I always show gratitude, in every situation," he smiled while placing his napkin upon his lap.

Vega's eyes danced around the romantic whimsical restaurant, admiring all of the happy couples, halting when her eyes met Altair's scowl.

63

"Vega." Stan interrupted.

"Sorry, what were you saying?"

"Altair was telling me of the Goddess of the Sea, and we were comparing your encounter with the known myths. Now, I know it was a hard day, but try to remember... did she have one tail or two?"

"Two." Vega answered immediately.

Stan exhaled before beginning, "She has gone by many names; Melusine, Goddess of the Sea, and now, it appears she has another: Deneb."

Altair leaned in, to shield his voice from the ongoing chatter of the restaurant, "So, this creature... say she did possess two rings at one point in time, when and where would she have gotten them?"

"I've read that this sea creature once lived here on Crete, only appearing to those whom she wished to aid. Perhaps that included the blacksmith Daedalus, and for one reason or another, she safeguarded his precious rings, and took them somewhere to her liking; somewhere safe."

"But where did Daedalus get the rings?" Vega added.

"My theory involves the original god of blacksmithing, Hephaestus, who was the brother of the fire god Apollo. Together the brothers created many great things, and I know I read a legend somewhere telling of rings that they made using Apollo's fire and Hephaestus' blacksmithing skills," Stan said.

Mirroring eyes focused on Altair's hand as Vega blurted out, "Where did you get your ring?"

"Deneb gave it to me. She found it off the coast of France during a dive."

"And the ring that she has, where did she get that ring?" Stan whispered while intently focusing upon the simple band wrapped around his finger.

"We found it together. Well, kind of... It was wrapped around a scroll that we found in a cave in France."

"Goodness gracious!" Stan furiously whispered.

"So, you think that Deneb, as this sea creature, may have somehow gotten these rings long ago and placed them somewhere so that we could find them in present time? I guess now I can see why she would have agreed to become this creature, so she could place the rings where they could be found."

Vega crossed her arms as she continued to puzzle over the story. "Sorry to interrupt, but how could a sea creature move a ring into a cave, located on land?"

"Well, maybe these rings have been passed through many hands."

"Right, but I suppose all that matters is that I have one of the rings, and if it works, then perhaps it can grant me access into the labyrinth."

"You mean us. Grant *us* access into the labyrinth," Vega corrected him.

"And just how do you think you would get there?" Altair rebutted.

"Each one of us was given a key to the doors of time," she leaned in closer towards the flickering light of the candle.

"So, are you telling me that you can get to the same place, using your song?" Altair questioned.

She playfully winked, "Different key, same door."

"Let's get back to our course of action shall we?" Stan said, receiving simultaneous nods of agreement.

"Let's say that the ring you possess, there, on your finger..." he paused while trying to fathom the historical magnitude of the artifact before him. "Right, so, let's say that this ring once belonged to Daedalus, and now, you possess the ability to open doors into the past and even into the Heavenly Market Enclosure, I mean labyrinth, where Deneb is trapped. Say you can do all of that...you both agree that just getting there is not enough?"

Vega immediately chimed in. "When I saw her she said, 'find the gold.' I think that somehow she offered a trade of gold to someone in exchange for her freedom. The shell that I saw in my dream, had the same symbol on it that appears on the gold coins of Crete. I think that maybe there was treasure here, with the same symbol on it, and somehow it made its way off this island. What I wouldn't give to know a pirate right now," she laughed.

"Did someone say treasure?" a handsome sounding voice interrupted their conversation.

"Wow. When I said meet us in an hour or so, you really held me to that didn't you?" Vega nervously laughed.

"And when I said I would be here, I meant it. I always keep my word." He smiled as he pulled out a chair from a nearby table.

"Room for a few more?" he asked, while abrasively scooting a table up next to theirs. A room full of discontented glances shot daggers at his hands as he continued to drag the table closer.

"Hope this doesn't bother you all?" he said with a cowboy smile, as he tipped his old baseball cap at the aggravated viewers.

"Come on boys, take a seat," he invited as he took his place beside Vega.

"No problem at all," Stan sneered, as he eyed the new guests.

"Know how I found you?" he smirked while locking eyes with Vega.

She nervously shook her head no.

"My ears were ringing," country twang mixed with a dialect somewhat unidentifiable cracked through his voice as he devilishly smiled.

"They were?" she fumbled for a normal response.

"Indeed they were," he winked at his buddies, "no one can even *speak* the word 'treasure' without me feeling it; I feel it in my soul!" He laughed while placing an exaggerated hand over his heart.

Stan, noticing Vega's odd incapacity for words, replied, "Well, you're just in time then. We were just discussing our next destination. First, let me introduce myself. My name is Stan, and I have spent a majority of my life in a similar venture as you all, both above and below water. I've been a scuba instructor for many years now, and in my previous lifetime I was an archeologist," he humbly smiled.

The men raised staggered glasses in his direction as Altair remained silent, observing the energy of his new companions.

"I'm Ben, and this here is Lance, and Boone."

All eyes turned towards Altair as he stiffly gazed into the candlelight.

"Ahem," Vega nudged.

"Right. Sorry. Altair," he nodded towards the group.

67

"Alright mate, nice to meet you," Ben said while returning to the matter at hand.

Resting his smile for a moment, Ben looked over the group. "I want you all to know that my crew and I have a deep passion for history, not treasure. We hunt, search, and seek places where important figures may have left behind remnants and every so often, we get our hands on something special. I don't know what you all are after, and frankly, I don't care to know. We are most likely headed to Rome for completely different reasons, but I find it amusingly pleasant that the prettiest girl on the island is headed to the same place as us, so we're happy to assist in whatever way we can."

Vega's cheeks flushed crimson as she scrambled to speak the fleeting words she had been rehearsing in her mind, "We're so happy you can join with us too."

Stan covered her awkwardly sparse words with a fresh idea. "So, cheers everyone. I am happy that like minds can come together in new unchartered territories and uncover everything our hearts desire."

"Let's hope so," Ben glanced towards Vega who sat silently kicking herself for her idiotic response.

As the plates of delicious food came and went, the stars announced themselves across the sky, pulling Altair's attention up to the brightest one.

"What's the matter," Vega nudged, trying to pull his mind out of the abyss it seemed stranded in.

"I'm not sure about leaving here Vega. I feel like I need to stay," he whispered directly to her; shielding his secrets from the rest of the table.

"Trust me, this is the right move. I'll show you more when we get back to the hotel room," she slyly whispered before shifting her full attention on Ben.

Before Altair could ask another question, Vega nodded towards the waiter, who quickly slid the bill presenter off the table.

"Thank you for dinner," Vega smiled while uttering her first confident sentence of the night.

"Wait, What?" Stan's eyes scattered over the table, searching for the bill presenter that he swore had not yet arrived.

"I'm a quick one," Lance winked.

"I wanted to pick up dinner... I didn't even see him drop the check on the table." Stan scrambled for his wallet as if he could change something.

The cold, dark eyed man attentively stood, "Maybe next time."

The warm light of the candles shown like gold upon Ben's face as he locked eyes with Vega. Stan interrupted the love-struck scene before her swooning could get the best of her, "Alright then, seems we should all head back to our rooms and pack. Our flight leaves in just a few hours."

"Yes, indeed," Ben's odd accent slipped through once more as he tipped the brim of his hat to the group before leaving the restaurant.

Vega watched in youthful wonderment as he slipped through the hallway of twinkling branches and out of view. A slight exhale escaped her stiff lips as she snapped back to the present and attempted to gather her thoughts. "Okay, so, it looks like we are all headed to Rome."

Stan remained watchfully vigilant as he studied the variety of emotions emanating from her. "Vega, we have a lot of planning to do. We can't become distracted on this voyage."

As the last trace of Ben's shadow escaped the room, Vega's focus returned. "I know that Stan. Don't think that I'm not taking this seriously. We need treasure to get Deneb back and they are treasure hunters. I know what I'm doing here," she huffed before storming ahead of them.

"Oh my," Stan said with concern.

"Don't worry Stan. I'll keep my eye one her and make sure that nothing distracts her from our mission," Altair patted his back as they exited the restaurant.

CHAPTER 7

Vega's luggage sat neatly packed by the door, as Altair walked into the unusually quiet hotel room. He followed the glow of the solitary light, to the bedroom where she sat, thoroughly still.

"Hey," Altair nervously entered, expecting her head to turn, or at least move in his direction.

"I need to show you something," she said sternly. "Hurry, we don't have much time before we leave for the airport."

"Okay, what is it that we're looking at?" He quickly sat down beside her, attempting to focus his eyes on the same empty wall.

She turned her body ever so slightly towards his, focusing on the simple band around his finger.

"I need to show you how Deneb and I opened portals, and you need to learn to do the same. The person seeking the gold for the trade is not in this dimension; not in this time; at least I don't think so. Once we find the gold, one of us is going to have to get to wherever Deneb is being held, and offer it. If for some reason I'm not here, or unable to travel, I need you to be able to go. You and I are the only ones capable of saving her."

"Now? We're going to try this now Vega?" Altair nervously fidgeted with his ring.

"We have to Altair. This is the only time when we know we'll be together here in Crete and who knows, maybe the doors that open here are different than the ones that open in Rome."

Altair jumped as a gust of wind flung the elegant white drapes into the room, followed by the fragrant smell of impending rain.

"Hurry. Now, where is the crystal?" Vega looked around the room for his bag.

"In the sword."

"Take it out," she insisted. "I think you'll need it."

"But it's hers. That's Deneb's crystal."

"Take it out and hold it in your right hand."

Altair rushed to the sword, cringing as he pulled the crystal from its rightful place.

"Now, place the crystal in your right hand, and wrap your hand that has the ring, around it."

"How do you know what to do?" he frantically questioned as he obeyed her directions.

"I don't. What I do know is that the Goddess of the Sea has energy coming from both of her hands. If the crystal is in one hand, then your source of energy must be in the other, which I'm thinking is your ring."

"And say we do open a door, or a portal, where are we going?" Altair's eyes sprung open as subtle vibrations began to shake within his fists. Before she could answer, he pulled his fingers open.

"Vega! What in the world was that?! It felt like a million buzzing bees within my palms; I could feel the vibration from the crystal seep into my soul, as if I was somehow vibrating at an extremely high frequency."

"Good. That means it's working. I feel the same way when I hum my song," she radiated with a happiness that had only shone from her when she travelled with Deneb, while she nodded for him to resume.

"You didn't answer my question, where are we going?"

"Just focus on the gold, and if our intentions are the same, then we'll be transported back in time to the place where we will find it," she said while relaxing on the bed.

"But there is gold all over the planet Vega. We need to be more specific," he interrupted her closing eyes.

She huffed in annoyance, "Okay, so let's focus on the gold coins that have the image of the labyrinth on them. Focus on those coins and then we will both wind up wherever they are, together. Do you want a blanket or something? You seem really nervous." She pushed the soft down comforter towards him.

"Thanks, somehow that does help," he resumed his fearfully strong grip around the crystal as the rain began to lash upon the glass doors.

"I'm going to shut those real fast okay?" She scrambled to the living room as thunder rattled the doors. The sound of rain spilled in through the open window she had forgotten about in the kitchen, as she called to Altair, "Be right there!"

Her socks slid across the floor as she dashed back into the room, smiling at the peaceful vision of Altair, quietly sitting with his eyes closed, feet on the floor, and fists tightly clasped around the crystal. She scanned the tightly locked doors once more as lightning flashed across the sheets of rain like mirrors sliding from the sky. Soft music slipped through her lips as she quickly laid her head upon the pillow, adjusting it so that she could keep a watchful eye on Altair. She kept her eyes open for a few moments longer, watching his shaking hands struggle to contain the crystal. The lightning danced through the darkness of her closed eyes, as she continued to hum, feeling the electric vibrations stir around inside her. In a moment of curiosity, Vega opened an intrusive eye, hoping to catch a glimpse of Altair's powers. As she slid one eye open, the light glowing from the fire hot band around his finger nearly blinded her, forcing her eyes closed and her lips together. A final jolt of lightening tore through the room, cracking the bedframe and sending Altair back through time. With closed eyes Vega carefully felt around on the bed near the place where he once sat, quickly pulling her hands back when she touched the burnt blanket he had just been wrapped in.

"What in the world?" she slowly opened her eye just a sliver, testing the safety of the room. Tattered fragments of the burnt blanket rained around her like singed confetti as she looked around in wonderment. "I'm right behind you," she thought to herself as she quickly laid her head upon the ash-covered pillow.

Her mind relaxed into the enchanting melody of her song, as the notes of antiquity rained around her. The energy of the peaceful music rocked her softly, side to side, as a hand slowly slid over hers.

"Are you awake my love?" whispered a masculine voice, sending Vega into a combative panic, and nearly capsizing the wooden boat. She furiously blinked, as she adjusted to the blinding sunlight shimmering down upon them. "Where am I?" she demanded while throwing a protecting hand to her forehead, bringing the familiar silhouette into focus. A halo of light basked around his muscular shoulders as his smile gleamed in the twelve-o-clock sunlight.

"Don't get up just yet; you've been asleep for quite some time." He placed a loving hand to her chest while she adjusted to the passing scenery.

74

"For a while?" she questioned while hoisting herself up a bit in the boat, and looking up toward the passing canopies of trees, layered with exotic birds and colorful butterflies. Quiet bliss trickled around them as they slowly pushed themselves down the river Nile, toward their destiny.

"Alexander?" she whispered while watching the muscles built by countless battles, contract with each row.

"Yes my love." His face remained anchored in the direction of the sun as he pulled the oars, one after the other, through the calm crystalline water.

"Where are we going?"

With a humble laugh, he turned his head ever so slightly, illuminating the sun glistening on his sweaty face. "To deliver the gold." He spoke as if to reawaken her to the mission she had slept through.

"Right, the gold." She sat up, more intently now, and focused her attention on the silhouette of a large chest, resting beneath the secrecy of a scarlet cloak.

"Remind me... where are we taking it?" she coyly smiled.

His smile washed from his face as he turned once more, "Every time I watch your eyes close, succumbing to the darkness of sleep, I fear a part of you disappears and returns back to another time where I'll never know you. One day I pray that you will stay here with me, basking in the light eternal."

Sadness twisted with lost memories as she struggled to find the proper response, "Perhaps one day, I will."

A tired smile returned as has he repeated his oft-repeated wish. "Perhaps you will."

Before another question could escape from her, he recapped their journey. "The island is not far from us now. The sun moves us towards the X, see there, overhead?" He pointed at an island just up ahead barely visible on the horizon.

"So, we follow the sun down the river, and when the rays shine directly overhead on those boulders over there, we stop?" She wrinkled her brow, as if she had never seen the tusk shaped island before.

"Yes my love, we follow the lines of light towards the island. These memories will see you once more," he hopelessly smiled.

"I'm sure they will," she smiled.

Rays of golden light glistened through the treetops of the primitive island ahead as Vega grabbed an ore and began paddling. Happiness replaced the wrinkles of sadness aged into his youthful face, as he joined her in synchronous strokes. Lush greenery surrounded the rocky cliff-side as they approached; searching for the trail, they had worn into the land. As they pulled the small wooden boat to shore, Vega's eyes fixated upon the scarlet covered chest as he heaved it from the boat.

"Why do you keep it covered?" she playfully asked while following close behind, right on his heels.

"We are not to look at the chest. You know this." He sternly answered while continuing to climb the rocky path.

She tumbled over her internal dialogue, reframing the many questions she wanted to ask but knew she should keep to herself.

"How many times have we brought this chest here?" she stopped to catch her breath, while looking up at the magnificent boulders lining the winding trail above them.

"Do you not remember bringing it here for the celebration of the sun god? On this day, when the sun burns the longest, we come here and align ourselves with the powers of fertility and fire, and absorb the light from above the well. From this day forth the sun will recede in the sky, day by day, so it is important that we come here on *this* day, and offer our gifts."

A pleasant smile spread across her face as she recalled a moment where she had intently listened to Stan speak about the Summer Solstice.

"I remember now," she said while pondering how to frame her next line of questions.

"Do you remember that the trail narrows just ahead?" he kindly reminded her.

"Of course!" Vega nervously turned sideways, inching along slowly behind him, around the curvy lip of the island. In an attempt to distract herself from the falling pebbles that each step fed to the water below, she continued with her questions.

"So -- we brought the chest all the way up here, and now what? We bury it?"

With a nod, he motioned to the clearing just ahead, bypassing her question altogether, "not much further."

Together they carefully walked around the final rocky turn, toward the sound of rushing water. Puzzled, Vega looked around through the dense greenery that surrounded them, which was devoid of water. Before she could ask about the source of the sound, he place a cautionary hand upon her chest, insisting she watch her step.

"Wait here." He smiled as he cleared away foliage from atop the well, naturally worn in an unnaturally perfect circle.

Vega's eyes opened wide and danced with delight as she inched closer to the gaping hole in the rock, daring to peer inside to the aqua depths below. The sun inched closer to its highest point in the sky, as Alexander stretched a careful hand to the inside of the chest, before quickly closing it again.

"Where'd you get THAT?" Vega whispered as she eyed the familiar artifact sparkling between his fingers.

"I've travelled far and wide to acquire the gold coins of King Minos," he said while tossing it down into the depths of the well.

"Why did you do that?" Heart ached; she watched it bounce off the rocky sides to the water below.

"Patience." He silenced her by nodding towards the watery hole where dashes of light began to flicker.

"She's here!" he whispered with uncontainable joy while running around to the other side of the well to get a better look.

"Who? Who's here?" Vega watched with perplexed eyes as the familiar lights of Melusine stirred beneath the waves. Her enchanting eyes squinted through the surface of the water up to the unmistakably recognizable fire red hair above.

"Why does she look at you like that?" he crossly asked, while stepping back abruptly from the well.

"I don't know. Why did you throw that coin to her?" she stammered back.

"Not now. There isn't much time," he returned his gaze to the sun and then back to the well, while grabbing hold of Vega's hand. Rays of sunlight slowly spread across the island, creeping toward the shadowy depth of the well as he squeezed her hand in a moment of anticipatory excitement.

"Are you ready? The portal is about to open," he whispered as the sun moved into alignment above the well.

"Yes" Vega uttered in sincere shock while the majestic transfer unfolded before her eyes.

Beams of golden light surged through the well, reflecting off the rapidly rising water of the Nile. The ground began to shake beneath their feet as the nearly blinding tunnel of light illuminated the porcelain hand reaching up from the well. Alexander reached his hand to hers as she pushed a large object to the surface. His face lit with glory as he locked eyes with the carefully receptive creature, and pulled the heavy metal plate from her fingertips. As the sun continued to inch across the sky, the water began to slowly recede, replacing the once brilliantly illuminated water with emptiness. Alexander's gaze remained fixated on the heavy metal plate resting within his triumphant palms as Vega's frantic eyes struggled to find the remnants of the portal.

"That creature," she interrupted his silent victory; "I've seen her before."

He slowly turned while heaving the metal plate under his arm, "Do you remember when I met you on the shores of Atlantis?"

Vega smiled, recalling what still remained as only a dream in her mind, "I do."

"When we travelled on my ship, back to my land, you used your song to shorten the time it took to transport us there. Although, when we arrived we were not alone. Somehow your song had resonated through the water and triggered something within that creature," Alexander paused, noticing the discontent on Vega's face.

"She is not a creature; she has a name."

He awaited the correction.

"Melusine, her name is Melusine."

79

"Okay then, we call her Melusine. After that point she continued to follow me every time I travelled through the sea, and one day, when no one was around she called to me, and I answered."

"What did she say?" Vega whispered, wondering if somehow Deneb had told him of the future.

"She said that if I could acquire the gold coins of King Minos from the island of Crete, that she would show me how to open the portals of time."

"And that, right there..." she motioned with wide, astonished eyes towards the now seemingly normal well, "that was the portal?"

He solemnly nodded while returning to his story, "Her only demand was that I give her gold coins each time that we met, and that we meet here, at the well."

"Wait, but why today? Why this hour?" she wrinkled her eyebrow, reminding herself for the first time how long she had been away from the present day.

"Today is a celebration to the sun god, and marks the day when the light outweighs the darkness and overturns the wheel."

"Right! The wheel!" Vega said, while trying to remember the precise directives of Stan's conversation on the 'wheel of the year.'

"Each year when the sun aligns over the well, we are promised rising water, rain, and fertility. This date denotes the perfection of the sun above, water below, and perfect balance of elements in between. I travelled far depths to find the gold of King Minos, and every year I return here on this day, offering coins to the two tailed lady, in exchange for a gift."

"A gift?" Vega eyed the metal plate hoisted up under his arm.

"In the beginning… there were more portals to open."

"Wait, so, there is more than one well? Or there is more than one portal?" Vega scrambled for words as anxiety overtook her.

"The wells *are* the portals my love, and in the beginning that was all that I sought. Once she opened the last portal to a place called Franca, I learned of the plates, and I wanted more. Trust me when I say, the plates of Apollo are worth their weight in gold."

"What is that shape etched into the metal?" She struggled to maintain her vision while eyeing the strange heavy plate.

"This is the Egg of Cygnus," he beamed, while heaving the heavy plate in front of his chest, revealing the unique carving.

"What is that? An egg?" she struggled to articulate the questions racing through her mind.

"It is." He smiled as pleasant splatters of rain began to fall around them. Each refreshing drop outweighed the next until the rain parading around them in blinding sheets making Vega realize the collective magnificence of the drops.

"Alexander?" she called out to the silhouette, now fading behind the watery wall surrounding her.

CHAPTER 8

"Vega?" Altair rattled her arm as he shook her awake. She sat up, scattering the remnants of the burnt sheets as she returned.

"What happened to you?" she winced in pain as she retreated to the pillow.

"What happened to *you*?" he frightfully looked at the sickly, pale girl.

"No, I asked you first." She coughed, while closing her tired eyes. She waited, listening to his heavy boots pace the room.

"We were only gone for fifteen minutes! How in the world?" his breath quickened as Vega painfully found words to calm him.

"Time is different there, than it is here."

"Where?" he instinctually blurted out before considering her condition.

"I'm sorry, you don't have to answer that," he exhaled, while trying to collect his thoughts.

"Let me tell you about what just happened! So, you know how we were both sitting here on the bed, and remember, we both agreed to focus on the gold. That's what you said, "focus on the gold" and we would both wind up wherever it was... together." She could hear the anxiety quickening his already shaken voice.

Her eyes remained closed as she calmly muttered, "mmm hmm."

"Right, so all of the sudden this simple ring, you know,... the one here around my finger; it became fire red and began glowing as if I had put it in a forge or something! Only, the light from the ring began to circle around me like a halo and I felt like I was inside of this bubble of light that was rapidly spinning, until all of the sudden -- there I was."

He paused, waiting for the usual interjection of opinions, but his recitation was followed by only silence. "So, like I was saying... there I was standing in a dark hallway of what I can only imagine was a castle. The thick grey stones loomed around me in stark silence as I pressed on toward the glowing flames at the end of the hallway. As I quietly approached the torches, I clearly heard the echoes of voices, and I realized I was not alone. As silently as possible, I peered through the arched doorway, looking down to the grand town hall below, where an election was taking place.

I listened intently as several judges who seemed to be members of some kind of council, took their seats upon a dais, and cast their votes on some kind of treaty. Then, as if someone had punched me in the stomach, I felt the rush of a secret within my gut. I knew that one of the men on the council was a knight, and that he had made his way into the council to overthrow the system. While the focus of the room remained on the council, something else caught my eye; a series of shadows moving through the arches, around the upper terrace where I stood. One shadow ran to the next, and then to the next, and then… a colossal man cloaked in shadowy emerald handed me four metal plates and told me 'the job was done.' Together we fled the castle and mounted our horses, disappearing into the depths of the forest."

"Wait, metal plates?" Vega forced the words from her aching lungs.

"Yes, and they were not typical metal plates by any means. These were hand forged, hand crafted metal plates with detailed drawings etched onto their faces."

"Where did you take them?" she painfully pushed herself up so she could look directly into his eyes.

Altair rushed to the kitchen to get her some water, hoping it would somehow ease her condition. His thoughts tumbled around in his mind, as he struggled to recall where they had actually taken the plates. He held a glass to her quivering lips, helping her to take a small sip of water, before continuing.

"There was a group of us; some came from the castle, and the others waited for us in the forest. Together, we rode for miles until we came to a cathedral with two pointed towers,

84

rising up toward the full moon overhead. I stared up in wonderment at the sheer beauty of the church, as speckles of rain began to fall. We silently walked toward the heavy cathedral doors, and as I reached for the iron handle, something yanked me back to the present. I don't know why or how, but somehow I was just sent...back."

"The plates, I saw them too, when I traveled. They date back to a time far beyond our original thought, back to the time of Apollo."

"Apollo? Like the Greek God of Fire and the Sun, Apollo?" Altair asked, somewhat in disbelief.

Vega corrected him, "I thought that Apollo was the God of Music and Healing through tones?"

While each silently contemplated their likeness to the ancient deity, a swift knock came from outside the door. Stan's friendly voice called, "Hey kids, I'm going to run a quick errand, I'll meet you down at the car in a half hour. Okay?"

Awkward, yet relieved, glances shot between the two as Altair replied, "Sounds good Stan. See you down there!"

"Are you going to be okay, you know, to travel tonight?" Altair cautiously whispered, weary of Stan's lingering presence.

"I'll be alright," she smiled while circling back to the fusion of their two stories.

"So, the plates of Apollo, what were they used for when you saw them?"

"Well, nothing, I only helped with getting them out of a castle. I don't really know what they would have been used for, or why we were bringing them to a cathedral." He paused, realizing for the first time that perhaps they had a value greater than any currency. "What did they do when you saw them?" he asked, hoping that Vega's experience held the answers to their questions.

"I traveled to the time of Alexander the Great, and we sailed down the Nile to an island, carrying a sacred chest of gold. We hiked along tight and winding trails until we came to a well… and, you are never going to guess in a million years what happened next. As the sun rose directly overhead, the Nile began to rise, and then Melusine appeared." Vega paused to take a breath as Altair grabbed her hands, in anticipation of her next sentence. She exhaled slowly while locking eyes in their shared heartbreak. "Alexander threw one of the gold coins into the well, as if offering her a token for her service, and then…" Tears began to overflow from her eyes as she recalled the vision of Deneb in her fishlike condition.

"It's okay Vega, continue when you're ready."

"During the fraction of time when the sun shone directly upon the well, there was an opening, for their exchange. He called it a portal."

Altair contemplated the precise timing of such an exchange. "What happened when the portal was open?"

"She reached her hands up through the water and handed him a metal plate," she whispered while simultaneously questioning the nature of their entangled stories.

"Then what?" he gripped her sweaty palms within his.

"Then the portal closed and it began to rain." She remained expressionless as the stain of the story melted into her mind.

"That was it? It just began to rain and then you were back here?" The anticlimactic ending loosened his grip on her palms.

Her stoic eyes glazed over as she recalled his face once more. "One more thing. He said that was the last of the plates and that all of the portals had been opened."

"So… the well… it was the portal?" he tried to keep up with the quickly moving tale.

She nodded in solemn agreement, "Yes, the wells are the portals."

"Wells? So there is more than one?"

"Seems like it," she pushed herself up on the pillow beside him. "You know, I can't help but wonder, if he had been throwing the gold coins of Minos into the well on that island, wouldn't she have it all by now? What gold are we supposed to retrieve?"

"Good point," Altair's mind remained consumed with the metal plates.

"What is it?" Vega brought his attention back to present.

"I find it odd that the men that I rode with spoke in French. Do you think that they spoke that way because it is my native tongue, or do you think that perhaps I was in France? The cathedral did look awfully familiar."

"If the portals are wells, then maybe there was a well somewhere within the cathedral and somehow they all link together? I don't know." Vega mused.

"Do you think that our Goddess of the Sea was somehow there, moving the plates from one location to the next?" Altair asked.

"I honestly don't know what to think at this point. I am sure she has something to do with moving these plates from one-time period to the next, but why? What is so important about these plates?"

Altair frantically looked towards his watch in a sobering moment of limited time, "We need to get moving! Stan is probably waiting on us!"

Altair threw a courteous arm around Vega, and attempted to shield her from the rain as they darted through the pelting drops toward the umbrella toting man standing next to the taxi.

"Altair and Vega?" the man hurriedly asked while opening the door to let them in. Stan's warm, pleasant face greeted them as they pushed their way into the back seat of the cab.

"Ah, good to see you both," he gleamed with excitement while looking at the rearview mirror. "I spoke with our friends, and I believe we are just waiting for one more."

Vega slowly turned around to look through the rear window, longingly gazing at the headlights following behind them.

"The treasure hunters, they're all in the car behind us? Wait, why are there two cars for the three of them?" Vega giggled as the giant of a man got into the second car, nearly weighing down the back. "Man, Boone is huge."

"Looks like we are all here," Stan informed the driver as they took off into the night. The car remained awkwardly silent, as Vega's anxiety stirred within her. She blurted out, "Stan, have you ever heard of the plates of Apollo?"

His wide, frightened eyes hushed any further questions, as he looked to the driver, then back towards her. "Perhaps we should discuss your questions on the plane."

She shamefully nodded, "Of course."

The smell of sea salt rain misted through the air as the cars rolled to a stop outside of the sleepy coastal airport. As others scrambled to grab their bags and escape the discomfort of the rain, Vega watched with hopeless eyes, licking the salt from her lips as Ben emerged from the car behind them.

"Vega?" Altair snapped his wet fingers in front of her face while pulling her bag from the car. "What's gotten into you?" he questioned the soaked girl who may, or may not, have realized how long she had been staring.

"Sorry," she said apologetically while wringing her hair out onto the slick tile floor as they entered the airport.

"Say sorry to yourself; you're the one who is going to be soaking wet for the next two hours," Altair shook his head at the accident she had unknowingly created beneath their feet.

"Kids, this way." Stan waved them over to the ticket counter, as Vega remained unmoved from her visual quest to locate Ben.

"Oh Vega, never would I have imagined I'd see this level of desperation from you," Altair jokingly whispered in an attempt to bring her back to the present.

"Oh please," she playfully smacked his unmoving bicep, nearly slipping on the slick floor beneath her.

"Kids?" Stan's insistent glare quickly shifted at the glimmer of their unexpected friendship.

"Coming." Vega delightfully attempted to push Altair onto the puddle beneath his feet as she presented herself at the counter. Together they slid their ID's across to the ticketing clerk, while continuing to playfully nudge one another, slipping and sliding on the chaotically wet floor beneath them. Like a watchful parent, Stan interrupted once more,

89

"I hope you both get whatever this is out of your systems. We have an awful lot to discuss on the plane."

They uniformly retreated into order, tucking their laughter into the sides of their bitten cheeks. "Everything is fine," Vega replied without looking for Ben for the first time.

As they filed into the comfort of their seats, Altair kept a watchful eye on Vega, ensuring that she was safely tucked between himself and Stan. For the first time he felt a brotherly bond between them, which seemed to dissipate as Ben entered the plane. His liquid eyes entranced her, as a smile slid across his face, which mistakenly could have been in her direction... or not. Altair inwardly cringed at her brimming excitement as he jabbed her down to his level. "He isn't smiling at you; he is smiling at the crowd because that's what men like that do; he's a showman."

"A showman?" Vega briefly smiled at Altair's attempt to dull the glow that her mind had created around him.

"Come on Vega; he's pompous, and men like that, they never settle down. They live for attention. It's what keeps them alive."

"You're just jealous," Vega huffed with a failed whimsical toss of her wet hair.

Altair's silent smile spread while he watched Ben joyfully greet the immediately swooning woman seated next to him. "Wow, a two-hour flight; I'm going to sleep, what about you Vega?"

She shot a childish glare towards the innocent woman, as she answered, "I'm not tired."

As the wheels of the plane folded beneath them, and the shoreline of the island faded, anxiety began to creep through her mind. She pensively watched as Ben conversed with the beautiful woman beside him.

90

"Hey Stan," she leaned in while attempting to occupy her mind from the story it was creating; "can we talk about the metal plates? I want to learn more about what these things are."

"Of course. First let me ask, how did you come to know of the plates of Apollo?"

She shot a permissive glance at Altair before revealing their story, "Well…. something happened while we were on Crete that we haven't exactly told you about." Before Stan could react she continued, "Don't worry, everything is fine. We, just… well, we just needed to figure out what Altair's real gift was."

"Vega?" Stan parentally ceased her rambling.

"Right, so, we conducted somewhat of an experiment." She glanced at Altair seeking equal responsibility for their voyage, triggering Stan to cross his arms.

She exhaled, "We both wanted to learn more about the gold coins of Minos so we did what we needed to do."

"And just what was that?" Stan's arms wound more tightly around themselves, fearing what would follow.

"I used my song to travel, and Altair used the crystal and… well, his ring to do the same."

"His ring?" Stan questioned, while looking at the plainly deceptive band.

Altair intervened, removing the pressures of consequence from Vega. "I needed to learn how to do what they do, and that was the only time that we saw fit to try it. We focused on finding gold, because that is what's needed to save Deneb, and somehow, we ended up in different places."

Stan's arms loosened as he turned towards the seemingly more reliable one. "Tell me, how did you use your ring, and where did you travel?"

"I don't really know exactly 'how' it was used but I held the crystal in my right hand, and then all of the sudden my ring began to glow like molten steel and this ball of light appeared around me, swirling faster and faster until I was just pulled through time."

Stan leaned in intently, whispering his next question. "And just where did you go?"

"It was as if I was just sucked through time and when I opened my eyes I was in the upper terrace of a castle, watching an election of sorts. I watched in silence as a group of cloaked men moved untraced through the upper balcony of the grand hall, and then, a giant man cloaked in green handed me these metal plates and told me it was done. We fled the castle and mounted our horses, which were waiting for us at the edge of the forest, where the rest of the knights stood guard. We must have ridden for hours toward what I remember was a beautifully enchanting cathedral. I looked at the plates, and saw these intricately carved symbols on them."

Vega inquisitively raised an eyebrow at this new addition to his story.

"Wait, you didn't tell me that," she said.

Sensing the hurt in her voice he quickly replied, "I didn't get that far, I was going to tell you but we had to leave."

"Fine." She huffed.

"Anyway, the plates, they had symbols on them; a frog, a dragon, and a snake."

"Wait, that's only three symbols, what was the fourth?" Stan asked.

"I didn't get a chance to see the fourth plate, and for that matter I didn't get to see the inside of the cathedral. It started to rain, and then it was as if I was just pulled back to the present."

"Right, the cathedral! Which cathedral was it?" Stan excitedly whispered while reaching under the seat to pull a book from his bag.

"Well, that's the thing. I believe it was in France, and I know I've seen it before, but I just can't place which one it is."

Vega interrupted his story, "There's more. We believe that this cathedral must have a well somewhere inside."

"Interesting, Vega. What leads you to believe that?" Stan's eyes lit up with wonder.

"For some reason, I travelled a bit further back in time, and found myself sailing down the Nile with Alexander the Great. We docked our small boat on an island, and carried a sacred chest to a well. As the sun aligned directly overhead, he tossed a gold coin down inside of the well. You know, I was relieved that you had taught me about the summer solstice, because I actually knew what he was talking about when he said, "Today is a celebration to the Sun God, and marks the day when the light outweighs the darkness and overturns the wheel." She triumphantly smiled.

"You don't say!" Stan brimmed with excitement while rapidly flipping through his book, deciding which page to show them first.

"Yes, and it was as if the sun over the water had something to do with the ability for us to open the portal."

Stan's fingers slid between the pages of the swiftly closed book, "Portal? What kind of portal?"

93

"Right, we weren't alone on the island. When I looked down into the well, I saw The Goddess of the Sea, otherwise known to us as Deneb. She looked up at me, as if she recognized me somehow, as the water quickly began to rise. As soon as she had the gold coin, the exchange took place. I watched as she pushed a heavy metal plate into Alexander's hands, only this metal plate had the image of an egg on it. When he pulled it from the water, he told me it was the 'Egg of Cygnus.' As you can imagine, questions began spewing from my mouth as I began to rationalize what had just taken place. I asked him about the plates and the portals, and he said "the wells are the portals my love, and in the beginning that was all that I sought. Once she opened the last portal, to a place called Franca, I learned of the plates, and I wanted more. Trust me when I say, the plates of Apollo are worth their weight in gold.'

Then it began to rain and it was as if I was just shot back to present time."

"Oh my," Stan exhaled in contemplation.

"What is it?" Altair reactively grabbed the armrest.

"Altair, what time of year was it when you were in France? Do you remember?"

"It was cold out, and we were cloaked in heavy garments. I remember looking up at the full moon directly overhead as we entered the cathedral."

"Okay and Vega, you said it was during the summer solstice that your portal was opened?"

"Mmm hmm."

Stan scanned through the precise wording of Vega's story, seeking his 'ah ha' moment. His eyes beamed with joy as he reopened the book once more, "Here. The Wheel of the Year.

The Wheel of the Year is broken down into eight segments, originally categorized by solar and lunar equinoxes. Observing the cycles of the seasons has been a celebrated, yet sacred occurrence since ancient times, though the original names and festivals associated have been masked and altered throughout the ages due to various measures. Each festival marks a significant universal cycle, and so, you'll see many holidays reflected today, that fall in line with what I'm about to share with you. The first festival, associated with the winter solstice, is called Yule. During this time, the days are the shortest, and the moon the brightest. The dark and colder days loomed heavily on the people who relied on the sun for many things, including the growth of food. The time of Yule is dedicated to the celebration of the sun, becoming reborn into the sky, announcing its reclaim of the wheel. In many ancient cultures, the holly tree is very sacred, and is said to remove darkness, so tradition would have it that sprigs of evergreen and holly decorated the hearths during Yule, until the day when the light would return. As you can imagine, grand feasts took place during Yule, and in Celtic tradition wine was poured onto the hearths as an offering to the light."

"Like a Yule Log?" Vega interrupted while pulling tidbits of her heritage through to the conversation.

"Yes, Vega, like a Yule Log. Tradition has it that a large log was carefully selected from the forest, and decorated with sprigs of evergreen and holly. Evergreen and holly both hold deep symbolic meanings; the evergreen remains green throughout the year and is associated with immortality, and the holly is a clearer of darkness. Good tidings were assured to those who placed a Yule log in their hearth, and oftentimes, offerings of wine, ale, and cider were poured over the log to help it burn a bit more brightly for the next twelve days. According to some traditions, time actually stood still for the last 12 days of the year."

"Okay, so the first part of the wheel is associated with the full moon, winter, and a grand feast where people drank lots of wine and celebrated the longer days returning, right?" Vega added in her own summary.

"I suppose that's close enough, yes," Stan nodded while turning to the next page.

"Now, February 1st is associated with a fire festival celebrating the return of spring, and honors Brigid, a Celtic Goddess of poetry, blacksmithing, ancient wells, arts, healing, fertility, serpents, and spring.

Here on the wheel you will see it labelled as Imbolc, which some say translates to the old Irish word *i mbolc,* which means 'in the belly.' Now, here is something I think you will find interesting Vega... during Imbolc, holy wells were visited."

"Wells were visited? Why?" her eyes gleamed at the roughly sketched image of Brigid on the page.

"When you think of fertility, you often think of something that can receive, and wells, were often the source of life; deep and full of nourishment for the towns around them."

"Wait, this image of her, why does she have horns on her head? Isn't that evil?" Vega pulled away from the book, pressing her shoulder blades into the back of her seat.

"On the contrary my dear. You see, in Celtic legends there are two main God archetypes, the Sun God and the Horned God who is the spirit of nature, animals, and connection to Mother Earth. If you look closely at some of the older images, the horns are actually antlers, and not devilish, modern day horns."

"Wait. So this festival actually celebrates a goddess who taught blacksmiths how to forge, visited sacred wells, and was connected to nature?" Vega gave her assessment of the festival.

A lusterless exhale escaped Stan. "It is much more than that Vega. This goddess is associated with one of the metal plates I believe."

"Wait? What?" Altair took his eye off Ben for the first time to reply.

"I think that the plates that you kids have seen in your travels correspond to the Wheel of the Year. Think about it!" Stan madly flipped to the next page labeled Ostara.

"The next part of the wheel, Ostara or Eostre, takes place during the spring equinox and celebrates the rebirth of the Earth after a long winter. The symbols associated with Eostre, are the rabbit and the egg."

"Like Easter?" Vega seemingly corrected him.

"Like I said before, you will see intertwined, similarities between ancient celebrations and holidays that you might be more familiar with. The point is, the symbol of Eostre is the egg. Did you not see an egg on the metal plate Vega?"

"I did, but then wouldn't the plates from Altair's journey also align with specific parts of the wheel?"

"Well, I believe so. It's our job to discover which plates are associated with the wheel, and more importantly, why."

"Well, the symbols that I saw on the plates were a frog, a dragon and a snake. You said yourself that Brigid is the goddess of blacksmithing and her festival is a fire festival. So, would she then be associated with the dragon, a fire breathing creature?"

"Perhaps. I do think we should be writing all of this down. Do either of you have something to write on?" Stan looked towards Altair's bag.

As Vega scrambled for a pen, Altair reached for Deneb's journal, knowing that somehow she would be okay with him taking up a few pages.

"Here you go," Altair handed it across Vega's lap.

"I'll take notes." Vega snatched the book, halting it from moving any further.

"Alright then," Stan agreed, unwilling to question her possessiveness.

"Okay, so, we have Eostre lining up with the egg, and Imbolc lining up with the dragon. Well, we have six more plates to match," she rested the pen in her lap attempting to think about the topic that she knew nothing about.

"Let's move through the rest of the wheel and see if anything resonates, shall we?" Stan flipped the page once more.

"Ah, Beltane, one of my personal favorites. This festival takes place between the Spring Equinox and Summer Solstice and is better known today as May Day. During this festival of flowers and fertility, rituals were performed to protect crops, cattle, and people, and to encourage growth for the coming season. Sacred bonfires were set ablaze, producing ash and smoke said to contain protective powers, and tales of old tell of magical songs played on the lyre as people danced around the maypoles by firelight. Holy wells were also visited during this festival, as it was thought that the dew of Beltane brought forth everlasting youthfulness."

"Like the fountain of youth?" Vega intruded on his whimsical tale.

"I suppose, yes. Like the fountain of youth."

"Wow, do you think that maybe one of these plates passed through the actual fountain of youth?" Vega's face lit up in wonderment.

"Haven't you already found it?" Altair privately whispered, referring to her green elixir.

"Let's move on," she smiled as she playfully jabbed his side with her elbow.

"Okay, so, the next we have Litha, otherwise known as the Summer Solstice which takes place on the twenty-first of June. This holiday is exactly six months from Yule, which is the Winter Solstice. This specific day, is the longest day of the year and is a celebration of light and all that is good in the world. As you can imagine, the sun was equated to growth and nourishment of all things, so the day that it shone the longest was surely a day to be celebrated. The full moon in June is known as the 'Honey Moon' as bees are making honey now, and people often celebrated with drinks of mead or honey wine. The Druidic name for Litha means *Alban Heruin* or 'Light of the Shore,' and suggests that the balance between the light of the Earth and the Light of water served some enchantingly magnificent purpose."

"Wait. So, when the sun was shone directly over the well, the portal was opened; do you think that other people throughout time knew about this...portal?" she fearfully asked while silently wondering who all knew about the sacred island she previously thought only belonged to her and Alexander.

"Funny you say that Vega. There are tales of two kings associated with the lighter and darker half of the year. The Oak King is associated with the first part of the year; when the sun shines the longest and governs sky, and then after Litha, he passes his reign over to the Holly King, who oversees the rest of the year; when the days are darker and colder. The Celtic word for 'oak' is 'duir', which means doorway. Also, not sure if this is related or not, but The Louvre also is said to have gotten its name from the French word *rouvre*, meaning "oak tree." So perhaps somewhere among these tales we regard as symbolic fables, there is real magic, and doorways we have overlooked for centuries."

Vega jotted down the words, "oak tree, Louvre, and doorway," onto the page as she yawned.

"Why don't you get some rest," Altair comfortingly patted his shoulder, triggering déjà vu.

"I used to do that for Deneb. She used to sleep on my shoulder almost every time we travelled, did you know that?" She looked at him as if he had just assaulted her.

"I'm sorry, I didn't know that. I just know how tired you have to be, and I thought I would offer my shoulder. Nothing more," he patted his shoulder once more with sympathetic eyes.

"I am exhausted," she smiled with relief while wadding her jacket up into a disheveled ball upon his shoulder.

"Just get some sleep, and when you wake we'll pick up where we left off," Stan humbly reassured.

The abrasiveness melted from the lines of her face as she quickly slipped into slumber. Her breath passed between her constantly moving lips in soft rhythmic movements as Altair whispered over her, "I want to hear more about the plates of Apollo."

Stan smirked at the continuation of their conversation, placing a silencing finger in the air while digging through his bag with his free hand.

"Ah... here. There isn't much documented in modern day literature, but this book was passed down to me by a great teacher and mentor, and inside these pages you'll see his notes and lifework." The apples of his cheeks flushed as he carefully flipped through the worn pages he had viewed so many times.

"I don't know why, but when you spoke of metal plates my mind immediately went here, to a page I've nearly memorized, yet seldom look at these days. I carry this book everywhere I go, and I used to study his words so intently that when excerpts of his studies are quoted, I know exactly where and what page the words are taken from."

"Must have been a great teacher," Altair whispered, cognizant of his tone.

"Indeed he was, as was his teacher before him, and the one before him," he winked as he lovingly placed his fingers upon the aged paper.

Altair squinted as he visually reached over Vega, "What is that? A shield?"

"As you probably know, shields have protected great warriors, kings, saints, and knights throughout the ages. Now pay attention son, because this next part is important. If you look closely, here upon the shield, you will see a familiar image," Stan tapped an insistent finger upon the drawing as Altair leaned in closer.

"What is that? An Eagle?" he whispered, fearful of awaking Vega.

"Precisely. An old legend, seldom written, but passed down through great orators tells of a trade that occurred back in the time of our master blacksmith, Daedalus. He was said to have received a gift from the god Apollo, a simple iron ring created by Apollo and his brother Hephaestus, which was able to breathe life into objects of stone, metal, gold, and iron. He had called upon Apollo in his darkest hours as he tirelessly built the Labyrinth under the light of the full moon, and Apollo answered with a mighty gift. The blacksmith was able to use his ring to create an unending maze, alive with twisted intentions."

"Well, what does the shield have to do with it?"

101

Stan smiled, "I'll get to that in just a moment. Now, once our blacksmith built this elaborately glorious labyrinth, something dreadful occurred. Fearful of losing the secrets of its construction, King Minos seized Daedalus and his son, and locked them both away in a dim and gloomy tower. At that time, the King owned every passage of Crete, both land and sea, so Daedalus had to get creative in order to escape. So, he fashioned a set of wings using the feathers of an eagle and the wax of bees."

"To fly over the sea?" Altair chuckled. "And, where would he get wax?" Altair laughed again.

A satisfied smirk crept upon Stan's face before he answered. "When Daedalus called out for Apollo's help a second time, he was answered, but this time he was offered a trade. He would help the man and his son fly from the tower using the wax from sacred bees and the feathers from an eagle, but they were only to fly on the day of the Summer solstice, when the portals of time were open."

Stan slid his finger along to the bottom of the page and tapped once more. "Here, I think this is what we are looking for."

'Legends tell of eight metal plates made in accordance to the wheel of the year, each plate signifying excellence and sacred immortality. Through these mediums great power was had, held, and transmuted. The Wings of the Eagle, the Lyre of Lyra, and the Egg of Cygnus were of the most powerful of the sun cross.'

"Wait... so these plates... Apollo made them but I don't see how they have anything to do with Daedalus' escape."

"Now, when Apollo and his brother brought forth into existence their molten creations, they decided to bequeath the plates into the arms of the one whom they trusted the most; a mere mortal; Daedalus. In his moments of fleeting hope, he called upon the gods and asked for help, and then as fate would have it, Apollo answered, and gifted him two metal plates. One baring the symbol of a bee, and the other, a shield. The stories of his flight seem to end with his landing on the island of Sicily, and it is there where he built a temple dedicated to the god Apollo."

"The drawing here; it shows an eagle on the shield. Is that to represent protection of the blacksmith?"

"I believe so. Do you understand the power contained within these plates?" Stan whispered, fearful of the listening ears of strangers.

"I... I'm not completely sure I do."

"The wax came into creation via the plate bearing the emblem of the bee, and the metal shield depicting the eagle, offered protective flight."

"So, the plates can come to life. But I can go to the store and buy beeswax, what's the difference between using these plates and sourcing it myself?"

"I don't think you fully comprehend what we are dealing with here. This is not just the wax of bees. Throughout time, bees have been the common symbol of faithful workers; people who would give their lives to save their queen. The bee is merely one of the plates, which symbolizes an eighth of the universal wheel. Can you imagine what would happen if someone got their hands on even one of these plates? It would mean that they control a portion of.... well, the universe and life itself."

"OK. So..., Apollo helped the blacksmith obtain the wax and the safety of flight, but what did he get in return?"

Stan nodded as he continued reading, "Apollo, born on the seventh day of the month on the ancient island of Delos, is

103

said to have been born with a golden sword in his hand, which he used in countless battles. Two dragons, one a male, one a female, often sought his demise, and appear in paintings, statues and stories, battling the sun god. Myths throughout the ages have labelled them as different fiery serpents but I believe Draco and Hydra have always been after the plates, which he entrusted to Daedalus. It is said that an oath was made, and Daedalus swore to Apollo that he would place the plates according to the Athenian calendar into the secrecy of sacred wells, where they would lay dormant until two pearls fell from the grasp of lions into the waters."

"Pearls? Like pearls from oyster shells? Are you saying that two simple pearls reawaken these ancient plates of Apollo?"

"Whether they are real pearls or symbolic pearls, I'm not sure. Additionally, if you look at most Guardian Lions, they have open mouths with immovable pearls inside. These Guardians, still to this day, stand firm at the gates of temples, palaces, and sacred institutions where you will see a male lion roaring and a female lion by its side, with one paw atop her cub. This balance of yin and yang represents the cycles of life, where the female lion is nurturing her cub and inhaling, and the male is exhaling, representing death and letting go. Through their unity and balance they form an immovable coalition, and deep within their mouths you will find their most precious gem, the pearl of wisdom."

"So, you believe the pearls of wisdom are guarded by two lions. Correct? Say we find these lions and are able to remove the pearls from their grasp, how are we supposed to know what wells to drop them in?"

"All good questions Altair; questions I'm afraid I don't know the answers to right now," Stan scribbled a note in his book reminding himself to look up other legends involving pearls.

They both refrained from their impeding thoughts as Vega catapulted into the waking world from some form of nightmare, which left her hands shaking and breath heavy.

Ben paused with the plastic cup of whiskey halfway to his lips, and pulled his eyes away from the red-lipped conversation that had occupied his thoughts for the past hour, and looked over at the heavily breathing girl.

"Everything okay over there?" He stood in front of his seat, demanding an answer for her condition.

Altair protectively leaned forward, shielding Vega's gaze from his. "She's okay, just a bad dream."

"Alright man," he smirked, sensing the hormonal standoff arising between them before sitting down.

Altair resumed his heightened focus on Vega. "Are you alright? What happened?"

She placed both hands to her temples before running her fingers back through her thick red hair. A sigh of composure collapsed her story to a whisper. "I had a dream, but, it felt so real. I was on the back of an elephant, decorated in fine silk and colorful flowers, travelling to see a queen. It felt like I was a prisoner in a way. In front of me was a monkey, guarding four heavy metal plates that were once mine. I peeked at the symbols forged into the metal, and saw an egg, wine, a shield, and....well...the fourth looked blank to me."

Altair grabbed her hand, as if squeezing reassurance into her being. "Then what?"

"I took the plates to what I thought was a Chinese pagoda, and walked silently through a perfectly manicured garden. I followed the sound of trickling water into a grand terrace where a beautiful fountain shimmered under the light of the sun overhead. There, among an army of servants the

105

queen proudly sat upon a throne of onyx. Her long beige dress rippled down the stairs as she adjusted the golden headdress covering the shadows of her hair."

"Child of Lyra, I have waited many moons to see your face. Tell me; are you happy to see me as well?"

I felt enchanted by her majesty, as if her power were something I longed to possess. Words slipped from my tongue as if in a trance, and I answered "I've waited long to see you as well." The black locks of her hair slithered around her beautiful face as she hissed, "Take your place beside the well if you have come here to give me what I've asked for."

"Cautiously I asked her, what is it that you wanted me to bring again?" Her laugh echoed through the temple as she replied, "Spill the pearls into the wells, or everything you love will be taken from you."

"Then I woke up." A tear spilled from Vega's cheek as she tucked herself into the appeasing arms of Altair, which immediately made her uncomfortable.

"Sorry about that." She wiped her eyes, immediately shifting her attention over to the peripheral display of ongoing affection between Ben and the mystery woman next to him. Vega's mind fled into a panicky place where she began to tear herself down with petty comparisons to the vixen. Was she thinner? Prettier? Perhaps she had more expensive luggage or a more established career. As her inner demons began to work up a downward spiral of lashings, Altair interrupted.

"Hey, don't worry about that guy. He doesn't know what he's missing. You're an incredible person, and it's his loss that he won't ever know that. Are you starting to see what kind of guy he is?" Altair jabbed.

She habitually reapplied her lipstick before responding. "I don't know why he affects me this much. I shouldn't feel this bothered by a complete stranger having a conversation with someone else, right?" She smacked her lips together before replying to herself. "I mean, I've only met him once, and we've never even gone out on a date. For that matter, we have never even been alone together. What in the world is wrong with me?"

Stan chuckled, "ahh, young love."

"Not love," Altair quickly corrected his verbiage. "This is infatuation, or from what I see, Vega nurturing the competitive nature of her own psyche."

"Whatever it is, I know I have bigger things to worry about," Vega stated, somewhat annoyed at the upheaval of her emotions.

Stan and Altair nodded in agreement before pressing on to the next topic. "So, while you were sleeping, Altair and I continued our conversation and I think that you might find it interesting to know that the pearls from your dream are extremely relevant to what it is that I believe we are after. I will try to summarize this as best I can to help bring you up to speed. Remember the blacksmith who built the Labyrinth? Well, he had struck a deal with the god of the sun, Apollo, in order to gain sanctuary from his captor, King Minos. Indebted to the fiery god for both his escape and the bestowed gift of his ring, he agreed to fulfill a list of tasks, which included finding safe havens for eight magical plates. The plates of Apollo are said to have been placed in sacred wells scattered across the globe, and on the day when two pearls fall from the grasp of lions into the wells, his plates will awaken."

"Whoa, whoa, whoa, wait a minute. Did you just say two pearls?" She massaged her fingertips over the deep lines of laughter she had only recently began calling wrinkles.

"Vega, you must be careful when you slip into dreams, if that is even possible. If each plate corresponds with a different festival of the year, then that means that we are looking for eight different wells, or better yet eight different portals around the world. If Hydra somehow has found out how to control these portals and open the doors of time… well, I don't even want to think about what she would do with the power contained within the plates."

With crossed arms and an equally annoyed eye roll, Vega said, "I'm a Leo, being careful isn't really my thing."

Altair interrupted. "What if the pearls we're looking for are not within actual lions? Could it be that two people, born under the sign of Leo once protected the pearls?"

"Wait just one minute…" Stan whispered to himself while scanning his memory for a story tucked away. "As I recall, there is a legend. I'll have to see if I can remember it entirely, but it involves tears being turned into pearls."

"Can we get back to the plates here for a moment?" Vega asked while pulling out her pen to take more notes.

"Right, the plates. So far, we have matched the Egg to Eostre, and the Dragon to Imbolc. I personally think of wine and great festivities around Yule, and you said you saw a plate with wine on it in your dream, is that correct?" Stan asked.

"I did. There were four plates with the symbols of the egg, wine, shield, and well, the fourth one looked blank."

"Right, so, while you were sleeping, I explained to Altair the importance of the shield. Let's focus on the legend of Daedalus and his son, who flew safely over the ocean by conjuring the magic of two plates, the shield and the bee. If you look closely, here on the page, you will see the shield has the wings of an Eagle upon it. This symbolizes the bond between the blacksmith and Apollo, and the sworn safety

108

that he provided. Now, I'm not sure what festival pairs with a shield, but perhaps you should write that down and we'll get back to it."

Vega nodded while scribbling down the following:

Yule = wine

Imbolc = dragon

Eostre = egg

Beltane =

"Wait, what was Beltane again?" she paused while scanning her memory, "Oh right, it was a festival of flowers where people played music on lyres and danced around Maypoles." She scribbled the word 'lyre' on the page before moving on to the next festival. "Okay, what's next?"

"After Beltane comes Litha; otherwise known as the summer solstice. On this day, the sun shines the longest and festivals of light take place. During Litha, bees are making honey once more and everything buzzes with creation."

Altair tapped the notebook resting in Vega's lap, "Write down, Litha = bees."

"But we haven't seen a plate with bees on it Altair," she pressed the pen to the paper awaiting his response.

"In the tale of the blacksmith, he used the honey from sacred bees, brought forth by the plate of Apollo. Even though you and I haven't seen this plate in our journeys, it doesn't mean it doesn't exist."

"Okay, fine," she muttered while scribbling the words, 'Litha = bees.'

Now, the next set of festivals begins our journey into the darker half of the year, when the daylight becomes less. On the first of August, the Celtic God of the sun, otherwise known as Lugh, sacrifices himself only to be born again at Yule. The festival is called Lughnasadh, and marks the date of the first harvest. To commemorate the sun god, who sacrificed himself to become something greater, people would collect the blessings of the harvest and create fresh bread, which would physically rise up, similar to the rebirth of Lugh. This festival truly honors the cycles of death and rebirth, similar to the image of the snake eating its own tale."

"Did you say snake?" Altair perked up.

"The snake, as you're learning, doesn't always symbolize something evil. When we get to Rome, I'll show you a particular statue, known as 'Sleeping Ariadne, long called Cleopatra,' this beautiful marble sculpture of the goddess remains a focal point to all who pass by it, however, many look right past what is wrapped around the upper part of her left arm, the serpent. The left side of the body is associated with feminine energy, and the serpent wrapped around her arm symbolizes something more than just a decorative cuff. The snake symbolizes the sacred cycle of universal life, death, and rebirth. The snake eats its own tail, feeding itself while synchronously killing itself. This karmic symbol has been celebrated throughout time as a praise to the cycles of the universe; light and darkness, sowing and reaping, birth and death. I believe our lady Cleopatra, who often was affiliated with this symbol, belonged to the same mystery school that worked not with serpents, but with the energy and the cycles that they represented. Some affiliate the symbols of two snakes with vitality; I'm sure you've both seen the symbol for DNA?"

Vega added to her list, speaking aloud to herself while writing, "Okay so we have..."

Yule = wine

Imbolc = dragon

Eostre = egg

Beltane = lyre?

Litha = bees

Lughnasadh = snake

"Now what?" she looked up at Stan, eager for more enlightening content.

"As we near the second harvest, otherwise known as the Autumn Equinox, a great festival of protection comes to pass. During this time, the berries have been picked, the grain collected, and the people are preparing for the coming months of winter. Gourds of plenty are stuffed with dried nuts, berries, and fruits, as a symbol of thanks to the Green Man of the Forest. The warmth of prayer elevates above the frosty chills of winter, offering thanks for the harvest along with prayers for shielding and protection. The Druids called this celebration Mabon, which means Mea'n Fo'mhair, and honors a man of the forest called The Green Man. During Mabon thanks is given for his bounty and all that has come from the last harvest of the year."

"So... Thanksgiving? You described Thanksgiving." Vega set her pen down once more.

"Remember that what I'm sharing with you comes from civilizations long before you and I."

"Okay, so... Then Mabon it associated with protection through the coming winter months?"

Stan nodded in agreement at the place where her pen sat idly upon the paper, "I'd say shielding is the more appropriate word."

As Vega added the next pairing to their list, "Mabon = shield," Stan continued on to the last festival of the year, Samhain. "Ah, one of my personal favorites," he smiled recalling the chilly autumn evenings of his favorite time of year. "October thirty first, more commonly known as All Hallows Eve, is known in Celtic traditions as the day of the dead, otherwise known as Samhain. During this time, the leaves have completed their colorful cycles and fallen back to the earth from which they came. This festival is not just a celebration of the dead, but also even more, a celebration of their lives. People often set an additional plate at the dinner table, honoring those who have blessed their lives, but who are no longer among them. During the time between All Hallows Eve and November first, the true date of Samhain, the laws of space and time become suspended, and the veil between our world and the spirit world is lifted."

A look of shame lingered on Vega's face as she held her remarks.

"What's the matter?" Altair nudged.

"Nothing, I just feel kind of stupid for not knowing any of this before. I mean, for years I just put on a stupid costume and went out asking people to throw candy in my pillowcase, without ever asking why I was doing it."

"Well, sometimes we do things because it's what we were taught to do. It does not mean that there is anything wrong with how you were raised. You just never stopped to question why you were doing the things you were doing."

"Did you?" she countered.

"No, I didn't either. I believe it's never too late to learn though," he playfully nudged her arm back towards the paper. She smiled, eager to complete their uncovered list, but paused when she realized she didn't know what to write next.

"Hold on. What is the symbol for the last one?" the blank space on the page taunted her with each passing moment.

"Did you know that frogs are among the few creatures able to pass between worlds of water and land? Some say that folklore involving witches spells often incorporated frogs because of their abilities to travel between realms and live in the oddest of conditions. For example, a frog can freeze in the muddy waters of winter and then magically thaw itself out under the warmth of the sunshine. Some say that the correlation between the frog's ability to scale between worlds, and escape death, link it to mystical spells of ancient lore. If I were to place any of the symbols you've seen with the festival of Samhain, it would be the frog."

"Okay, so that's it, right?" Vega gave the complete list a once over.

Yule = wine

Imbolc = dragon

Eostre = egg

Beltane = lyre?

Litha = bees

Lughnasadh = snake

Mabon = shield

Samhain = frog

"Okay, so now that we know the times of the year that are associated with these magical plates, it still doesn't answer the question of what the plates actually *do*, and better yet, where they *are*?"

113

"Right, when we get to Rome, there are a few places that I want to visit. Specifically, the overlook from the Dome of St. Peter's Basilica. It is something you need to see firsthand in order to fathom what it is we are working with here. Through the ages great constructs were created in the consideration of the universe, and it is in that specific place where you can see the magnitude of love for the cycles of the universe that were incorporated into its foundation."

Vega leaned over Stan's lap, trying to sneak a premature peek at the twinkling lights below.

"Don't worry Vega, I think tomorrow morning when the sun rises over St. Peter's Square, you'll see the beauty you're searching for."

"Sunrise?" Altair winced at the early plans.

"Oh come on Altair, it's not that bad." Stan gave a fatherly wink.

"Well what are we looking for when we get there? I want to know what to pay attention to tomorrow," Vega insisted.

Giving in to her impatient urges, Stan reluctantly answered. "My description of this sacred place is only meant to lay the groundwork for what you are going to experience okay?"

Simultaneous nods answered him. "Have you all heard of Leonardo? Or perhaps the mechanical lion of the Louvre?"

"Maybe…" Vega answered with a questioning tone.

"Da Vinci?" Altair smugly grinned, "Of course we have… right Vega?"

Their judging eyes forced an answer. "Of course."

"Okay, well… Leonardo was known as a great artist of his time and still considered to be so today. He is credited with creating the mechanical lion, and many other countless pieces of artwork, for great kings and queens. He created a piece of such discrete magnificence that it is still studied and discussed among scholars. It is said that Leonardo inspired many architects with his genius, including the man responsible for creating St. Peter's Square. Not only does the layout of the square resemble some of Leonardo's work, but more importantly, it follows solar and lunar patterns that you will see illuminated when we look down from above."

A sensual voice from the overhead speakers spread through the cabin. "Ladies and gentlemen, this is your captain speaking. We are beginning our final descent into Rome. Please return your tray tables and seats to an upright position. Flight attendants, please prepare the cabin for landing."

"Oh man, I don't know why I'm so nervous; or maybe I'm excited; but it feels like nervous." Vega's manic eyes darted between not-so-secretive glances at Ben, and the approaching sight of land just outside the window.

Altair amusingly smiled at her chaos, "Just calm down, we'll get to our hotel soon enough. Speaking of, where are we staying Stan?"

He looked appeased before he answered. "I found a beautiful hotel just a few blocks from the Trevi Fountain." Blank stares again greeted his words.

"Jeez guys, come on. You don't know anything about Rome do you?"

"Hold on now, I know about the Colosseum! That is where gladiators fought, and I heard that they even filled it up with water, and ships would battle one another inside of it! See, I know a thing or two," Vega confidently raised her eyebrows.

115

"This may come as a surprise to you Stan, but I know a lot about the architecture of Rome. I've read a few books about the evolution of art, and as you know, much has been derived from Roman culture."

"Well, that's reassuring. There will be so much for you to see in the little time we are there, so I want you to pay attention tomorrow and just keep your wits about you. We don't know who or what could be waiting for us there."

As the plane came to a stop, all of passengers eagerly rose to their feet, scrambling ahead to the long awaited exit. Ben's accidental stumble forced his hands around Vega's shoulders as he leaned in apologetically. "Forgive my hands; people behind me don't seem to have much manners."

Butterflies stirred her words as she replied with a quick, "That's okay."

"Since I've got you, I want to make sure that I get a day with you to myself, while we're here. My team and I are booked for the next two days, but what do you say three days from now, you and I go hiking on one of my favorite islands; Capri."

"That sounds incredible," she blushed.

"It's a date then." He whispered in her ear before grabbing his hand-stitched leather bag from overhead. As they entered the busy airport, Vega mindlessly followed after him, only to be yanked back by a pull on her backpack.

"Not so fast," Altair smiled, as she hopelessly watched Ben disappear into the crowd.

"Why'd you do that?" she sighed.

"Well, one of us had to or you would have followed him like a puppy all the way to his hotel."

"You mean *our* hotel," she smiled. "We're all staying at the same place right Stan?"

"That's the plan. He attempted to tame her impatience while hailing the nearest cab. They zipped through the busy city, weaving in and out of the lines of cars, until at last they stopped in front of the entrance to the magnificently regal hotel.

"No way!" she stammered on as they walked through the promenade of marble pillars towards the towering wooden doors, still equipped with the original iron doorknockers from centuries ago.

Their eyes scanned the building in wonderment, silencing their voices as they entered the old palace, now transformed into a modern day hotel. White marble lined the floors, complimenting the dainty gold leaf furniture, most of which was labelled 'do not sit.' Vega's eyes locked on the oversized mirror behind the front desk, as she attempted to quickly fix her disheveled hair.

"Checking in?" the astute man adjusted his designer glasses as he looked up from his computer.

"Yes. Reservation is under Stan."

Prolonged silence followed several clicks, as he searched for what seemed to be a missing room.

"We do have a bit of a problem sir. It appears that we booked one of your rooms in our penthouse suite, and the other two are the single rooms you requested. The price for the Penthouse Suite is much higher, but due to our error, I can give you the suite for the same price as the regular rooms."

Before Stan could answer, Vega interrupted. "How about Altair and I take the suite again, and you can just cancel the third room? I'm beginning to enjoy his company anyway," she smirked.

"It's perfectly fine with me," Altair assured.

"Alright then, we'll take just the two rooms," Stan said while the attendant slid two heavy bronze keys across the counter.

"Well this is different." He looked up and chuckled to the unamused man behind the desk.

"There are many pieces of the palace that we chose to keep intact; one of which is the exquisitely carved wooden doors, though we have updated the keys and locks."

"Wow! Just think of the history here!" Vega's eyes lit up as she scoured the room for artifacts. The man slid his glasses down his nose a bit, looking down towards her wide curious eyes, "You'd be surprised at what you'll find here."

Before she could consume more of the busy man's time, Stan interrupted. "Well kids, we have an early morning tomorrow, so how about we have an early night tonight, and meet tomorrow for our sunrise tour of St. Peter's?"

The three of them made their way through the sumptuous, dark palace halls, carefully dragging their luggage across the long ruby carpet to their rooms. Each door seemed to grow a tad taller than the one before it, until at last they reached the largest door at the end of the hall.

"Would you look at this place?!" Vega whirled her bag across the marble floors, looking up towards the intricately painted, vaulted ceiling. Her fingers danced across the silk curtains that surrounded the king size bed, as she twirled in the direction of the bathroom, gasping at the site. "The entire bathroom is covered from floor to ceiling in mosaic tile, and there's a fountain in the wall! I've never seen anything like this place," she said while running her fingers through the water spitting from the mouth of the stone lion.

"It is pretty nice. He walked out to the balcony, overlooking the hotel gardens. The details of the ironwork sent shivers through his body, as he traced his fingers across the balcony.

"Something feels familiar here," he called over his shoulder.

She stepped beside him, and settled into an unusual moment of silence. "It does, doesn't it?"

CHAPTER 9

The three of them lethargically made their way to the top of the dome, twisting through the compact, narrow stairwell up to the dwindling flickers of starlight above.

"Not much further," Stan informed the agitated, tired group.

"Thanks for letting us know we would be climbing hundreds of stairs this morning," Vega jabbed as they neared the top.

"Man, I haven't been up to see the sunrise since... " Moments of silence passed as Altair scanned his memories.

As they took their places at the top of the dome and gazed down upon the monumental design of the grand square below, the sun began to peek through the morning clouds.

Vega squinted a curious eye at the towering obelisk in the center of the square, casting the first shadow of the morning. She held her tongue, respecting the moment of serenity. Instead reaching her hand into the pocket of her jacket, searching for something that seemed important, if only for that moment.

"I see what you are looking at Vega. The obelisk?" Stan observingly whispered, halting her fidgeting fingers.

"I didn't want to ruin the moment," she smiled, "Glad you did it for me."

"The Egyptian obelisk is essentially a marker for a significant source of energy. Now, this is interesting. If you look around the square, you will see sixteen markers, denoting specific compass directions, which if followed, lead to key locations around the world. Each marker is about

18-20 degrees apart, and I say that because the compass rose of St. Peter's Square is not oriented to true north. Now, if you read the literature here, it states that these markers are simply to denote the directions from which the winds come, but I personally think that the architect of the square designed a compass which points directly to other places of historic relevance."

As mighty rays of gold covered the square, all eyes remained focused on the simple obelisk at its center.

"Did you say eighteen degrees?" Altair asked, reflecting back to prior dreams.

Stan nodded while intercepting Vega's next line of questions. "And the statues that you are staring at -- there, at the base of the obelisk -- are lions."

"Wait, a minute, you said this obelisk is from Egypt? What is it doing here in Rome?" Vega squinted, trying to identify the lions below.

"That, I don't know." Stan surprising even himself with momentary lack of facts.

"Interesting." She fidgeted with her small phoenix figurine, nervously flipping it between her anxious fingers.

"What do you have there?" He nodded towards the figurine, silencing her stirring.

"Oh, this? It's just a gift from a friend," she smiled. "I find myself carrying it everywhere. I don't know why but somehow it brings me peace of mind."

"Happy it helps."

"So. Where do the lines of this sundial point?" Altair asked while shielding his face from the morning sun.

A moment of shocking clarity widened Stan's eyes, "St. Chartres Cathedral is one of the locations. Do you realize what this means Altair?"

"I know that cathedral very well, but I'm afraid I don't see the relevance Stan. Sorry, maybe I need more coffee?"

"What? The 200 stairs didn't jumpstart your morning?" Vega laughed.

"Chartres Cathedral is a sacred temple in France, with a labyrinth of gold etched upon its floor. Across the ceiling spreads a depiction of the wheel of life, and somewhere within the confines of its ancient grounds, lies a well."

"It all makes sense now! Why didn't I recognize it before? I have been to that very cathedral many times," Altair said, recalling childhood trips.

"I suppose that time has a way of changing things doesn't it?" Stan said, triggering an unwanted image of Melusine in Vega's mind.

"So what? This obelisk points to places we see in our travels." She made quotation marks with her fingers while emphasizing the word travels.

"Don't you see Vega? This very place where we stand has something to do with all of the metal plates, and better yet, has something to do with Deneb coming back to us. This isn't a coincidence."

"But what about the dream that Deneb had? You know... about the circle of stars here in Rome? How are we supposed to find that?" Altair asked.

"Perhaps we should do some sight-seeing today. I have just the place to show you." He hurriedly grabbed the neatly folded map from his pocket as Vega rolled her eyes.

"Of course you have a map of the city on hand," she laughed.

"You never know when you'll need it," he winked. "When you said the words, circle of stars, I immediately thought of a place called Villa Farnesina. There is something there that I think you kids needs to see."

As the morning sun defined the shadows below, the three of them made their way back down the swirling stairs and out into the waking streets. Together they walked through the large, yet small city, brimming with historic landmarks they had no time to stop at, and continued toward a well-landscaped garden, surrounding what appeared to be a beautiful, old, two story home. Stan's finger pointed out each unique characteristic of the house as he excitedly presented the historical site. "See the outdoor archway that lines the entire first level there? That was designed specifically to give this villa an airy 'summer home' feel. And the clean-lined row of windows along the second story facing out to the garden? That too was not typical of the Renaissance period. See, most palaces designed during that era, faced roads and entryways. But this designer had different measurements in mind when he built this palace... I mean ...villa. Come, there is so much to show you!"

They walked briskly past the slowly moving tourists, and through the perfectly manicured gardens, where they stopped to admire the fragrant flowers of the numerous rose bushes. Their hurried feet seemed to slow to the pace of the other lackadaisical visitors as they neared the focal point of the garden, the fountain. Entranced, Vega looked into its meditative waters, "I feel like I've been here before...," she whispered to herself as she reached into her pocket for the phoenix.

"More important things await us inside." Stan interrupted her trance-like state as she continued to flip the figurine between her fingers.

123

Altair quickly nudged her as Stan trudged ahead. "Hey, this place... I feel like I have been here before too. I don't know how or why, but I think when we get back to the hotel we need to talk about it."

"I think there is something here; something that we won't see in present time. Think about how much has changed since the time of the man who built this place. I feel like we are in the right place, but the wrong time," she mused.

He nodded in agreement and quickly switched the subject, feeling Stan's heavy eyes hone in on their secretive conversation.

"Everything okay?" Stan eyed Altair, then Vega, as they quickly responded with a uniform, "Yes."

Silently they entered the historic villa, taking in the breathtaking frescos and golden accents that covered the arched ceilings. Vega's eyes remained on the floor, as she watched her simple sneakers cross the perfectly polished marble.

"Vega, what are you looking at?" Altair interrupted.

"Nothing. Well, I don't know. Something here is bothering me, like nails on a chalkboard. I can't place what it is..."

"Remember, things happened on this land thousands of years ago. So even though this palace was built in the 1500's, much more has taken place here than we know. Maybe there is something here that you are somehow picking up on?"

"True." She lifted her eyes from the floor for the first time and gazed at the brilliant painting, studying the face of the golden haired maiden and the weeping servants arranged beside her.

"Are you okay?" Altair noticed the frozen look on her face as she gazed up in perplexed wonder.

"Betrayal encased in paint," she whispered, as her eyes began to swell.

"Vega?" Stan leaned in, careful not to interrupt the unusual state of her focus.

"Have you ever been to the symphony?" she abruptly turned and asked.

"Yes," Stan replied, "many times."

"You know the moment when you finally connect with the sadness of their story, their angelically beautiful song? That is what I feel when I look at that painting. What is it?"

Stan exhaled in wonderment, "This painting is known as *The Wedding of Alexander and Roxane*, and depicts the celebration of the marriage between Alexander the Great and his princess, Roxane. Many say that Alexander longed for the Orient, and went on to conquer Bactria, which was nestled within a nearly unreachable mountain fortress. It is said that when he reached the top of the snowy mountain and took his captives, one woman, although an enemy, won his heart. His love for her outweighed his victory. So, you see that here, during this marriage celebration, most are weeping, when he hands the golden crown to the breathtaking maiden."

"Golden crown?" Altair squinted towards the painting as if it had lips to answer.

"Yes. Well, some say that the man who commissioned paintings such as this, was completely enthralled with the constellations, and the act of handing over a golden crown to the woman stood for far more than a material crown."

"Could she somehow have been involved with gaining control of the Northern Crown, or better yet the labyrinth of time associated with it?" Altair strung together pieces of previous conversations.

Vega quickly turned away, fleeing to the next room.

"You read my mind!" Stan called behind her. "The room that I wanted to show you is over there."

"Are you okay?" Altair wrapped a protective arm around Vega as her eyes melted towards the ceiling. "Vega? I've never seen you this emotional..."

"I've never seen such beauty." She gawked in wonder at the intricately painted chariot, flying across the dark and starry hues of the painting above. Slowly she spun in a circle, captivated by the painted representations of celestial beings, circling around the chariot above, while temporarily leaving her heartache in the previous room.

"Ah, this is the painting I wanted to show you. It was created by an artist named Baldassare Peruzzi, who was widely known for his mysteriously brilliant paintings. Some say he created illusions based upon where you stood while viewing his work. This is one of my favorites -- a celestial wonder some say. Now, see there -- in the center of the ceiling -- there are two central images; a chariot pulled by bulls and the woman with snakes emerging from her head, being slain. Now if you look just above the snake-headed beast, there is another painted image." Stan waited in silence as they looked up at the celestial figure holding an illuminated triangle above the clouds.

"Is that the Summer Triangle? Painted on a ceiling? From hundreds of years ago?" Vega asked in choppy fragments while her mind dissected what her eyes were studying.

"It very well could be. Furthermore, I think it is of great importance to study the surrounding images that circle around the chariot and the dragon."

"What is that?" Vega pointed to the painting of a beautiful woman with two twirling strands reminiscent of DNA hovering over her head, and a scorpion behind her back, as Altair focused on another, more eye-catching image.

"And that one too… what is that one?" He whispered in awe as he studied the image of a man thrusting a torch at a multi-headed serpent, beside the swan of Cygnus.

"I think you're reading a story, that is painted here, upon the ceiling," Stan suggested as they studied the circle of constellations.

"Who owned this palace again?' Vega leaned her head back, gazing up at the image of the lyre, which was directly above her head.

"Known to many as 'the banker' he was a man of immeasurable wealth. In his garden, he grew exotic herbs and fruits, which he traded to scholars and artists for their time and inspiring presence. Gold, silver, and jewels flooded into his possession, though his passion was not with material goods, but with the knowledge and wisdom of the arcane. Some say that he and his dinner guests once ate from golden plates, almost as a mockery of wealth, and one night he stood on the bank of the river and threw them all into the water. His fascinations were not for material things, but rather for the spiritual. Stars, the measurement and timing of the universe and the zodiac enchanted his mind, so he hired great artists to bring to life the constellations that he favored, within the walls of his famously unique summer villa. Painted above you are the traces of stories, passed down through trusted scholars, depicting the lives and battles of universal energies. Legends; encased in hundreds of years of paint."

127

Vega rolled her eyes at the group of people passing by; each lost in their phones, texting blindly, as they mindlessly meandered beneath the lost meaning of magnificence.

"What are we to make of all of this Stan?" Altair asked with unmoving eyes, locked upon the twisting, snake-like strands painted above the beautiful woman.

"You were searching for a circle of stars in Rome, and I believe you've found it."

Their eyes simultaneously raised up to the heavenly scenery above, silently searching for their affiliated depiction."

"Wait. In the dream, the gold was below the circle of stars," Altair said as he quickly looked down at the soles of his heavy boots.

"I think we should head back now." Vega sternly said while guiding Altair by the elbow.

"We just got here Vega...." Stan called behind the quickly moving duo. "Did you see the Swan of Cygnus, the Lyre of Lyra, and all the other constellations that seem to intertwine with your stories? Vega?" he scurried across the slippery marble floors after the headstrong girl, struggling to keep up.

Hastily she whispered chaotic thoughts to Altair as she dragged him through the romantic gardens towards the fountain. "I feel like this is all connected! If we can somehow go back to the time of the banker, then maybe we can change things! We need to go back!"

"Whoa! Hold on Vega!" Altair yanked his arm away from hers in a momentary attempt at sanity.

"I know you're excited, but we can't just leave people behind every time we find a clue. We have to do this together, okay?"

128

"Okay. I'm sorry." She stared into the fountain as Stan caught up.

"Is everything alright?" he wheezed.

"Everything is fine. Vega just got a little carried away. I think it best we go back to the hotel and perhaps discuss our thoughts over dinner?" Altair looked to the group for agreeing nods.

"Good. Shall we?" Resuming a normal pace, he extended his arm towards Vega once more.

She smiled and latched on, "Sorry about all that. Sometimes I get a little carried away."

"I know." He smiled down at the larger-than-life girl that could easily fit beneath his arm.

"How can so much intensity fit within a body of your size?" he joked.

She shrugged. "I shock even myself."

CHAPTER 10

"Just a few more minutes. Sorry," Vega called through the steam of the bathroom.

"No problem," he yelled from the balcony, as he admired the architecture of the hotel; studying each twisted branch of iron artistically wrapped around the terrace. A gust of wind rustled the heavy crimson curtains that fell from the vaulted ceiling behind him, as he quickly turned, shocked at the vision in front of him. Vega nervously fumbled with her necklace, which hung nearly to the waist of her knee length, sapphire colored dress of silk and satin. Her eyes darted around the room as he looked over her like a child seeing his first snow.

"How do I look?" she asked already knowing his answer.

He struggled to formulate a cohesive sentence, "Amazing. You look amazing. Where... where did you get that dress?"

Bashfully she whisked a shawl around her shoulders, feeling the heaviness of his eyes. "I actually bought this is France when we had a free day. That was the day when..." she stopped herself from continuing.

"When what?"

"When Deneb took the train to Paris with Eltanin. There were other places that I wanted to see, which happened to include a cute little boutique in Marseille where I found this dress."

His eyes gleamed at the mention of his hometown.

"Oh that's right! I forgot that you are from there! Come on! We need to get down to the restaurant and meet Stan."

She rambled as they walked through the warmly lit hallways toward the heavy bronze elevator doors. "You know I feel really bad about just running away today, and leaving poor Stan behind."

Altair smiled down towards the pint-sized beauty. "You didn't feel even a little bit bad for leaving me behind?"

"Well, technically I did grab you by the elbow and yank you along," she giggled as they walked arm in arm into the lobby.

Silent eyes matched admiring whispers as they entered the fog like ancient ghosts, drawn to the glowing lights of the romantic city. Noticing the prolonged silence, Vega asked, "So, how far away is this place? I'm starving."

"Not too far; I think it might be that white building up there," he pointed towards the warmly lit, two story building ahead.

As they entered the restaurant, their slow steps echoed off the cathedral ceilings, announcing their presence to the patrons of the cozy, upscale lounge. Vega's eyes delightedly danced with the crystals dangling from the overhead chandelier, watching as the angelic lights radiated against the shiny copper walls that surrounded them.

"What a place!" Her eyes sunk into the long hallway of recurring French doors, each festooned with whimsical ivory curtains. Sensing his lack of agreeable response, she nudged her unmovable friend, whose eyes remained locked on the ornately carved lion in center of the bar.

Vega slid onto the old barstool, playfully turning the chandelier into a quickly spinning kaleidoscope. As her stool slowed to a stop, Altair's eyes remained fixated on the mighty wooden king, "I need to figure out the significance of the lion. The old man in Crete had a lion on the top of his cane, and introduced me to the tale of the Serpent Goddess. Then Stan tells me of the blacksmith that made a deal with the god Apollo, whose plates reawaken when the pearls from two lions fall into a well. Now, here in Rome, we see two lions at the base of the obelisk at St. Peter's square. There is something important about the symbol of the lion that is somehow escaping me."

Vega quickly grabbed his arm, pulling him through the galley of whimsical curtains, and into the secrecy of a quiet room. She looked around for any bystanders, before whispering. "I don't know if you know this, but there was a moment in France, when I saved Deneb from drowning. She had swam out past a large boulder, hoping to return a necklace that Eltanin had given her to the sea. Before he could join her out there, she dove down beneath the waves and found a ring... your ring. I don't know what happened out there, but she said he tried to grab what she had around her neck, which was the crystal and the ring, and that was when she got pushed into the rocks. You look confused. Have you not heard this story?"

132

"I heard about her dive, but I wasn't aware that there was ever a potential for them to be together."

"Well…. I don't know about all of that. I just know that when I brought her to the surface, she had a ring and we sat there on the beach and studied it intently. Have you…. ever… you know… *looked* at the ring?"

"I've never taken it off."

"Well, if you did, you'd see the image of a lion, etched into the underside of the band," she whispered as her eyes glistened with wonder.

"No way," he reached for his ring as she quickly intercepted his hand.

"Wait. Not here. Later -- when we get back to the hotel. Come on, we need to find Stan."

Silence overtook the usually chatty girl as they entered the busy dining room, and were captivated by the exquisite stained glass window, which spread from floor to ceiling. "Am I in a fairytale? Look at that window… each small pane of glass looks like a feather, fluttering in the light of every candle. Together their eyes lovingly melted into the scenery of illuminated glass wings wrapping around the dining room, as a waving hand came into focus.

Stan beamed with joy as he flicked impressive glances around the room. "Can you believe this place?"

"Incredible" they responded in unison as the waiter slid warm bread and three glasses of red wine upon the table.

"I hope you like wine. We are in Italy, after all." Stan tilted his glasses, while holding the menu up towards the candlelight, and then adjusted them once more to make sure his eyes were not playing some sort of trick on him. "Well, Vega, I must say you look simply lovely this evening."

His compliment triggered immediate fidgeting. "Thanks." She quickly picked up the menu, searching for a new topic of conversation.

"Well. I think I'm going to have some sort of pasta." She decisively set the menu back upon the tablecloth and quickly picked it up again, to make room for the savory plate of mozzarella and carpaccio that the waiter placed between them.

As they placed their orders of truffle infused pasta and ricotta stuffed ravioli, the conversation shifted to more important matters.

"I have to say, I've been wondering all afternoon what had you in such a fury today Vega?" Stan dipped his bread into the aromatic dish of olive oil and herbs as he awaited her answer. She leaned in, as to conceal her reply, and joined in with the delicious dunking of bread. The warm glow of the candle highlighted features of her face that Altair had never noticed before, as she scarfed down another ill-mannered bite of bread.

"A few things," she answered between chews. "I looked at the image of the woman with the DNA over her head, and the scorpion behind her, and it felt like there is someone else that we don't know about; some other villain just waiting for us. Most of the images painted on the ceiling I recognized... well, except for the chariot in the center -- and the scorpion."

They silently waited for the real reason to be revealed, stirring her into discomfort. She sighed. "Then there was the painting of Alexander and Roxane. In all of my travels involving him, he has loved me, and only me. I guess I felt somewhat betrayed looking at a famous painting of his wedding with someone else." Emotion fueled her tone. "Furthermore, I don't know why he would go to China. I mean, why would he go there and seek some sort of mountain fortress? And then... " she laughed while angrily shoving more bread in her mouth, "He gives away a golden crown to someone that is supposed to be his enemy?"

Stan answered before Altair could attempt to calm her down. "Vega, you must consider the fate of the man you follow. He changes sides every 500 years. Perhaps his intentions changed, somewhere between his conquest of the Orient and his taking of it. I believe that the paintings inside Villa Farnesina hold far deeper meanings, but they also carry a common theme, one of celestial nature."

"So, we just need to figure out what his plans were and go there now, and then we can stop it! We can stop them from being together!" She scowled at her own emotions. "I'm sorry, I just feel like we're wasting time sitting here drinking fancy wine and eating delicious food."

Stan reassured her guilt-filled mind. "Travels like this require planning, patience, and a hearty meal, I might add. I know you are upset by what you saw today, but may I remind you that the task remains focused on Deneb. Neither Altair nor I are here for a vacation, or to try fancy food and wine. Trust me when I say, I have seen the world -- many times. My work has sent me to the depths of every sea, and to places in this world that even the finest archeologists are not permitted to enter. I have been studying the history of this planet for most of my life. I am not here to slow you down; I am here to help. For example, if you were to go back to the time when that palace, I mean villa, was built, you would want to be dressed in accordance with the royal class of Rome in the 1400's. Do you even know what that would be?" he raised an inquisitively triumphant eyebrow.

135

Her eyes lowered towards the table as she shamefully shook her head no. "Sorry Stan. I just care so much about getting her back, and I know that the gold we seek is somewhere beneath the circle of stars that we saw today."

Altair momentarily drifted away from the conversation as he pictured their masquerade. "So... Say we go back to the time of this illustrious banker... What are we supposed to do while we're there? If we go, we need to make sure we do it right."

"You mean when we go..." Vega corrected him, while looking over his shoulder at the shadowy face of a tall dark haired man, courteously extending his hand to his black haired companion. As she rose from the table, spinning her long textured dress of black lace up over her spiny heels, she turned ever so slightly, flashing a smile of seductive darkness toward the eyes she knew laid heavily upon her.

"Vega?" Altair interrupted. "What's the matter?"

Startled, she looked quickly back at Altair, and then back to the empty table where only a simple candle burned, awaiting its next set of dinner guests.

"Nothing. I thought I saw someone..."

"To return to our conversation... I believe that when you go back to the roaring moments of Villa Farnesina, you'll find what it is that you are looking for... which is?" he looked at Altair for an honest answer.

His head turned to Vega, seeking the answer he wished he had. She sternly said, "We won't know until we get there. I believe there is something of significance buried near the fountain, but honestly, I want to go back there because of what I felt, when we were there today."

"So... Then we leave tonight; when we get back to the hotel."

"No, not tonight. You'll need to look the part." Stan leaned back as the waiter set their piping hot meals before them, silencing their conversation with steamy scents of savory herbs and spices.

"This looks incredible! Thank you for inviting us here Stan." Vega humbly folded her hands upon her lap and bowed her head.

Following suit, Altair folded his hands, cringing at how easily his fingers slid between each other, devoid of any burns or calluses. Stan swallowed his emerging smile and quickly spoke a few words of admiration for the moment that time had allowed for them to sit there together. As they ate in silence, each contemplating their collective journey, Vega's mind drifted toward thoughts of the dark haired man and his shadowy woman. Her hauntingly familiar smile spread across her mind like an inkblot. Her mind wandered in the shadows of who was there in Rome with them, causing her to jump as Altair shook her arm.

"Um Vega? You okay?"

"I'm fine. I just... I think I want to go back to the room. Is that okay?"

"Of course it is!" Stan assured, as he savored the last bite of his delightful meal, while eyeing the nearby cart of enticing desserts.

"You can order dessert Stan," Vega giggled.

"No, it's quite alright. I'll partake another night."

As they duplicated their path back into the foggy streets, Vega remembered something she had been meaning to discuss with both Stan and Altair.

"Hey Stan, do you remember when we were in France and Deneb had the incident out by the rocks?"

"How could I forget? I still don't know how you saved her that day."

"I think people are capable of far more than they give themselves credit for," she smiled. "Anyway, before she was pushed into the rocks, she had found a ring on the ocean floor."

"You didn't tell me that she was pushed into the rocks, Vega?"

"Oh man," she tumbled through her thoughts, trying to remember what version of the truth she had actually told him. She continued past her mistakes and resumed the story. "Well, while everyone else finished their dive, we sat on the shoreline under the shade of a pine tree, catching our breath, and collecting our thoughts. I remember it like it was yesterday. She pulled a ring from the water logged pouch she wore around her neck, and slowly held it up to the sunlight, examining the faint image of a lion etched on the inside of the band."

Altair grabbed one hand protectively around the other, as if the universe had heard his secret.

"My question is... do you think that the lion in his ring has something to do with the lions containing the pearls?"

"I believe there are no coincidences in life. If Altair's ring has in fact descended from Apollo and his brother, then I'd say there is a good chance that the lion in his ring is connected to the pearls in some way."

Let me do some reading before you kids go shopping tomorrow; we can discuss it over breakfast."

"Shopping?" Vega cringed.

138

"We need to find both of you suitable outfits for your travels. I know of a vintage thrift shop that might have something right up your alley!"

"Sounds like a plan." Vega happily reached for the front door of the hotel, just as three men scrambled through the lobby, in a moment of belligerent chivalry, attempting to open the door for her. She awkwardly edged past the plastered smiles of the admiring men as they neared the elevator.

"You kids get some good sleep tonight okay, and I'll see you both down here in the morning for breakfast." Stan stepped off at his floor, as they continued towards their suite.

"Don't you think it's weird that we keep getting these incredibly beautiful rooms?" Vega pushed open the door only to be greeted by a fresh bottle of champagne on ice, chocolate truffles and berries.

"I'm not complaining!" He popped a truffle in his mouth while kicking off his shoes. "It's kind of nice, feeling like royalty every once and awhile." He walked barefoot across the expensive Moroccan rug to the bathroom, admiring the fresh salts and rose petals lining the tub.

"I might take a bath or something," he yelled from the bathroom to the unusually quiet girl.

"What are you doing out there?" he called out to the sound of pages flipping, which instantly stopped when she realized he had asked her something.

"Nothing. Hey, can you come here for a second?"

Failing to contain his laughter at her 1990s hyper-color pajamas, he replied, "Yeah, what's up?"

She pulled the comfort of the covers around her as she revealed her insecurities." I saw someone tonight...at the restaurant. Something about her struck a chord with me. I

139

watched her move across the room like a timeless vision of darkness, as she admired how easily she had captured the attention of everyone who laid eyes on her. There was something horribly frightening about her, but still I stared, trying to figure out why her mere presence radiated a frequency that still seems to haunt me."

He flipped through his memories of Hydra. "Don't worry Vega; I'll be right here, okay? Nothing will happen to you."

"That's the thing. When I fall asleep, it's like I just get up and go wherever my heart desires, and I'm scared that somewhere in my psyche she connected with me. I don't want to answer the call that I know I will hear when my eyes close."

"So, what do we do?" He paced the bed like a lion stalking its prey.

"Will you lay here beside me, and stay until I fall asleep? I just want to make sure that I do not go anywhere. You are the only one I trust to keep me from...well, myself."

As guilt and the word 'betrayal' sunk into his heart, he quickly answered. "I'll tell you what. I'll sleep on the floor, right next to the bed. That way, if you start to go anywhere, I'll bring you back."

"You'd do that for me?" she smiled as she tucked herself beneath the covers.

"I'd do anything for you. You're like a sister to me." He threw a few blankets and pillows down, and took his place on the floor.

"Good night Altair," she said as she stretched across the king sized bed.

"Good night Vega," he folded his hands behind his head, gazing restlessly up at the ceiling. Hours passed as he laid faithfully beside her, watchfully waiting for any moment of intrusion.

As she slid into slumber, an entrancing voice echoed through her dreams, "Vega, it's me, Lan. I've missed you." She blinked her heavy eyes, as his different, yet unmistakably familiar face came into focus. "Where are we?" she blinked once more as the twinkling garden, fresh with gardenias, bougainvillea, and poppy, sprung to life around her. "It's beautiful," her words echoed through the misty morning fog as the sun graced his refreshingly handsome face.

"We're in the market enclosure," he smiled.

"It is a garden? I thought it was a maze." Her words lethargically slid from her tongue, as if the world had slowed almost to a standstill.

"It is," he whispered in her ear while leaning in to kiss her lips. "How I've missed you. Come, I need to show you something."

She followed him through the maze of misty, golden light up to a large wooden altar. Instinctually, she looked behind her, realizing that others were quickly moving through the labyrinth of light behind her.

"What are they carrying?" Her whispers seemed confined in the secrecy of the fog.

"Take this; you will need it to sever the bond," he urged while placing a rudely welded metal dagger within her tiny hands.

"Wait! What are they carrying?" She squinted through the fog toward the familiar dark haired woman, unnaturally floating through the passages of the maze behind them.

141

"She has the plate; the Egg of Cygnus! You must hurry! Pass the dagger through the well!" He lovingly caressed her face as his essence began to evaporate into the misty light of the morning sun.

"Lan?" She ached for just one more moment with him, as she fell to her knees on the wooden altar, looking out to the eerily quiet cathedral. His departing words softly echoed through the cathedral like church bells, sinking in her heart as he spoke, "Remember, I am within you now... but I am not with you then."

"Lan!" she screamed, as Altair quickly stood up and rushed to the bed. The embrace of his arms instantly slowed the rapid rising and falling of her chest.

"Are you okay?" he asked the clearly shaken girl.

"I'm fine." She frantically wiped the tears from her face while kicking the blankets to the floor.

"Want to talk about it?" he asked, already knowing the answer.

"I saw Lan, but he looked different...maybe because it was a different time period." She paused trying to recall the versions of Lan's existence before continuing. "At first we were in the heavenly market enclosure, which looked like a majestic garden. It was one of the most beautiful places I have ever seen. Each flower transmitted a bright light, which shone through the morning fog. Hand in hand, he led me through a maze of golden light up to a wooden altar. I could feel a presence behind us... an ominous female presence."

"Then what?" Altair squeezed her tiny hands within his.

"He placed a metal dagger into my hands, and begged me to pass it through the wells. He said it was the only thing that would sever the bond. It looked familiar, like the dagger that I found at your workshop when I found you that day," she sighed while recalling the previous triumphs of Hydra.

"You found me there?" he moved to the bed beside her.

"Yeah, well, we kept Deneb in the car because we didn't want to freak you out," she laughed recalling the only humorous part of the solemn memory.

"Well, what happened to the dagger that you found?"

"I kept it. I keep it with me always." She smiled while nodding at her canvas bag on the floor.

"It's there? In your bag? Now?" He let go of her hands for a moment and dug frantically through the treasures of her old bag. He picked up the tattered plaid shirt, wrapped tightly around the jagged dagger, and returned to the bed.

"You know, I kept it because it had symbols on it that only I seemed to be able to see. As it cooled from molten hot to … well, what you see now, symbols appeared and disappeared on the blade.

"What symbols?" he asked while carefully placing the bare metal into his hands.

"At first it was a snake with many heads, which then turned into a tortoise, and then a tiger and finally, a fiery bird."

"Interesting," he said as he moved the heavy dagger from one hand to the other. "What the?" He jumped, nearly dropping the blade, as a spark erupted between his ring and the dagger.

Vega jumped up on the bed in a combative stance, just as the light of the encounter fizzled out.

"What was that?" she demanded with amazed eyes now glued on her newfound muse.

143

"I...I don't know what that was. It was like my ring did something to this dagger."

The delight of revealed mystery illuminated within Vega's soul as she inched closer to Altair. "Do it again," she whispered.

Slowly, he shifted the blade into his left hand, coursing heavy pulses through his veins. As a magnificent glow illuminated the room, small shapes began to take form upon the blade.

"What the..." Vega stared at the molten hot dagger that he painlessly held within his hands, as the etchings began to move, ever so slightly.

"Did that just...move?" she screamed as the fiery eyes of the snake illuminated on the blade. "Altair, you better put that thing down! NOW!" She scrambled across the bed, reaching for her old tattered shirt to confine the once simple dagger. She lunged across his lap, knocking it to the floor, and breaking whatever had held him so entranced.

With shaky arms, she pushed herself up from the floor, attempting to catch her breath. Her eyes landed heavily on the wadded up shirt, wrapped around the now seemingly normal dagger.

"What...what just happened? It was as if your ring caused it to go back to its original form of creation. That is exactly what it looked like when I found it, except, you know, the eyes of the creatures on it weren't staring at me!"

"That was so intense!" He paced with eerie vigor.

"We need to keep that blade away from you until we know what it is, and more importantly what it does. Sorry to burst your bubble Altair, but the objects on that blade are bad. According to Chinese legend, those are the four Guardians of the Directions, otherwise known as the four members of the underworld, or the Four Beasts. Hydra's constellation spans two of the directions, which represent the Azure Dragon and the Vermillion Bird. They both appear right there on the blade as a multi-headed snake and a phoenix."

"Well, I thought that the phoenix was good. You know, all of the stories I've heard tell of a being that experienced death and rose from the ashes to be reborn again."

"When you killed Hydra, did she not disintegrate into a pile of black ashes? I can answer that for you: she did! Now she is back, risen from the ashes, born again. Look, I don't know if this dagger is good, or bad, but it certainly seems like it's bad to me. I do think it has value though, as Lan said, it destroys some sort of bond," Vega joined his pacing as they continued to circle the shirt.

His heavy footsteps ceased as he paused, "You said there are four beasts. What are the other two?"

She sighed, scouring painful memories. "The tiger opposes her, which is why 'she' cannot exist without him."

"You mean Lan?" He cringed as he spoke his name, forcing Vega to recall the unfortunate balance of their bond.

"Yeah."

"So... then, what is the fourth... who is that?"

"Good question, the symbol is a tortoise. Thus far, we haven't met anyone who represents that symbol."

Altair resumed his pacing. "Okay, so say this dagger *does* control these four beasts. Maybe the bond that it severs is between Hydra and Lan?"

She sat back on the bed and pulled the blankets around her like a cocoon.

"Can I ask you a question?" She blinked a few times, struggling to stay awake.

"What's up?" He whispered to the sleepy girl, while tucking the bound dagger back into her bag.

"Will you hold my hand while I sleep?"

"Umm… sure." He settled into his makeshift bed and extended his hand up to hers, resting his wrist on the edge of the mattress. As he wrapped his protective hand around both hers, he felt a shift within her, and for the first time, heard a breath of relaxation escape her lips.

CHAPTER 11

Knock, knock! Stan's joyful tone radiated through the door as Vega scrambled to reach the bathroom, nearly tripping over Altair.

"Get up!" She yelled over the rushing shower water, hoping Stan hadn't heard her.

"Just a second!" Altair shoved one leg into his jeans as he hopped towards the door.

"Everything okay in there?" Stan pressed his eye to the peephole, as if he could somehow see inside.

"Just fine." Altair charmingly smiled as he yanked the door open, causing Stan to nearly topple in.

"So, how did you sleep?" Stan's eyes scanned the room, inquisitively stopping at the site of the oddly made bed on the floor.

"Just fine." Altair wrapped a friendly arm around him, steering him out to the privacy of the balcony. They stepped out onto the terrace, where beautiful hanging flowers spilled over the balcony, taking in the morning sunshine.

"What a view you two have up here!" He inhaled the crisp air.

"It is breathtaking isn't it?" Altair peeked back inside to see if Vega was out of the shower.

147

Vega's absence evoked hurried words from Altair. "So, last night, Vega sort of disappeared into a dream where she seemed to think that she was in a cathedral of some kind. She described a labyrinth of light, with darkness within, and a woman who carried the Egg of Cygnus on a metal plate, following closely behind her. When she woke, she told me that Lan had brought her there, and hurriedly told her to take the dagger and pass it through the well. He said that it would destroy a bond of some sort."

"Forgive my rusty memory, but what dagger are you talking about?" Stan said with shameful confusion.

"The dagger that was found in my workshop; the dagger that Hydra made."

"Ah, I remember now. Go on."

"Ever since that day, Vega has carried the dagger. I believe the images that she saw transforming on the blade frightened, yet intrigued her, so she kept it under her watchful guard. Last night, after she awoke from her dream, we unwrapped the dagger, and...something spectacular happened."

Stan's eyes screamed with excitement as Altair continued.

"Once my ring touched the blade, it was as if it was brought back to life; back to its original, pure form. Together we watched the creatures that were firmly etched into the metal come to life. I felt a connection to it -- so powerful, that it was if this primitive life force somehow merged with my soul. It wasn't until Vega dove across my lap, knocking it to the floor that I disconnected with the blade."

"When you say disconnected, what exactly do you mean by that?"

"I could feel the energy of the four symbols, all of them... as if they were speaking to me through the fire."

"Oh dear! Altair! We need to be careful with this dagger. I feel very nervous about you having it anywhere near you! If it had that much of an effect on you, who's to say what would happen if you held onto it longer. I think it best that Vega keep watch of it for now, at least until we figure out its purpose."

"One more thing…when Vega told me of her encounter with Lan, he said something that continues to haunt me, 'I am here with you now, but I am not with you then.' What do you think that means?"

"Well, the white tiger that opposes Hydra changes allegiance every 500 years. So, perhaps he meant that he was able to help her then, but not in the present day."

Vega's sneaking footsteps quietly crept across the floor, as her shadow slid between them; betrayed by a creaking floorboard, she returned their intrusive looks with a bashful giggle, "Hey guys."

"How long have you been standing there?" Altair's leisurely question contradicted the alarm on his face.

"Not long." she joined them on the balcony, extending her gaze across the ancient, now modernized city.

"We were just talking about your dream last night. Stan thinks it best that you hold onto the dagger until we find out what to do with it."

"Sounds good to me. Who's ready to shop?" she whisked the doorway of drapes behind her as she exited the balcony, heading for the door. Stan and Altair scrambled behind the headstrong girl, who was already halfway down the hallway.

Vega walked through the lobby as if she were royalty, grabbing the complimentary coffee that awaited her, just before striding past the arms that held the door to the street open. She slid her overtly glamorous Chanel glasses onto her tiny face, lined her lips with a layer of plum lipstick, and stepped out into the sunshine of her day.

"Thank you, sir." She tucked a few euros into the man's pocket, creating blushing cheeks behind the closing door.

"Vega?" Altair interrupted her sensational exit, holding the door as Stan hurried behind.

"I don't know why, but I'm excited to go shopping today. You know, thrift shops are my favorite!" Before she could raise her arm to hail a cab, the doorman rushed to an approaching car, and pulled the door open for her.

Stan and Altair traded glances of shock as they followed the favored vixen into the car.

"Where to miss?" The driver dreamily looked in the rearview mirror at the reflection of what seemed to be the only passenger in the car.

"To...well... Stan?"

Stan, happy to be of use, answered, "There is an old costume store, famous here in Rome! We'll go there!"

Silent moments passed as they zipped down busy streets, passing historical structures, which seemed tucked somewhere between the modern world and ancient history.

Vega tilted her sunglasses, allowing her eyes to take in the magnificence of the royal fountain of Trevi.

"Isn't it weird to think that this ancient fountain is just *here*... sitting in the middle of a city and that we are driving our modern day cars past? Think of the history all around us, and here we are, just driving in a car past a fountain that is thousands of years old. I mean, could you imagine if you were the creator of this fountain, and got a glimpse into the future to see the modern-day world that now surrounds it? No one could handle that," she laughed.

150

"Well, similarly, do you think that most people could handle glimpses into the past?" Altair asserted their own journey, evoking a rewarding smirk.

"Ah, here we are." Stan instructed the speeding driver as they neared the easily missed shop, tucked within the confines of a slender alley. They walked single file through the alleyway, each lost in their own mental voyage. Vega fantasized about the costumes awaiting her behind the heavy velvet curtain of the entryway, as Altair walked slowly behind her, wondering when he might have another moment alone with the dagger. Stan, lost in his own unusual thoughts, basked in the imagined memories of footsteps that had echoed through these streets long before him, losing himself in the moments of time beneath his feet.

"Coming?" Vega, sensing Altair's distance, grabbed him by the arm, and yanked him through the curtain into the magical land of costumes. Every era and genre hung neatly upon the enchantingly disorganized racks, scattered floor to ceiling within the surprisingly enormous shop. Together they disappeared into the ruins of clothing, passing by silk embroidered gowns, Egyptian heiress dresses, crowns, cuffs, and jewelry until something sparkling caught her eye. "What in the world is that?" She whispered to herself while dipping through the racks of overstuffed gowns toward a simple silk dress, hanging alone on a rusted metal rack. Her cautious fingers danced upon the embroidered patches of beads, which extended like armor over the shoulders of the deep blue dress, as her heart connected with its essence. "This dress…"

"Vega?" Stan said, causing her to jump into the clothing rack behind her. "Sorry to startle you, I found something that I think you might like." With eyes locked on the mysterious dress that called to her, she reluctantly followed him through the store towards a stone staircase, where a beautiful Egyptian gown stood underneath a single beam of sunlight. Hand forged, matching golden cuffs spiraled around the forearms of the mannequin as Altair leaned in, noticing her frozen expression. "Hey! I picked up that dress you were just drooling over. I must say your taste in gowns is far better than your taste in men."

"Funny," she replied, as her eyes remained fixated on the elegant Egyptian dress that magnetically drew her near. She carefully traced her fingers along the sheer train of the dress, which flowed down the staircase, as if awaiting its queen. Like a parent getting their child ready for their first dance, Stan bounced around collecting accessories to compliment the outfit he knew was destined for her. "Here, try this on," he pushed a golden headdress her way, which lay heavy in her hands. Lovingly, she extended it in front of her, turning it the way that it would be placed upon her head. The fragile strands dangled from the frontal stone, wrapping over her head like a hairnet of gold. She giggled as she placed it over her head, feeling the heavy, cold emerald come to rest just in the center of her forehead, as the strands of gold dangled through her hair.

"How do I look?" she looked down the stairs at Altair as Stan rushed off to find a store attendant.

"Try on the gown!" Altair dashed up the stairs to help her remove the dress from the mannequin.

"Wait one moment!" The flashy store clerk rushed up the stairs, yanking the dress from her hands. He struggled to catch his breath between annoyed pants.

"Sorry, but this dress is very, very old. Only a professional handler like myself can remove it from the mannequin. Okay?" he smacked her hands away, evoking a subtle giggle.

"Something funny?" He demanded with hands firmly placed on his hips.

152

"Sorry, I've just never seen anything like this dress before. Most of my clothes are from thrift stores, but…." she smiled towards the dress.

He relaxed his demeanor, realizing that the boyish girl in front of him had probably never even tried on a gown before, and grabbed her by the hand. "Come, let's try this on. I want to know all about why you are buying this." He yanked her through the crowd of clothing and into a private dressing room lined with velvet curtains. As she entered the royally decorated dressing room, her eyes scanned the vaulted ceiling above, noticing the heavenly painting of angels that watched over her.

Noticing her admiration for the space, the store attendant said, "I see you like the dressing room. I tried to make it feel…timeless in here."

"Well you did a good job. It's nice to feel special; even for just a moment on my birthday," she smiled while stepping behind the curtain.

"Oh! Is this dress for your celebration? A theme party I presume?"

"Well, ummm… yes! It's a theme party set in the time of…" she struggled to fabricate the details "It's set in the time period of the 1400's, and the party is being thrown to pay homage to the great artists of the Villa Farnesina."

His rapid pacing outside of the dressing room came to a complete stop.   "Oh! I see! How fun for you!"

"I suppose so," she smiled while slipping into the dress.

"Let me know if you need help getting into the dress!" he called from outside, as she disappeared into a private moment with the piece that she felt might whisk her away in that very moment. Quietly, she pulled the silk garment around her and draped the long sheer train behind her.

153

In response to her admiring silence, the shop clerk interrupted, "Do you know about the Villa? Long before it was owned by the banker it belonged to Julius Caesar; well the land at least. Whatever era of its history you are attuning yourself to, I hope you have a marvelous time!"

She paused, reflecting on his words, 'whatever time she was attuning herself to.'

"What do you mean by that?" She yanked the heavy curtain back, searching outside of the dressing room for the eccentric man.

"Vega?" Altair called out, while slowly entering the lavish dressing room. He inched past the heavy velvet curtains, gold framed paintings, and a large stone fountain in the center of the room toward the sound of her jingling headdress.

"In here!" she peeked her face through the curtain, laughing at his awkwardness.

"You okay? You just kind of ran off?"

"Yeah well, there was a man that..." she stopped noticing his crazy stare, "Nothing."

"Can I see what you tried on?" He smiled as she stepped out onto the royal blue carpeting.

"You look like Egyptian royalty," he smiled while reaching his hand up to adjust her headdress, just as Stan entered the room.

"Oh my," he whispered to himself. "Vega you are a vision!" Stan handed her the gold cuffs for her arms, and fluffed the beige train of the dress.

"You must get this dress!" Stan insisted as Altair draped the other dress over his free arm.

154

"What do you have there?" she nodded towards the stack of billowing shirts, trousers, silk jackets, and scarves layered over his arm.

"I've got to look the part too, and it's good to have options," he smiled.

"You're right, I need options! You know, in case we need to go somewhere else." She cringed, realizing for the first time that she was enjoy dress shopping.

"I'll meet you up front!" Stan exited the dressing room, and Altair quickly followed.

The store clerk painfully wrapped up what was easily his favorite garment in the store, and lovingly placed both dresses into her hands. "I want you to be very careful with the cream dress, and above all, have a very happy birthday."

"Gosh I feel like I'm getting ready for a ball or something," she blushed while taking hold of the hanger.

Puzzled glances followed her as they made their way back to the hotel. Avoiding the birthday topic altogether, Vega asked, "Stan, when we go to the time of the banker, how exactly are we supposed to fit in with these people? I mean, do I bring a gift of some sort to the party?" Questions flew around her racing mind.

"You bring up a good point Vega. I do believe you will need an identity, as well as a gift of some kind upon your entrance. Hmmm," he paused to think.

"What would be considered a really outstanding gift for a man of his time, who had almost everything?" Altair added, "And speaking of gifts..."

"Time!" Thoughts sparked within Stan's mind. "The gift of time! A watch."

155

"Wouldn't he already have a watch?" Vega asked, skirting around the topic of her birthday once more.

"No, the timepiece was not invented until the 1700's. Sure there were scientists working on various mechanisms to tell time, but nothing like the modern day wristwatch."

"Wouldn't that mess with history? Giving someone something before it was invented?" Vega asked.

"That is why it is important that you take it back before you exit the party. It will be up to you, to decide how you do that."

"I think we leave as soon as we both are dressed; what do you think Altair?"

His head nodded in agreement as his mind traveled to a distant place; his future, set some time in the past. Abruptly he reminded his eager counterpart, who was already laying her dress out across the bed, of the real mission. "Remember, we are going there to see the circle of stars on the ceiling, and find the gold that is buried beneath."

She shot a high-school glare his way while arranging her hair into spirals. "You don't think I know why we're going there?"

"I just don't want you to get too caught up in the glamour of it all," he responded.

She placed the curling iron onto the counter, "I'm the last person on this planet that is in any way concerned with glamour," she laughed with an exaggerated hair toss.

Stan interrupted their banter, "Now, I need you both to remember a few key things. Back in the time of these lavish Italian parties, people tried herbs, oils, and liqueurs to heighten their experiences. I do not want either of you to be lured into trying anything that seems suspicious."

156

Vega laughed once more, "You guys really are something! Stan you think that I'm going to try drugs and Altair... you think I'm going to become so consumed with my own vision that I'll lose sight of our mission. Is that what I'm hearing from both of you?"

"No! That isn't at all what we meant!" Stan cowered at the thought of his presumptuous words.

"I'll be fine," she said.

"We'll... we'll be fine."

"Alright, then I suppose I'll leave you both to get changed. Vega, let me go fetch you a timepiece...and dessert with candles for later," he quickly added. "Shall I return in say, 30 minutes?"

"Perfect," they replied in unison.

As the door slowly closed behind him, Altair addressed the elephant in the room.

"You know, even though you're away from your normal life, we can still celebrate your birthday."

"I don't know. I just don't want to draw attention away from Deneb. That's all I care about right now," she sighed.

"Tell you what -- when we get back, we'll have a personal spa day. Whatever you want!" He gestured toward the flower petals scattered around the bathroom, which was fully stocked with facial scrubs, salts, and oils.

"Deal."

CHAPTER 12

Vega fidgeted with the pink diamond watch, strangling both her wrist and character as she walked through the labyrinth of flowers and manicured bushes toward the sound of conversations emanating from the villa ahead. She paused, adjusting her headdress, feeling the soft strands of gold trickle through her hair as she gathered her confidence. The subtle splashing of the fountain eased her nerves as a familiar voice called from behind.

"Fancy seeing you here!" Altair's deep voice triggered a smile, as the last of the sun's rays illuminated her face.

"You look..." she refrained from giggling, "awesome."

"You look stunning." He extended his hand toward the villa, as together they entered the party.

"Wait," Vega subtly yanked on his long silk jacket, "what is our plan?"

"I figured we would enjoy the party, and you would somehow find this banker and trade him the watch for a look at the place under the stars?" He raised an eyebrow, awaiting her reply.

She shrugged as a glass of champagne floated into her hands, pulling her inside toward the lively scene.

"Would you look at this place, and look at that! We just walked right in," Altair whispered while sipping his beverage.

"Careful. Remember what Stan said about spirits and oils!" she paternally scolded while he delighted in the refreshing bubbles.

"It's just champagne Vega." He hushed her as his fleeting eyes danced through the party, admiring the extravagant ambiance of the grand ballroom, finely decorated for a private dinner. The table, covered with fine embroidered silk running down the center, exploded with decadence in the form of golden cups, lavish cocktails, fruits in bronze bowls, and finely carved wooden chairs lining each side.

"There are only six places at this table Vega," Do you know what this means?" he whispered.

Busy plucking grapes from the passing silver tray, she paused, "What?"

"There are only six dinner guests here, which means that they will know that we are outsiders!"

"Don't worry. The servants will notice that we're here and set two additional places, trust me."

She swallowed another grape while raising her chin in lady-like confidence, striding towards the man who she deemed

159

the best dressed. Before she could speak to the person, who she was sure carried the title of 'banker,' a dainty hand grabbed her arm, laughing while pulling her into the parlor. She barely understood the language, thankful for the few years of Italian she had taken in college. Clouds of smoke surrounded the figures of feather-clad women, giggling as lemon scented liqueur flowed over their dainty, clinking glasses. Panic consumed her mind with every moment she was away from Altair, until suddenly a calm overtook her. The sultry, feminine laughs wafted through the hazy clouds, as her mind slowed, allowing her to both admire and study the royal females she sat among. Heavy was the weight of the headdress, as she studied the headpieces of the others. Lace, silk and feathers tied between braids and veils, accented the vivacious eyes that spoke to her through the clouds of smoke. Something felt familiar, as if she had sat here before; many lifetimes ago, clinking glasses with this group of heroic women she now knew nothing about. They spoke of grand ideas, life, astronomy, and the concepts of time that they had infused into the minds of their assimilating counterparts.

"The banker is about to give a tour," one of them giggled while pointing toward the light of the doorway, where Altair's shadow briefly passed behind a short, well-dressed man. Their swarm followed heavy on the heels of the man, proudly pronouncing his presence across the echoing floors as they entered the ballroom. He was nearly across the room, standing proudly with his fingers wrapped around the heavy silk curtains of the doorway, which led outside, when something caught Vega's eye, holding her feet to the floor like glue. Her abrupt stop sent the woman behind her crashing into her back, halting the group altogether as she stared in shock at the bare, white ceiling overhead.

"The ceiling... where is the artwork?" she asked as casually as possible.

"Ah, the ceiling, the topic of our discourse!" he jested for the group to follow him out into the garden. "I suppose I am waiting for the right inspiration," he paused, admiring the magnificence of the stars.

Puzzled looks passed between Altair and Vega as the man, rich with wealth beyond their dreams, pointed towards the sky, speaking exuberant phrases about the constellations above. Trying her hardest to memorize his words, Vega moved closer, careful not to interrupt his grand speech.

"Here on the night of the lion, we gather together, beneath this circle of stars, honoring the god of the fire sign. May the rising of our glasses conjure the falling blessings of Hephaestus, and ignite a fiery passion within our souls." He raised his intricately carved cane towards the stars, illuminating the emerald eyes of the lion that sat atop.

"I don't mean to interrupt, but where did you get such a brilliant walking stick?" Altair boldly interrupted.

The banker chuckled, "This comes from the Orient, passed through the hands of time, to mine. It is said the god Hephaestus, once shunned for his deformity, used this very walking stick. It has travelled through sacred hands to reach me, which is where it belongs."

"The brother of Apollo made that walking stick. What deformity do you speak of?" Altair recanted.

"It is true. The god Apollo had a brother who was gifted in blacksmithing and ironwork. Although gifted in his trade, he fell short in a physical sense, and so he walked with a cane. Legends say he was thrown from the heavens for his deformity, but what he seemingly lacked in physical stature, he graciously made up for with his talents. He was a true god of humility. Some say his physical weakness is what likened him to man; and aided him in finding the mortal Daedalus, his beloved student."

161

As he concluded the conversation, the banker joyously slid a vial of liquid from his coat pocket, holding it up in the air towards the starlight. Altair watched in shock as the man rubbed oil on his lips, and passed the vial between the graceful fingers of his friends. Vega's eyes, completely missing the scene that was unfolding right in front of her, sneakily slipped through their passing hands, and quietly made her way beside Altair.

"The circle of stars from Deneb's dream is either the circle of stars above us now, or the circle of stars that it yet to be painted upon the ceiling here. I don't see any wells here, do you?" She looked through the garden and toward the rushing sound of the river. "But maybe she knew all along that if we came here under seeking a circle of stars, we would somehow find the gold."

He shushed her. "I think they are doing some kind of drug, look, they are passing around an oil and rubbing it on their lips and teeth."

Awkwardly frozen, and not wanting to oust herself from the tribal vibration of the group, she faked her dosage and passed the vial. Once the oil had made its way back into the hands of the banker, the royal gathering of inspired guests joined their golden cups together in a toast to the stars. As their challises remained raised to the full moon above, another man chimed in, "Perhaps you should have the ceiling painted to reflect your most favorite constellations; a true reflection of the eternal glory of the gods!"

The banker scowled. "Bring forth the name of another constellation that embarks such majesty as Leo, and surely I will paint it! Come, let us eat!"

The well-mannered group slowly melted into roaring, celebratory union, spilling forth legendary stories as they continued to consume the delights around them. As all inhibitions seemingly washed away, Altair studied the guests of the banker, none of whom wore clothing of fine silks and tailoring. Alternatively, they all resembled artisans, cleaned up for an evening of swanky delights. All accept one, a calm, yet rigidly pensive, Chinese man who seemed to mirror the gestures of the lively group of artists, scholars, and astronomers. As the night unfolded, the personalities of the guests revealed themselves, showing the banker's true taste for company and heightening Altair's suspicions of the unusually quiet man. Lemon liqueur continued to flow as another round of toasts were tossed across the lengthy dinner table. "To great company!" the banker wobbled while raising his cup, "and to the artist who will paint the breath of life eternal upon the ceiling of my home, Villa Farnesina."

As he patted the back of the gentleman seated next to him, who humbly took a sip of his savory cocktail, Altair and Vega synchronically realized whose company they were in; the actual artist of the ceiling yet to be painted. Before Altair could speak his inspirational words of what *should* be painted on the ceiling, the servants began placing heavy plates of gold before each of the eight dinner guests.

The banker wriggled in excitement as he stood proudly before the table. "Tonight, we dine on golden plates pulled from the depths of the sea! You see, the treasures that I hold dearest to my heart lay not with golden splendor, but here with you, my most precious friends. To wisdom! The true treasure of the world!" He sloshed his wine upon the table as he raised his glass in another celebratory toast.

Shock stuck in Vega's throat as the very same golden plates adorned with the same symbols she had only seen in dreams, circled the table of exemplary dinner guests. She kicked Altair under the table, speaking out of the corner of her mouth so that only he could hear; "Are you seeing what I'm seeing? These were metal plates when I saw them. Now they are gold plates! This has to be the same thing right? Or are there two sets of plates?"

163

"I don't know Vega, but if it's gold we're looking for, it looks like we've found it," he brought up a valid point as they resumed normalcy.

Delightful conversations circled the table as the courses came and went, followed by spiced tea, and various cakes for all to try. As the party began to wind down, panic struck, and Vega kicked Altair under the table once more, forcing him to his feet. He stood awkwardly gazing over the table of pleasantly stuffed dinner guests, as he mustered his courage, "I have an idea for the ceiling; the constellations Aquila, Cygnus, and Lyra are among my favorites."

Laughter erupted from the scientist, banker, and his muse as they disappeared back into their conversations. Noticing the looming presence of the servants, poised to clear the golden plates and toss them into the river like all the others the banker had previously dined upon, Altair leaped to extremes.

"I see that does not amuse you. Perhaps you are unaware of the power of the Summer Triangle?" he waited in silence as their eyes lifted to meet his.

The astronomer provided insight to the group, "The Summer Triangle is comprised of the three brightest stars in the sky, Deneb, Altair, and Vega. The power of the three stars has conjured great myths and legends; most prominently seen in ancient scrolls and songs. The constellation trio is indeed a magnificent display."

"Go on," the banker said. "What more do you have to say about this Summer Triangle?"

All eyes remained locked on Altair, as he took a sip of champagne, triggering a disapproving shake of Vega's head.

"The Summer Triangle is the collective power of three of the brightest stars in the sky, their light representing the glory

164

of creation, creator, and all that exists in this world. With its beginning rooted in the Garden of Eden, The Constellation Cygnus, holds the key to life itself. The symbol of the white swan, pure in its essence, is embodied in the symbol of the egg, representing the beginning of life, and the birth of creation." He pointed at the golden plate inscribed with the egg, as the servant scurried to hand it to him.

"Now, the constellation of Lyra is associated with musical tones said to enchant and entrance great kings, noble knights, and powerful wizards. This song has been entrusted to the second point in the triangle, Vega." The servant rushed once more to grab the golden plate depicting the lyre on it, and handed it to Altair. "Now, the third, and some might say the most important," he winked at Vega in a moment of humored arrogance, "hails from the constellation of Aquila, the Eagle. This constellation is also affiliated with blacksmithing and the arts. It is said to contain powers of creation as well, only in a different way..." Vega sat wide eyed and pressed into her chair, anticipating a moment she feared she could not avoid. "Now, banker, before I show you this display, I'd like to propose an idea, if I may?"

Captivated by the potential show that awaited the starry-eyed group, he quickly replied, "Certainly."

"If you are moved by the delights of this show, you will paint the constellations of the Summer Triangle in great expression upon the ceiling."

He gave a favorable head nod towards the golden plates, awaiting his impression. Vega slid her fingers into the silk lining of her top and subtly pulled her golden figurine out, in an attempt to console her racing mind.

"With this ring, passed down by the God Apollo to the legendary blacksmith Daedalus, I call upon the force of the

Summer Triangle, to awaken the elements here before us." As his final words left his lips, flashes of fiery light began to swirl around his finger, evoking gasps, giggles, and an interrupting question.

"Is this magik the work of the oil?" one of the women giggled while looking over her own jewelry to see if it too was dancing with light.

"I assure you, what you see is real." Altair triumphantly continued, as the swirling light danced around his finger, illuminating the emerald eyes of the lion sitting atop the banker's cane. As the eyes glowed brighter, a glowing bubble of light expanded around Altair. A heavy mix of fear and delight enveloped the room as he calmly placed his powerfully unsure hand to the plate depicting the egg, sparking the attention of the quiet Chinese man in the corner. As the glowing egg began to fuse with his presumably less than human hands, panic overtook him. He dashed outside to the fountain, as the captivated party guests rushed after him, giggling and gasping. He stood at the edge of the fountain watching in awe, as the swirling water quickly moved in accordance with his energy, as if magnetized by the golden plate. Entranced by his own magic, Altair lowed the egg towards the swirling water, evoking a pattern of twisting strands of watery light, moving faster with every inch as he moved the plate closer.

"I don't believe we've met, young man." A deep voice cut into his concentration, slowing the water to dull waves. The Chinese man, cloaked in shadows of black silk, countered his position at the well, holding the other plates under his arm. Altair frantically looked for Vega, whose shadow seemed to be slinking behind the backs of the surrounding guests.

"Who are you, and what do you want with the plates?" Altair demanded on behalf of everyone present.

166

"My name is Ma Qiang, and I have travelled from a far, to collect what is rightfully mine. Now, drop the plate into the water, and I will be on my way," he casually instructed.

Noticing the anger consuming his adversary, the man spoke once more, "Don't think about trying anything brash Altair; it is my time to rise," he said as he pulled back one side of his silk jacket, revealing a long silver spear. The frightened guests cowered within the grace of each other's arms as the banker stepped into their midst.

"Tell me Ma Qiang, from whence do you hail?"

A devilishly proud smile slid across his pale cheeks, as snatched the cane from beneath the banker. "Auriga."

The banker pondered the familiar constellation of the charioteer, as he grabbed hold of a nearby guest, to keep his balance.

"Now give me the egg Altair!" Ma Qiang demanded. Empty of any grandiose idea for action, Altair slowly lowered the egg to the water, triggering an unexpected vortex-like portal, spinning quickly within the fountain.

As he contemplated his next move, the shadow of a familiar object rose from behind the man, creating both a longing for the object, and fear of what she might do with his beloved dagger. Vega fearlessly lunged towards the man, chaotically knocking the egg from Altair's hands, and sending herself, the man, and the plates into the quickly disappearing spiral of water below. Altair watched his precious dagger fall from her hands, landing in the dirt beside the fountain, as the dismantled tornado of water fell around the quickly closing doorway like raindrops. With mere seconds to decide, Altair jumped into the vortex, calling her name as he fell.

"Altair?" Vega choked for air, pulling herself out of the frigid water of the enormous lake. She frantically wiped her eyes with one hand, while straightening her heavy Egyptian gown with the other. Her hands frantically searched for the small treasure tucked within her breast, sighing in relief as she gripped the small phoenix. The heat of the morning sun burned her pale cheeks as she trudged towards the shade of a mulberry tree, where she surrendered to the comfort of the land. The thick trunk supported her back as flickers of sunlight tunneled between the leaves, casting shadowy snowflakes upon the grass. Not quite ready to get up, yet eager to explore her surroundings, she leaned forward, caressing the soft blades of grass through the tender tips of her fingers. Her mind, still adjusting from travel, pondered the elongated shadow eclipsing her own.

"You need not be alarmed," an angelic voice called from behind, as Vega forced herself to her knees, only to fall once more.

"Shhhh, do not speak. I am here to help restore you to health," the woman hurried into the shade of the tree, as Vega raised her head to assess her new companion. Her face was white as a ghost, and looked as if it had never seen the sun until this very moment. Her linen dress, dyed with stains of burgundy, was tied tightly around her waist with a sash of beige silk. Two whittled twigs held her shiny black hair back into a slick bun, except for a few graceful strands that the wind had carried. She placed her cold hands around Vega's, as she knelt down to meet her.

"I can heal you." She looked across the field of yellow wildflowers, nodding toward the mouth of a cave at the base of a snow-capped mountain. "I will help you walk," she said as she hoisted her small yet powerful arm around Vega's waist, and helped her to her feet.

Together they walked through what seemed like miles of wild flowers, until at last they reached the small cave, which now showed itself to be a simple home. A crackling fire quickly warmed the room, as the woman combined fragrant mixtures of herbs and aromatic flowers that she boiled into a tasty tea. The small, handmade teacup warmed Vega's once shaking hands, while the effective tea rapidly reawakened her youth. As her energy restored, Vega looked past the shadows of the dingy cave, admiring the simplicity of the woman's lifestyle.

"Are you alone here?" She posed the first question of the day.

"In a sense, but not."

Vega smirked at her evasiveness. "Well, thank you for saving me. I am really far from...home," she pondered which method had taken her the furthest from home, space or time.

The woman took a seat beside her, stirring petals of dandelion into her cup of steaming water. "Your journey need not be measured in lengths of simple men."

Vega shook her head in agreement, while trying to figure out just where she was. "There is a man, who stole something that belongs to me. I followed him, and ended up here. I don't intend to leave until I retrieve what is rightfully mine."

"As the sun passes through the sky, your body deteriorates. You must hurry to find what it is your heart seeks."

Alarm wrinkled across her youthful forehead. "How do you know of my condition?"

Casually, she sipped her tea before responding. "I know all, for I am the Magi. I heard your tone, as it is my own."

"Magi?" Vega traced the words back to the origins of her past, "As in magician?"

She nodded in agreement. "You may call me Magu. We do not have a lot of time, for there is another place that you must see."

Vega took a few steps toward the mouth of the cave, as Magu called from the darkness behind her, "This way."

As they walked through the tunnels of the mountain, etched into the memory of the anciently wondrous woman, Vega posed a question sparked from what few words the woman had said.

"You said that you knew my tone, as it is your own, what did you mean by that?" She carefully followed the footsteps of the light-footed woman into the darkness.

"It is my song that vibrates within your being; I heard your soul crying, like a siren who sings from the waves of a rocky island."

Trying her hardest to squint through the absence of light, Vega called into the tunnel, "Is the ocean nearby? I hear water."

"Do you know why this tunnel was carved between the Holy Lake and the Devil's Lake?" The looming silence urged her to continue. "Today, on the day of the Axis, the doors of time will open, sending forth light from the mountain."

"The lake that you found me near, what is it called?"

"The Holy Lake," the woman answered.

"And am I the only person to have emerged from that lake?" she called into the darkness.

"From that lake, yes," Her response invited more questions.

"Why is the other lake called Devil's lake?" She cringed, fearing the answer.

"A snake-headed beast is said to have emerged from the once pure lake. The beast transformed its essence with a stagnantly foul element. Since its rebirth, the lake has been named Devil's Lake."

"Is she the only being to emerge from Devil's Lake?" Vega's pace, driven somewhat by fear, quickened.

"Until today, yes."

"And of what importance is this day of the Axis?" Vega grabbed the cavern wall as the sound of Magu's footsteps ceased.

"On this day, The Celestial Axis illuminates its connection between sky and earth where the four compass directions meet, allowing for travel and communication between the higher and lower realms. Breathe, you who dwell in the light, so that you may shine your light into the darkness of otherworldly realms and gain possession of the cool waters which open the gates of time."

"The gates of time?" she asked as a flicker of light emerged in the tunnel.

"It is said that those who make songs may enter, holding steady to a tethered cord, to fetch back what is theirs and return to their time. Be warned that the portals of time are only open when the sun passes over the cool waters. If you decide to make this choice, may your hands be steady, your legs move swiftly, and your soul rejoice."

Vega pondered the hidden meanings of her phrasing as the light expanded in the distance of the tunnel.

"Are you ready to open the door?" the woman whispered.

"Now? We open it now!?"

"If you are ready, we shall shine forth from the mountain."

171

As the song slipped through her lips, instinctually, Vega cringed in combativeness; thinking for mere seconds that she had been robbed of her soul's only secret. As the majestic tune of her livelihood echoed off the sacred walls, she joined in, watching as the harmony of their existence ripped open a doorway of light from the darkness of the cave. In silent confidence, they stepped through to the other side, as the sound of the hymn ceased and the tunnel crumbled behind them. "Silence, we must move like ghosts, as that is what we are now."

They slipped from the mouth of the once sacred mountain, into a silvery scape of futuristic wealth. The lavish multi-level pagoda beamed with light from the overhead sundial, casting rays of gold off the sleek, silver walls inside. Directly below, a simple fountain stood, devoid of any fixtures, lights or accents. Vega cast a curious eye across the balcony, trying to place where she had seen this all before.

"How the..." Vega thought, as she locked eyes with Magu, who suddenly appeared beside the fountain. Silence seemed to emanate from her eyes as she urged Vega to join her, before slipping away into the shadows of the nearby garden.

Hurried footsteps echoed along the shiny labyrinth of slick silver balconies, stacked around the fountain, extending up to the opening above. A familiar man cloaked in black silk made his way down through the levels, approaching the simple fountain below. Her eyes centered in on the man, who she knew carried the treasure she had travelled through time to retrieve. She slyly inched her way over to a set of stairs. The safety of the shadows shielded her from the man, as he lowered his hood, and stood proudly over the water.

A quick gasp escaped her, as she stared longingly towards the only man she had ever loved. Turmoil traveled between her head and her heart as she contemplated stepping into the light of his presence. Decisively she stepped forward, and quickly retreated, as another approached.

Another man, similarly dressed in black silk, bowed before joining him. "Emperor -- on this day of your eternal celebration, I'd like to offer you what I know your heart desires."

Fury boiled within, as she watched the thief present the stack of golden plates to Lan. His eyes, once kind and loving, flashed with greed and power as he proudly took the plates from the man's hands.

"This, she will be most pleased with." He smiled as he gazed down into the water. Timing favored another move, as Vega quickly slid behind the backs of the occupied men, who were fixedly looking into the waters of the fountain.

Just as she was about to foolishly pounce on the armed men, a soft voice whispered from behind.

"You must wait until the time is right. The portals are not open. Search the room; do you see anything familiar here that calls to you?"

"Besides him?" Vega smirked.

She waited as Vega peered across the room, stopping when her eyes met a copper vase sitting high upon an ornately carved jade shelf.

"That vase; I've seen it before in an underwater cave."

"Do you see how the future can impact the past?"

"We are in the future?" Vega winced.

Magu nodded. "Seize the moment when the portal is open, and remember that sometimes the gold of a deed is heavier than the sum of any treasure."

The sunlight of the autumn equinox shifted over the sundial, illuminating the slowly churning waters of the once simple well, duplicating the roar of the crowd outside the palace walls. Beams of gold flashed over the well, as she waited eagerly with watchful eyes alternating between the face appearing in the water, and the copper vase, which she knew contained her green elixir.

Magu's words pounded through her consciousness as she moved silently toward the simple vase, which vibrated from the sound of the chanting hoards outside. She placed her steady hands around the simple vase, while all eyes remained fixated on the face she knew was emerging from the watery doorway. Startled by the passing shadow of the sun, the word doorway suddenly caused rampant thoughts, "was this quickly closing doorway the only way out of here?" As she tucked the vase under her arm like a football, something fell from her wrist. Never in her life had she heard something so tiny make such a loud noise.

She scowled at the dainty pink watch, as she stepped forward into the light of the quickly fading sun. The powerful words that so seamlessly slipped from the royal emperor's tongue froze upon his lips like a winter's spell as he stared at the ghost of his glory.

"I can handle this," Ma Qiang stepped in front of Lan, slinging back his cloak, pulling forth his silver spear. Vega's frightless, love-struck eyes remained locked with Lan's as she stepped toward the arms she longed to feel embrace her once more. The melody of her song, though not from her lips, vibrated around her as she moved closer to him once more.

"You." He stepped powerlessly towards her, as she slid the copper vase behind her back.

"You." Tears slid down her cheeks, and splashed into the well. She tore her eyes from his, for mere seconds, as she

174

caught a glimpse of Deneb, reaching through her watery ceiling for the gold she was destined to place within the chest of her fate.

The water spiraled faster, perhaps energized with the hope of her freedom, as Vega capitalized on the intimate moment between her and Lan, and tossed the vase to the water below.

"Deliver it to the depths of the sea! To a place where no one will find it!" she yelled, knowing in her heart just where it would safely end up. Deneb's hands, soft as silk and white as snow, poked through the waves towards the vessel, feeling the freedom of their world, if only for a second.

As the shadows of the autumn sun swept across the water, Magu continued their song, suspending the silver spear of the charioteer in the air, mere inches from Vega's chest. Noticing the tiring woman struggling to continue their tune, Vega joined her; relieving her from her efforts. Magu appreciatively exhaled, and caught her breath; unintentionally sending the silver spear directly at Lan, nicking the side of his face. While he tended to his bleeding cheek, Vega scrambled to grab as many plates as her arms would allow.

"Follow me!" Magu screamed, as their song echoed like a royal cannon throughout the entire temple. Together they fled through the palace gates, to the gardens below, where a swarm of chanting people met them. Vega paused, realizing her outfit had caused somewhat of a silent commotion, commanding attention from all.

"It's her! The Queen!" The crowd erupted. Vega suddenly stopped on the steps above the sea of people who were fixated on her, as she looked out at the snow-capped mountain from whence she came, and the Holy Lake to which she longed to return. Vega demanded that the sea of buzzing people part for her ascension, as together they ran through the quickly collapsing pathway. Treasonous calls tore the crowd apart once more, as a fleet of silk clad man raced through the resuming cheers of onlookers, chasing the fleeing women, charging towards the Holy Lake.

As they neared the water's edge, the voice of her once faithful lover shattered her concentration. "Vega! Stop!" His voice fell like rain upon the quiet sea of people.

Seeing the sadness that caused her to pause, Magu insisted, "There isn't much time my dear. You must choose. Do not worry about me. I agreed to my destiny long before I came to this planet... written into the stars," she winked. Sadness overcame her, as she reminded herself of the words he had spoken to her while in his purest form. "I am with you now, but not with you then." Perhaps he knew that she would meet him again, and would need to be reminded of who he was, and who he was yet to become. In another sense, her heart felt bound to the woman who remained tied to the eternal mountain, emerging through the portals of time only at the most critical moments of her existence. Was she but a ghost? And what did that make Vega?

The last fragments of sunlight shimmered like white caps upon the Holy Lake, as Vega waded out into the waters of autumn, and drowned out the calls from her lover, echoing behind her. Fragments of his voice spun like a tornado of memories as she submerged herself into the secrecy of the waters. The sound of her song spun the walls of water around her as she closed her tear soaked eyes, longing to leave a place and time she was yet to determine. The spiral of water quickly solidified, as she grasped her shaking fists around what was now a whirlwind of sheets tangled around her.

"Vega!" Altair raced to her side, sweeping the wet, freezing girl into the warmth of his arms. Tears streamed from her eyes as she tucked herself into his chest, quietly sobbing in agony from the mental and physical ailments that now overcame her.

Her once elegant headdress was now tangled in a turmoil of red knots, and matched the state of her not so elegant waterlogged gown, as she struggled for words.

"What can I do?" He sprinted towards the bathroom, yanking the oversized white bathrobe off the hook. She coughed. "Water, I need some water."

"Are you sick? What's the matter?" He threw the robe next to her as he slid across the floor to the kitchen.

He placed the cup of water into her shivering hands, as she whispered between slow sips, "Where's Stan?"

"He went back to his room for a bit. We sat here for hours waiting for you to return." Before she could open her mouth to share the story of her journey, he interrupted.

"Hold on. Before I call Stan, I want to know why every time you travel, you come back in this condition. It only seems to be getting worse!" He sadly scolded.

She paused, while trying to find the best way to explain. "So, the travel seems to impact each of us differently. Deneb was able to travel as many times as she wanted, and remained unaffected by it, but I however have a very different experience."

"How so?"

"Every time I travel, and it doesn't matter what time period I visit, I grow… older. Time seems to change me for the worse each time I slip through it. By the time Deneb and I travelled back to Egypt to confront Hydra, I was hundreds of years old… then…in that time."

177

Noticing his silent confusion, as he searched for wrinkles on her youthful face, she replied, "When I arrive back in present time, the physical aging is gone, however the debilitating effects of it remain. At first, the sickness I felt lasted only a few hours, but the more times that I go, the worse it gets."

"Oh Vega, I'm so sorry. So the last time that you and I travelled, you felt sick when we returned?"

She shamefully nodded. "It wasn't that bad. We were only gone for fifteen minutes and it seems that my body healed rather quickly that time."

"Interesting. Wait, is that why you felt so awful after your dive with Stan, in Crete?"

"Honestly, I still don't know what happened there, but I suppose that would make sense because I know that I travelled... somewhere."

"There's more that we need to discuss. Stay right here." She rolled her eyes to communicate that she could not physically go anywhere, even if she wanted to.

"Right, sorry, be right back." He slowly walked into the other room to retrieve Deneb's journal. He flipped to the page she merely regarded as a dream, and waited quietly while Vega read.

Dear... journal. I am using this moment as somewhat of a confessional. I have travelled without Vega. I feel she is growing too sick to go, and there are things that call me in the night that I need to answer. Last night I dreamt of the pirate, Anne Bonny, who I have seen in dreams before. However, this time, when I dreamt of her, I travelled through the depths of the sea, to actually meet her. The dream began with somewhat of a birds' eye view, as if I were part of the fog looming over her ship.

Anne laid back on the old wood boards of the deck, unknowingly synchronizing the rising and falling of her chest with the sea beneath her. Her mate took his rightful place beside her, for what had become somewhat of a nightly ritual, aligning his gaze with hers upon the magnificence of the sky. With clasped hands, they silently lay in wonderment, admiring the beauty that returned without fail, night after night. Unknown to them, this night would change their existence and ripple through time. Just as Anne looked away from the sky, and turned to press her chapped, seafaring lips to his equally rugged face, something smacked against the side of the ship. Simultaneously, they sprang to their feet, each drawing their weapon of choice; Anne a dagger, and the knight his sword. They inched apart, across the creaking floorboards, so they could attack from opposite directions to defend against whoever had dared to make an attempt at their ship. Despite the petite frame that months at sea had given Anne, the courage of a lion still roared from her eyes as she pressed her hands to the bow, leaning over to confront whatever waited on the other side…, which somehow was me.

"What is it Anne?" the knight called from the opposite end of the ship, as the vision of the creature she had only heard of through fireside tales, consumed her. Her majestic eyes interlaced with mine, as twisting trails of light flickered through the darkness of the waves below. Unmoved, Anne spoke to me, and said, "What be ya business here creature?"

As I looked up at her, I replied, "I am here to make you a trade. I will give you 100 weight in gold, if you bid me one favor."

She sneered, but not before telling the knight to stand back, as she leaned over the bow a bit further. "Ya got me attention creature, tell me what ya bid me do."

Offended, if only for a moment, by the word creature, I continued the conversation. "There is a map, a ring, and a crystal in your possession, and I need you to give me that crystal, for only a day's time. I give my word, that before you reach the shorelines of Franca I will return it to you. You must promise to follow the coordinates on the inside of the ring to a cave, and bury both the map and ring together and mark the place of secrecy with an X."

"Why?" she snarled through her tobacco stained lips.

179

"Because the future of your soul depends on it."

Caring more for the gold than her soul, she replied, "Where is the gold? I need to see it."

"If you agree, I will meet you at sunrise with the gold coins of Minos, on the last island before you reach the coast of Franca."

"I make ye trade, but tell me this, are there more of you?"

I paused, wondering if she meant people like Vega and me, so I answered, "Yes."

She reached a celebratory hand up in the air, spilling her rum in rhythm with the rocking ship, as she yelled to the open air of the sea, "I be blessed by de gods tonight! And tonight we drink to gold!"

The heavy footsteps of her regal companion quivered across the deck of the ship, as the shadow of his golden sword rose alongside her teetering glass. Celebratory songs echoed across the water as they lowered their weapons, and merged their two shadows into one.

I swam from the boat, looking out at the light of the nearly full moon, as the word 'creature' began to torment my mind. The water swirled beneath me as I began my dive, down to the place where I had long been hiding golden coins, planning for this precise moment. I inched through the debris of many failed voyages, to the remnants of one lonely, unmarked ship, and uncovered centuries worth of golden coins. Then I woke up."

"When did you read this?" she asked.

"I had some time to myself before you returned. Do you see what this means?" He pointed to the last line of the entry, 'then I woke up.' "This simple journal confession was no dream, it was a premonition of her future state, somewhat intertwined with the consequences of her past." He closed the journal.

"I didn't know she had travelled without me," she mumbled in a hurt tone.

"You didn't?"

She shook her head while recalling the entry, "Do you know what this means? If that pirate kept her word, which, judging by where you found the map and the ring, she did, then it means that Deneb somehow borrowed the crystal for a day, and traded all of the gold coins that she collected from Alexander. That also means that all of those gold coins are together. Speaking of gold...."

She excitedly sat up, winced in pain, and fell back onto the pillow.

"You're right. We need to figure out how the metal plates that you and I saw, became the lavish golden plates that we dined on," he attempted to anticipate her sentence.

"Altair, help me remove this heavy, wet dress, "she said while unwrapping her robe.

"I'll help you Vega, but I just don't feel right seeing you that way."

"Of course you don't," she painfully laughed. "But I need to get this thing off of me, and more importantly, I need to show you what I brought back, which is uncomfortably beneath me."

Somehow, their mutual excitement for her acquisition made it less awkward. He lifted the waterlogged dress up and over her head; shutting his eyes as it rose above her knees.

She giggled at his chivalrous attempts, while she slipped into her sweatpants and oversized t-shirt, and returned to the comfort of the cozy white robe.

"Can I open my eyes now?"

"Yes, open them." She smiled as she battled gravity to prop the heavy golden plates up onto the pillow.

181

"Where are the rest of them?"

"For real? You aren't even impressed that I managed to get three of the eight?!" she laid back with an agitated huff.

"No! I'm impressed that you somehow managed to even get one of the plates! I know you're tired, and probably don't even want to talk about the whole trip, so why don't we just take it easy tonight, order in, and talk about whatever your heart desires."

"For real?" she raised an eyebrow; "Whatever I want?" she sat up, nodding towards her bag of spa-like goods.

Altair laughed, "Yes, whatever you want."

"You're full of it... you're too...."

"Too what?" he raised an inquisitive eyebrow while playfully crossing his arms.

Her face flushed with a hint of embarrassment as her headdress slid down over her eyes, "I don't know, too macho I guess."

Defending his pride, he dove into the bag of facial scrubs, essential oils, and clay masks, arrogantly arranging them neatly upon the table. She laughed while pushing the golden accessory out of her eyes, getting a better look at him.

"I've never done this before, so you're going to have to help me. Hold on a sec -- I think I know what I need." His dashing smile caused her face to light up, as he disappeared into the bathroom.

In the moments of solitary silence, she slid her careful fingers over the deep outlines on the golden plates she had managed to bring back. The swelling pride within her battled the sorrow that vibrated through them, as she tried to occupy her mind with thoughts of the future, which ultimately seemed to lead her right back to Lan. Deep emotions overcame her composure as she fell to the bed, silently sobbing over the only physical trace of him, which she had stolen.

"Ta Da!" He emerged from the bathroom in a matching robe, expecting to see a completely different sight.

"Oh man, you okay?"

The enormity of her sorrow overcame her as she painfully sobbed. "I saw Lan, but he was different. Somehow, even though he was devoted to Hydra, he saw me... he felt me."

"Oh Vega, I'm so sorry. You don't have to talk about this now."

"But I do," she shamelessly walked towards the presumptuously romantic pyramid of candles protruding from the walls, overlooking her bed.

"I need to come to the realization that the love of my life is not in love with me in this lifetime, and more so, I need to mentally prepare for what he might throw at me, knowing that I have always loved him unconditionally. These golden plates must be protected, and I think that somehow you need to be in charge of them."

Nonchalantly Altair opened the jar of fresh sea salt face scrub as he lit the candles she was scowling at. "This is our spa night Vega. How about we just relax and talk about all of the heavy stuff tomorrow."

She smiled, and then gasped; realizing for the first time that she had plans for the following day.

"Oh my god. I have a date tomorrow with Ben!" She rushed to the bathroom, and gripped the doorframe as her legs failed to synchronize with her enthusiasm.

"Whoa! Easy does it!" Altair swooped in behind her, guiding the falling girl to the edge of the tub. "How about you sit here, and I do all the work?" He kicked the hot water faucet; in an attempt to steam the room as he twisted open the jar of facial scrub.

"Okay," she smiled, admiring his attempt at easing her mind.

He squinted a skeptic eye at the wording of the jar, "This scrub will leave your face glowing as if you've just drank from the fountain of youth. Oh, speaking of cheesy wording, a letter showed up for you today," he chuckled. "Don't worry, it basically said 'you're so beautiful, I can't wait to see you, meet me in the lobby at 8 am to hike near the Blue Grotto, blah blah blah, Ben."

"Very funny." She extended her hand, and yanked the washcloth from his hand, quickly spreading it across her face. Moments of silence passed as he watched the tired girl soak her sorrow away into the rag which rose and fell with each breath. Foreign to the schedule of spa night, Altair mirrored her actions, placing a warm wet washcloth over his face, wondering for the first time why he had never done it before.

Hours passed as they moved through layers of salt scrubs, masks and oils, wiping away the memories of the day, as she opened up and talked about her travels. At last, when their faces were glowing, and their hands and feet were lathered in lavender, Altair realized that she needed much more than what he or perhaps anyone, could obtain for her.

"Hey, what's the matter, you look sad?" She flipped open the room service menu, eyeing the various pasta options.

"Nothing, I just, I was just thinking about... " The relaxed state of his body made it impossible for his mind to fabricate anything other than the truth. "I didn't realize you had been through so much. I see my own sadness when I look at you, I guess."

"We've both been through a lot, but you know what? We need these trials because that is how we become who we are supposed to be."

"You think that we needed to lose the only people we've ever loved, to somehow make us stronger?" he snatched the menu and flopped down on the couch.

"Do you remember that vase that I found in France when I was diving with Deneb?" She pulled the menu back as she sat down beside him.

"Mmm hmm," he looked over her shoulder as they shared the view.

"I know this sounds crazy, but I think that Deneb is the one who put it there for me to find, but only because I chose to save the vase over the gold. What I'm getting at here is that I think that our future is already written into the stars."

"How so?"

"Well, I've already found the vase in present time, which means that I had already made the decision to save the vase over the gold, even though I hadn't done it until today. Because Deneb is this timeless being who can jump, or swim, or whatever she does, through these portals of time, it means that it is all connected. Like all of our actions have already somehow happened or something."

"I don't know Vega. You had the choice to save the vase or grab all of the gold. You made that decision on your own. It isn't like you were forced to do one thing or the other. Who knows, if you had opted for the gold, maybe that vase would have still somehow ended up where it did. You do bring up a good point though. If Deneb is able to move things from time period to time period, then why did she borrow the

185

crystal from the pirate? What could she possibly have used it for during the precise time that she had it?" Altair solemnly stared at his ring, as if it held the answer.

"More importantly, what was so important to her, to justify trading decades of saved treasure for an hour with the crystal?"

"I don't know, but what I do know is that I'm starving." Altair nodded back towards the menu.

"Right, how about you order us some pasta, and I'll open up a little wine for us. What would a spa night be without it?"

As Altair picked up the phone, he immediately realized his failure to call the one person he had promised to call as soon as she had returned. "Oh no! Stan! We forgot to call Stan!"

"Oh man! Well, you better order a lot of food, but call him first!"

After hanging up, Altair quickly dialed the lobby, ordering up a spread of pasta large enough to feed a family of five.

A sharp knock followed within moments of the phone hitting the receiver. "You kids in there?" His voice rang out as he burst through the door in anticipation. He scurried in, beaming in excitement at their healthy glows.

"Smells wonderful in here," he inhaled while observing their white bathrobes. "Did I miss the memo?" he chuckled.

"Sorry Stan. Vega was in quite the state when she returned so…"

"And what about you?" Stan joked while nodding towards his bathrobe.

"Fair enough," he smiled. "We just ordered some dinner. We'd love it if you could stay and join us?"

As they wolfed down bite after delicious bite of savory, saucy pasta Altair shared the details of the only part of the story that he had witnessed.

"So, Stan, you wouldn't believe what happened! We went to a swanky party at the Villa and guess who was there! The artists who created the very paintings that cover the walls, which by the way were bare when we were there! They dined with us, while discussing their thirst for knowledge, science, and understanding of the universe. It was incredible. They had zero interest in the wealth of common men, and shared a deep passion for the arts, science and of course the stars. Now, that is not even the craziest part! The banker led the intimate group of us outside to gaze upon his most favorite constellation, Leo, as if to spark the inspiration for what was yet to be painted."

Stan's eyes and mouth remained frozen in gaping disbelief as he continued.

"After discussions of stars, constellations, and our favorite muses, we sat for dinner, and you wouldn't believe what we dined on…" He waited, only to be answered with a puzzled head nod. "The metal plates that we have seen in our visions, they were gold, and… we ate off of them!" Several moments of silence passed as Altair waited for his words to erupt the many maddening questions that he saw were visibly causing discomfort in the man.

"Do you mean to tell me that you ate from the plates of Apollo? And not only did you eat off of them, they were gold?"

"There's more to the story," Vega interrupted. "There was a man there that didn't seem to belong with the group of stoic artists. He silently dined with us and seemed to be almost studying our every move. His appearance and clothing were Chinese in nature, and he went by the name of Ma Qiang."

187

His very name sent tension up Stan's spine, abruptly changing the mood of his disposition. "Do you know who you have just encountered? Did he hurt you? Either of you!?"

"No, he didn't, but he tried." Vega revealed the rest of the story, and her attempts to fearlessly challenge the spear-clad warrior she knew nothing of, with a simple dagger.

"So you jumped through the portal after him, and Altair, you jumped in after Vega? Is that correct?"

His question suddenly yanked Altair's mind away from immediate thoughts of the dagger's whereabouts, as he asked again, "Altair? You jumped together but ended up in different places?"

"Yes. I mean, I know that where I landed was different from her. Which was where … Vega?" he shifted the questioning back to her as thoughts of the dagger consumed him once more.

"Describe it to me Vega, and I will try to tell you where it was that time took you."

"Well, I emerged from a lake into a field of wildflowers, and crawled into the shade of a mulberry tree. Thankfully, there was a woman there, who came down from the mountain, and saved me. If it wasn't for her…."

"This woman; what did she look like? What was her name?"

"She was beautiful; fair skinned, and appeared radiant, as if her body had never experienced impurity in any form. Simple sticks held her shiny black hair back, and her dress was simple yet elegant. She said that she found me because my tone was her own… she knew my song, and I knew hers, as it was one and the same. We both had learned from the same guide, Lyra, and she introduced herself as Magu."

188

Stan stood and began pacing the room, interrupting her story, "Vega, the woman that you encountered is a primal goddess from the ancient realms of the Orient. She is the bearer of fruit and protector of women, said to appear only to those in trouble, or who are celebrating a birthday. Myths have placed her in many places at once, able to navigate portals of time, only visible to those that she allows to see her. Often called the magician, or Magi, Magu gets her name from the various acts of heroism and magic she has used to out-maneuver her enemies throughout the ages. What a gift to have encountered such a being. She is affiliated with the mountain, standing between the Holy Lake and Devil's Lake in China."

"Wow, if I had known all of this going into it..." she paused wondering just what, if anything, she would have changed.

"The more important question is, where did she take you?"

"This will sound a bit crazy, but we entered a cave that was carved into the base of a snow capped mountain, and walked through a dark tunnel until we reached a glowing light at the end. It was as if we walked through the mountain into a time altogether different. The future."

"Just how far into the future would you say you went?"

"Oh, I don't know! Is there currently a silver temple there dedicated to Lan? If so, then maybe not too far," she said with a snarky tone.

"Wait; say that again, you saw a temple there? Between the lakes?"

"Yes, there was a temple that was vainly reflective, with silver walls, jade accents, and heavy wooden doors. The most important feature of the entire seminary was a simple fountain, which stirred to life as the golden plates came closer to it. I guess I should add, the man who stole the plates from us at the party, jumped through the well and

189

was also there, presenting them as gifts on what he said was a celebratory day, specifically for Lan."

"Like a birthday?" Altair interrupted.

"I guess so, but it seemed more important than that. Wait, so is there a temple there or not?" Vega asked.

"Not presently." Stan resumed his pacing as he shared his thoughts. "There is a festival that takes place during the Autumn Equinox dedicated to the Green Man. Historically speaking, if we look at the existence of the immortal man who once drank your green elixir, we can tie him to the livelihood of the Green Knight, as well as others of the same hue. I think though, that it would be worthwhile to look at other aspects of the Autumn Equinox, which celebrate the aspect of reaping what you sow, and the cornucopia shaped tunnel filled with offerings. If we compare your experience to the tunnel, where within you found a tie to your own gifts, we could shine light on the reasons why you were there in the first place, to reap what you have sewn."

"When would I have sewn any of the things I witnessed there?" she abrasively said, trying to steer her mind away from the vision it kept forcefully replaying.

"Don't you see? Because you shared your elixir with him, you essentially made him immortal. And here in the future you are confronted with the actions of your past."

"So it is all my fault?" she crossed her arms and began to circle the room in the opposite direction.

"No, Vega. I am simply saying that the symbols associated with the Autumn Equinox represent the celebration of rebirth and an undying crop. People celebrated their harvests, and praised the shielding aspects of Mother Nature, knowing that even though the winter would come, Her promise for rebirth would remain true for the spring. The opposite symbol on the calendar is the Egg, so, I would imagine that in some fashion you were shown the colder side of life, something that you would need to have faith in believing could be revived."

"So is that why Altair was shielded from this? Because it wasn't his battle?"

"Honestly, I don't know why Altair ended up in a different place, but I do want you both to know that the person you encountered, Ma Qiang, is a dangerous man. He carries what is known as the four spears of the wind; dangerous primal weapons controlled merely by breath and intentions. He is in tune, so to speak, but in a darker way. You see Vega, every light casts a shadow, and for everything that has been created in this world, there is an equal and opposite creation. He is a lot like you in a sense..."

"Wait, when I asked where he was from, he gave an answer. Auriga."

"Well, Auriga is the constellation of the charioteer, though in all of the legends I've read the charioteer is of noble bearing. You both saw the ceiling at Villa Farnesina; there was a charioteer painted in the center of the most important constellations. Actually, some legends say that Auriga is the son of the god of blacksmithing, Hephaestus. Perhaps the ring you wear was once promised to him, and was given to another."

"Maybe someone promised him that they could help him get it back..." Vega added.

"Interesting thought," Stan added. "Maybe you're onto something here. Maybe he was once noble, but turned dark at some point."

Vega stopped pacing. "You know...Lan changes every 500 years, maybe there are others who have somehow fallen into the same predicament? Furthermore, maybe the dagger that Lan told me could sever bonds somehow severs their alliance to Hydra!"

"Let's hope. However, I think it wise to assume that Hydra seeks an army of those that can change sides, from light to dark; people she can easily control. Maybe she used the ring as leverage over him?"

"Speaking of the connections between the light and the dark, or as you say it, the higher and the lower, Magu said something about the mountain itself being a **Celestial Axis, which she explained served as a** connection between sky and earth where the four compass directions meet, allowing for travel and communication between the higher and lower realms."

"Perhaps the Autumn Equinox provides a time where those of light and dark can meet."

Vega looked at the clock. "Oh my gosh, I need to go to sleep soon. I have a big day tomorrow."

Stan placed his hands on his hips, assuming a fatherly position as he scowled, "You've already had a big day today Vega. I think you should be taking it easy tomorrow; don't you agree Altair?"

"Wait, what?" he cringed at the thought of teaming up against Vega on the subject he clearly agreed on. "I... I think she is old enough to make decisions for herself. She knows better than to put her body through something that perhaps it can't handle." He tried to say it with a straight face. "But in all seriousness, I think Vega needs to decide for herself what she is up for tomorrow."

"Which is what exactly?" Stan pushed for more information.

"Well, since you both are so interested in my social life all of a sudden I guess it wouldn't kill me to tell you what his note said," she sighed while walking over to her bag, where she had hidden away the precious keepsake of what would be their first date.

"If you're wondering why the note is creased in different places, it was folded up like an origami bird before I read it," Altair confessed.

Daggers shot from her eyes to silence his heckling. "The note says: Vega, I feel like I've waited lifetimes to have our first date. I promise I will not disappoint. Meet me at sunrise in the lobby, for a day of hiking on the beautiful island of Capri."

"You guys are going to Capri?" Altair sulked, "I wanted to see that with you."

"Well, I'm sure that you and Stan can go see it, or something equally as cool. Hey! Pompeii isn't too far from here either."

"Do you know much about Capri? I assume you will be taking a foil boat to the island."

Guilt created a shameful smile as she answered, "I know it's an island made famous by legendary myths of sirens who lured Ulysses in the epic tale of The Odyssey."

Stan gave a shrug, disappointed that she knew nothing of the magical Blue Grotto, Roman castles, or other historical destinations, but knew tidbits of fabled mermaids and their triumphs over men.

"Siren? What's that?" Altair asked, evoking an equally annoyed response.

"You don't know what a siren is? You of all people?" Vega huffed while looking to Stan to explain.

"Oh Altair. Sirens are mythological creatures, said to have beautifully captivating features from the waist up, and the tail of a fish below."

193

"So, a mermaid?" he interrupted.

"But much more deceptive; evil some say. Sailors were warned to stay away from certain islands, fearful of the beautiful, enchanting songs, which would lure them to their rocky demise. It is said that sailors plugged their ears with wax, to avert the risk of hearing the entrancing tunes, carrying through the heavy fog of loneliness."

"And here I thought Vega was the only one with a dangerous song." He nudged the already swooning girl, whose mind seemed preoccupied with the simple folded note, each crease in the paper a thoughtful move to create something beautiful just for her.

"Well, I'd better get to bed." Vega slowly stood up from the comfort of the couch.

"Not so fast!" Altair smirked, as he dashed to the kitchen to grab the oversized piece of chocolate cake they had so skillfully kept hidden from her. A flick of the lighter sparked an immediate smile, as she realized that someone had actually remembered her birthday.

Noticing the awkward silence and bittersweet stares as she blew out the candles she laughed, "I'm pretty sure we all just wished for the same thing."

"Well Vega, I hope you and Ben have a nice time tomorrow. If you can, try to find out what it is they are looking for here in Rome. It might serve you well to understand his underlying reasons for being here."

"Funny you say that; I was actually thinking the same thing," she yawned.

"Ah, we better get out of here and let you get some sleep." Stan quickly winked at Altair, insinuating he had some sort of secret to share with only him.

"Right. Goodnight Vega," Altair said as she disappeared into the bedroom. Eager eyes waited for darkness to emerge from the bedroom before conversing.

"So, I didn't get to ask... you said you landed somewhere different than Vega, but you didn't' say where it was that you went."

Altair sighed, hesitant to give the full story. "She's been through so much, and I didn't want to add to the stress of her day."

"Do you mind sharing now?" Stan whispered, careful not to speak too loudly.

"It started in a tunnel...."

CHAPTER 13

Soot and darkness filled the damp tunnel Altair found himself in, as he wheezed, struggling to breathe in the thick, musty air. Flickers of half-burned candles lined the walls, serving as a guide to whomever frequented this secretive place. The faint sound of careful voices stirred from a glowing room down the hall, as he fearlessly walked toward the people he was destined to meet. The golden hues shining from the room seemed warm and inviting, as he carefully snuck a careful eye around the corner.

Laughter echoed off the walls of a perfectly pleasant workspace, filled with gadgets, paintings, beakers, test tubes full of steaming surprises, and piles of what looked like golden hay.

Noticing the similar dialect, Altair called out, "Pardon?"

Frightened eyes mirrored silenced conversations as the great inventors shuffled to hide papers, and whatever they deemed important, behind their backs.

In an attempt to ease their nerves, he introduced himself. "My name is Altair, and I am somewhat of an artist as well. I am a blacksmith, and work with metal and fire. Can I join you?"

Receptive, appeased glances loosened the energy of the room as a man dressed in an off-white, loose fitting top, worn brown trousers, bare feet, and disheveled hair from repeated head scratches, stepped forward.

"Has the king sent you to live here with us artisans?" he humbly smiled.

"I'm not sure yet. Perhaps this is just a trial to see if I belong here with you."

Uniform nods of agreement circled the watchful men as they opened their arms to invite him in.

"Each of us was brought here by the king, and given a wonderful place to stay while we create his favorite things. As you can see he has a taste for the arts, but he also goes through phases of taste and distaste," the painter nodded towards the stack of familiarly famous oil paintings, discarded in the dark corner of the room.

"If you don't mind me asking, what are you working on now?" He looked towards an awkwardly stacked object, concealed in a scarlet scarf.

196

"This is somewhat of a private project that takes a lifetime to achieve. Aside from our intense love for the arts, we also strive for transformation of body, mind, and soul. I believe that you were sent here for a very special reason. Perhaps you are the key to our transformation. Your arrival comes on a day of significant importance. Care to join us?"

Altair gave his consent to the illusive plan that he felt held the key to his destiny, as the man with the disheveled hair quickly picked up the secretive object and shuffled to the door.

"We must leave now," he sternly demanded.

The scribe tucked his scroll and quill up under his arm and grabbed a candle to guide them through the darkness of what seemed to be miles and miles of never-ending tunnels, only to stop when the stones in the walls changed to that of arched, thicker bricks. The clockmaker raised his monocle up to his eye, searching for a marking on the wall. His thick grey eyebrows lifted in excitement as a small emblem of a double axe appeared in his simple, yet extraordinary lens. Together they hoisted the man up into the air, and as he pushed his hands against the deceptively solid ceiling, a trap door opened, raining autumn leaves of red and gold down below. One by one, they climbed out of the tunnel, and up into the forest, where nothing but an autumn rainbow of serenity surrounded them for miles. The forest floor, lined with fallen leaves, crunched under their feet as they neared the familiar cathedral ahead.

Trying to contain his excitement, Altair asked, "Why this cathedral?"

Silence followed his question as they neared the simple stone steps. The scientist of the group paused, ransacking his deep pockets filled with useful trinkets, searching for a simple vial of liquid. They quickly removed their shoes, and set them outside on the stone steps. One by one, they

197

rubbed the secretive oil onto the soles of their feet. Joining them in their ritualistic activity, Altair followed suit and began rubbing what smelled like Frankincense into the soles of his feet.

As they entered the temple, the serene sound of trickling water echoed off the privacy of the stone walls. Silently, each man walked in a counterclockwise circular path, starting near the outside walls, and slowly making their way to the center of the room. Again, not wanting to ask the reason why, Altair followed the men as they meditatively pondered their individual journeys in life as they approached the center of the room.

The men stood in a small circle facing one another, as the scientist placed the heavy object he had been carrying onto the floor, and slowly pulled the silk away.

Struggling to contain his urge to grab the metal plates, Altair began nervously twisting his ring. As he touched his anxious fingers to the band once more, a shocking jolt of energy rushed through his entire body, shaking the ground beneath them. He wondered, was it his ring, the plates, or perhaps Deneb's crystal that he continued to carry that sparked the reaction?

"What was that?" the scribe apprehensively positioned his feet into a wide, protective stance, assessing the sound of rushing water below.

"The well, something has triggered the well!" the scientist gleamed as all eyes focused on Altair.

"Those metal plates, why do you bring them here?" He jumped at the opportunity to ask a question.

"We believe that through the initiation of the elements we can transform the sacred plates of metal into gold. We bring the plates here, today, on the celebration of Mabon, to bless them with sacred waters. We have been trying to find the right balance, the right formula, for decades, and today it seems as if something has changed."

As they inched toward the small opening in the floor, Altair cast a curious eye toward the rapidly moving water inside. The scribe quickly offered his candle, as if Altair knew what to do with it. Noticing his hesitation, he whispered, "Shine the white light over the well, and see if she comes."

With a shaking hand, he held the feeble candlestick over the water, knowing he would give anything just to see her again. His heavy heart pushed an unsuspecting tear from his eye, falling to the water below. Fearful of the gargling emotions welling up inside him he quickly rubbed his eye on the sleeve, teetering the candle just a bit.

"What was that?" the scientist exclaimed while eyeing the sparkling water.

"Nothing, I just..." Altair began to answer, but swallowed his words as a tornado of light began to spin below. As he gazed into the depths of the well, two familiar eyes emerged, looking inquisitively towards his. He flashed back to the dream he had told Stan about; where he looked longingly into a lake at what seemed to be an enchantingly beautiful being under the water. Their eyes mirrored one another as he leaned in further, extending the dripping candle towards her face. Irrational thoughts funneled through his mind; could he just jump into the well and be with her once more, and would he somehow change if he did? Or was she even there? Perhaps this was a figment of his imagination, due to his lack of experience in time travel.

Her deep, loving eyes sparkled as the light of her essence swirled upon the surface, nearly blinding him. The temperament of the water intensified, swirling faster around her, as if she herself were the eye of the storm. Her lips began to move, though no words were heard as she pointed towards his hand, and then, in a violent rush of departure, she vanished into the crashing water of the now simple well.

Sadness overtook him as he turned around, towards the ghost white strangers he had temporarily forgotten were there.

"What did she say?" the scribe belted out while reaching for his quill.

"I... I know her lips were moving, but I couldn't hear what she said." His eyes returned to the still waters below, praying for her return.

"Well, then what was exchanged?" There is always an exchange when she appears."

"I gave her nothing..." he questioned even his own response.

"She does not show unless an exchange is made. It is part of her being. Everything about her is balanced energetically; thus she does not give without receiving."

Puzzled he wondered what he had given... a tear? He expelled his somewhat altered secrets, "her beauty was so breathtaking that I cried into the well. It was only after my tears touched the water that she spoke."

"Tears? You gave her tears?" the scribe recorded quickly.

He nodded while eyeing the ink quickly filling the scroll.

"What did you receive in exchange for your tears?"

He bit his lip to divert his emotions from sadness to that of pain, which unknowingly was the same thing. "She pointed at my ring as she spoke words my ears did not receive."

"Oh my..." the scientist clenched the metal plates tight to his chest as he ran towards the heavy wooden doors. They hurriedly ran down outside towards a simple stone fountain.

"Hurry, there isn't much time," the disheveled scientist quickly flung the silk from on top of the metal plates and set them carefully around in a circle on the bottom of the large stone basin. His watchful eyes squinted up at the harvest moon, rapidly rising in the sky.

"Within these sacred waters we place these simple offerings, giving thanks for all that Mother Earth provides, asking humbly that the fires of the hearth be ignited, and the unity of male and female transform our offering for the betterment of mankind."

As the moon cast its light upon the water, Altair stepped forward and placed his hands upon the immersed plates. Shrieks erupted from the faithful men beside him, who painfully hid their eyes from a moment they had waited lifetimes to witness. Altair watched in wonderment the miraculous transformation, as flakes of metal began to peel from the archaic plates. Instinctually, he slipped the ring from his finger, illuminating the face of the lion within the shimmering waters, speeding up the process unfolding before him.

 "Keep your eyes hidden! This light blinds even the purest of heart! Blacksmith? Where are you?" The voices of the men trailed off in distant echoes as the last of the metal faded to gold. As the midnight clouds rolled over the moon, the gift of vision returned to his friends once more.

"Blacksmith?" the scientist called out again, blindly wandering towards Altair with one hand flailing, and the other sealed stiff to his eyes.

"It's okay, you can open your eyes," he said while standing proudly over the circle of golden plates resting at the bottom of the fountain.

"What have you done?"

"I...." Altair refrained from speaking, as he was still uncertain of the answer.

"Was this not what we wanted?" the artist questioned his companions.

The scientist stiffly paced around the fountain, "Hurry! Seize the gold! We cannot tell anyone of this -- not even the king."

Spatters of autumn rain began to fall from the swarm of clouds, as they quickly ran through the darkness of the forest toward the place that all but Altair had memorized.

"Wait!" he yelled through the sheets of rain as he chased behind their fleeing shadows.

"Wait! I need those plates!" He stopped, placing a defeated hand to his knee, and bent over to catch his breath. The only response to be heard came from the rain, pelting the dried leaves gathered around his feet. Then, for a moment he begged his mind not to create, he thought of Hydra. Moments of their time together flipped through his mind like a comic strip, on a waterlogged newspaper with stuck-together pages unable to turn. Her deceptively enchanting eyes of emerald burned into his mind as he pictured the two of them riding together through the forest, approaching his workshop. As if she were part of the forest he was lost in, he could feel her arms tight around his waist as she whispered her confession, her secret lust for fall. The sound of slithering snakes rustled the leaves around him, as he frantically turned, searching the seemingly empty forest for any sign of her.

"Hydra?" He yelled into the darkness, secretly hoping that the darkness wouldn't answer back.

Her sultry laugh shook the rain as she hissed through the creeping fog. "I've missed you."

202

He could feel her presence like hot breath on his wet skin, as he squinted through the heavy clouds of grey toward the sticky reminder of her triumph over him. Realizing his lack of protection, he responded the only way he saw fit. "I've missed you too."

An eerie silence lifted the fog, revealing the distant outlines of her voluptuous, predatory silhouette, standing silently, waiting for her prey to make just one fateful move.

"Do you miss me now, because I've enslaved your love?" Her voice caused the hairs on his arms to stand straight up, as he pondered her involvement in Deneb's disappearance.

"I was under the impression that a trade was made. She traded her existence in the present for a lifetime in the past." He remained firm in his conviction.

She laughed while triumphantly striding towards the man she knew she could easily capture again, if only her heart didn't long for more. The sound of quickly moving snakes slipped through the layers of dead leaves around his ankles as rage began to fuel his mind. With every attempted kick towards the leaves, her ivory smile grew wider, gleaming under the harvest moon.

"Wait," she said to herself, silencing the leaves. As the moonlight graced the evil beauty of her face, she leaned in and asked, "How do you say her name? Is it Vega?" A delightful cackle slipped through her lips as the smell of rotten fish steamed from her mouth.

The only answers he had prepared involved his ring, or his fake love for her, but not once did he think that she might ask about Vega.

"I think you're confused," he whispered with disdain.

She sneered with delight as her slivered eyes leapt towards his. "I can hear your heart racing, just as I can hear the thrill of her vibration. Deneb can be easily traded, for there is something new that I seek…a student."

Altair observed the silence. "What has changed? Why would you want her?"

Ignoring his question, and confirming her exit, she closed her eyes and deeply inhaled while slowly lifting both arms up over her head. Growls of thunder answered her energy, as the rain grew heavier. Fearfully, he looked up at the near bursting clouds, as if she were holding back the rain she had conjured, and called to her again, "Why her?"

With an irritated growl she flung open her eyes, and whispered in a painfully deep tone, "Because she is destined to be one of us."

As Altair concluded his story, Stan's eyes remained fixed on the closed bedroom door, where inside, the new focus of their journey lay resting.

He slowly whispered, "Altair, what sign are you?"

He replied, while mirroring his watchful glare, "Leo."

He nodded, confirming his growing theory. "And Vega? Leo too I presume?"

Altair eyed the half-eaten birthday cake. "Yes."

"I believe it's time to revisit my theory about the pearls and tears. Let's reconvene tomorrow once she returns."

CHAPTER 14

A whimsical exhale escaped Vega's lips as she stood on the balcony looking out to the city built on legendary love stories and heroic battles. Her eyes were like sponges, soaking in every age-old courtship that had ever taken place in Rome, as she thought of what Ben had in store for her.

"Right! I better get in the shower!" she ran inside with a girlish skip that surprised even her as she did it and zipped around the room, pulling clothing from her bag in a frazzled attempt to select her most flattering outfit. After lathering on her best soaps, salts, and oils, she wrapped herself up in a luxurious robe and began applying darker than normal eye makeup.

Her eyes sparkled in the mirror as she applied shaded depths of mystery around them, exhaling a steamy cloud across her reflection. With a hurried hand, she wiped the mirror, gasping in horror at the vision that replaced her own. Two enchantingly beautiful eyes glimmered back at hers through the quickly closing circle of steam. In a moment of curious confidence, she wiped the mirror once more; revealing the vision of the beautiful woman. Her dark eyes shimmered with wonder, though the focal point of her essence was the golden headdress draped through her thick black hair, and the hypnotically familiar emerald pendant dangling in the center of her forehead.

"Vega...." The woman's whisper spilled tears down the mirror.

"You need to listen to me. I am here to offer you a trade. I see your intensity... your talents. Join me. Join us. You can be with him forever. Wouldn't you like that?" she devilishly licked a drop of honey from her fingertip as she smiled.

"Who are you? What do you mean a trade can be made?" Vega pressed her eager fingers to the mirror.

"It is simple. Lay down your life for 500 years of servitude, and I will free your friend, and allow you to be with Lan forever. Don't join us, and the world as you know it will begin to shatter." Her psychotic laughter sent jagged cracks through the mirror as she delighted in her madness.

Vega rushed from the bathroom, slamming the door behind her. Madly, she looked for Altair, who surprisingly was already gone.

In a panic, she scribbled on a piece of paper, hoping that Altair would be able to read her chaotic writing.

"Something happened. Don't go in the bathroom." Realizing how weird that sounded she crossed it out, and wrote again. "Evil queen shattered mirror in bathroom. I am off to hike the island of Capri with Ben... I think we're going on a trail somewhere near the Blue Grotto!"

Vega's footsteps echoed off the reflective marble tiles as she slid through the lobby, and disappeared into the privacy of the hotel gardens. Her worn sneakers ignored the manicured grass shooting up between squares of white stone, as she walked towards the hideously innocent face of a cherub, delightfully shooting water from its mouth. She inched closer, carefully admiring the busts of marble men staggered around the garden, as if they had once been there admiring the fountain, but had somehow become trapped in an eternal moment of stillness.

Two warm hands covered her eyes from behind, as instinct led her to duck, simultaneously punching the assaulter in the stomach.

"Oh my God! I'm so sorry!" She rushed to aid her now wounded and hunched over date.

He laughed while pushing himself upright. "Wow, you pack quite a punch for such a tiny girl."

She cringed, "Sorry about that, I've had kind of a weird morning and I'm a little on edge. No biggie though! I'm ready when you are."

"I hope you don't mind a little travel today. The only way to get to Capri is by boat, and the quickest way to the boat is by train," he said as they headed through the city to the train station. Hours passed as they exchanged stories of travel, diving, and of course, treasure. Together they moved from train to boat, and finally, boat to land, where the towering Island of Capri welcomed them to begin their journey.

"You ready to hike?" He grabbed her hand, which was pressed to her forehead, shielding her eyes as she gazed towards the peak of the primal island.

"That sure is a big cliff. We're going up there?" she cringed while at the same time, admiring the challenge.

"Well, not all the way up, but trust me -- the views are worth it. The trail has a gradual ascent, and before you know it, we will be on the top of the island, at the edge of the sea. Trust me, it's safe, I've walked it a million times," he winked.

Her stomach growled as she laughed, "I don't suppose we could grab a quick bite to eat before we begin the hike?"

"This is your day my dear and I know the perfect place."

Sun-bleached pathways overrun with fragrant, colorful wildflowers guided them through groves of lemon trees as they made their way to a quiet restaurant nestled within a garden. The simple thatched roof contradicted the lavish

207

décor of the patio overlooking the sea. Samples of meat, cheese, and pasta came and went, followed by espresso and just a nibble of dessert as the two of them disappeared into a long awaited conversation.

"You know, I thought you'd be different." Vega poked at the content, well-stuffed man.

"How so?" he smiled

"You just seemed … and please don't be offended, kind of pompous," she giggled.

"Fair enough. When you've been around as long as I have, you tend to think you know everything."

"What do you mean by that?" Vega finished off the last of her espresso.

"I just mean that I've seen a lot of the world," he quickly answered.

"That's an odd way of saying it," she smiled. "Stay right here. I am going to run to the ladies' room. Be right back!" She blissfully hurried up the stone steps, stopping to sneak just one more glimpse of the breathtaking view. Slowly, she retreated down the stairs, stopping to assess the oddities of her unattended date. She silently watched his strange behavior, picking up her cup, scraping what looked like a sample from the side, and then setting it back down.

"Something the matter?" She awkwardly laughed while returning to the table.

"Nope, I'm all set," he replied, completely ignoring the oddities of his actions. Moments of passive silence agitated her as different scenarios played in her mind of what he might have been doing.

"Ready to go?" he interrupted her stirring thoughts.

"Mmm hmm," she watchfully replied.

His uncanny charm, mixed with the fragrant distractions of colorful flowers made it easy for Vega to follow along behind him through the winding hills of the island. As they neared a small wooden bridge, she suddenly realized just how high up they actually were, halting her steps.

"Something the matter?" He looked back, noticing her fright mixed with awe, as she looked down at the aqua waves crashing on the rocks far below.

"No. I just didn't realize how high up we were. I guess I was so lost in our conversation and the beauty of the island that I forgot to look down."

"It's beautiful isn't it?" He squeezed her hand as he walked out onto the slender wooden bridge. "Come on out here; it's where you can see the best view."

Carefully she inched along to stand beside him, as he wrapped his arms tight around her waist. "I got you." He lovingly looked into her eyes, as he leaned in for a kiss. Before their lips could touch, she pulled back.

"Where'd you get that scar on your face?"

Puzzled, and a bit frustrated that the moment had passed, he answered, "Believe it or not, someone I love did this to me, a long time ago."

Sensing his pain, she leaned back towards his lips. "I'm so sorry to hear that." As her lips pressed to his, the fear from the void beneath her feet diminished, while the familiarity of his soul overwhelmed her heart. Sensing the awkwardness of their fiery connection, she pulled away, and blurted out a question. "So, what's the coolest thing you've found so far, you know, while hunting treasure?"

Bashfully he turned a sly eye her way. "In all of my years searching for gold, artifacts, and lost cities, I've never found

209

anything quite as interesting as you. I'd search the world through all eternity, to find you."

She squeezed his hand while laughing. "Come on now, that's crap. What's your real answer?"

Somberly he answered, "Alright, if you must know, it was a watch."

She wrinkled her brow. "A watch? Come on, that can't be the real answer; and if it is, what was so special about it?"

He reached into his pocket and pulled out the pink diamond watch, still equipped with the broken clasp from when it had fallen off her wrist. Her feet staggered backwards, as the wooden bridge began to sway.

"Where.....where did you get that?" Fright caused the words to stick in her throat as she forced them out. His serious glare sent chills through her body, as he stood silently, watching to see what action she might attempt to make.

"I should have known." Anger replaced her fear, if only for seconds. "I've only felt this way about one person in all of my life, and that was you. But this... this is some new version of you that my soul feels bound to... but shouldn't. All this time, you have been following me. Am I the treasure you've been hunting?" she railed at him, once again rocking the bridge.

"Vega, I've told you many times, over thousands of years; I change. I am this way because of you. I continue to exist because of you; and though you think this is your first time here on the planet, you have been with me, in all of these past lifetimes... Wait. I'll correct myself; the lifetimes where I am free from the obligations of my servitude."

"Servitude?" She reminded herself, as she reached into her pocket for her figurine. As her shaking fingers caressed the small golden phoenix, she attempted to relax her racing mind.

"In this life, I am bound in the confines of her grasp, and you are what she instructs me to secure. Trust me when I say, the dismantling of human civilization is upon us, and you can either join us or perish. I suggest you join us."

Anger mixed with disgust fueled her next move, as she fully realized for the first time that for the next five hundred years, his soul would belong to another woman. Her mind raced back to the painting of Alexander with another woman at the Villa Farnesina, which was the real reason she had sprinted out of the museum that day. Reactively she stumbled backwards, catching her foot between the slits of the wooden planks as she tumbled over the side of the bridge. His paw-like hand gripped her arm, as she helplessly dangled over the water, eyeing her simple figurine, now resting at his feet.

"Lan, pull me up! Please!" she begged.

"Say you'll join us." He soullessly replied.

For seconds that lasted an eternity, she stared at the golden phoenix, lying at his feet, and found comfort in its essence; something so strong that it could face even death and be reborn to fly another day.

"Never." Her last words echoed off the rocks as she fell to the waves below.

The sound of peaceful, flowing water entered her thoughts and woke her, while she tried to adjust to the electric blue light that enveloped her. Between slow, groggy blinks, she attempted to discern her surroundings, as soft fingertips pressed into her back, guiding her floating body through what seemed to be a cave of watery light. Her injuries inhibited any sudden movements, so she settled for a glance at her feet, which appeared to be floating on top of the glowing water. Startled, she wondered whom or what was guiding her, and more importantly where she was being taken.

Painfully, as she approached the white light that shone from the mouth of the cave, she whispered a few words. "Where am I? Am I dead?"

Two familiar eyes rose through the stillness of the water as Deneb answered, "You are not dead my friend, you are in Grotta Azzurra."

"The Blue Grotto?" she attempted more questions, but had to stop to catch her breath.

"Yes. I don't have much time before I need to get the crystal back to the pirate."

Her eyes felt heavy once again, as she struggled to remain conscious. "The crystal? You borrowed your crystal to save me. How?"

"I needed it to jump through time, as currently, it's neither solstice nor equinox." Her insightful eyes swirled with mystery, reflecting the radiant pool that surrounded them.

"You traded all of that gold? For me?" A tear slipped down her cheek. "How do we find you?" Vega whispered her final words, as the weight of her eyes gave in to the pain.

"Use your song, but protect your lips. Something evil lurks in these waters. Find the blacksmith and leave. Time is running out."

Sea foam stained with blots of red washed up beside her, as the heartbreak of Deneb's words thundered through her mind. Carefully, she pushed herself up to a seated position, looking out across the vast ocean; her blood the only sign of life to be seen.

She slowly walked for what seemed like miles, along the sparse coastline, devoid of lavish Italian villas, or any form of life for that matter. As her vitality slowly returned, she altered her course, turning inland, toward the quiet coastal city. The familiar aroma of lemons haunted her senses, reminding her of Lan's betrayal, and she wondered, was he not far behind?

Nearing a busy market, she pulled a silk cloth from a window, quickly concealing the fresh wounds on her head. Decorated women danced through the streets, carrying piles of grapes stacked high upon planks of cedar. Following behind the dancers, men and women blissfully played the lyre as they made their way through the white marble streets. The parade energetically drew in more and more people as it moved through the town, past the bustling markets, and arrived at a beautiful amphitheater.

As the festivities continued, gladiators moved into the center of the ring; surprisingly unarmed with any of the typical weapons, but instead held props used for mere training. People filed into lavish marble seats that surrounded what appeared to be a diminutive version of the well-known colosseum, cheering on the prized warriors as they trained.

"Excuse me." Vega nudged an avid viewer, who was deep in thought. "What is it that they are training for?"

The unpretentious old man smiled, nervously flipping a coin between his fingers while keeping an eye focused on his prized warrior. "They train for the day when they will fight in the Amphitheatrum Flavium, where they will battle great warriors and beasts for the entire world to see."

She refrained from asking any more questions, knowing it would expose her as an outsider. "Thank you." She bowed and ducked into the passing crowd.

Moving through the lavish town, equipped with steaming bath houses, markets brimming with fragrant herbs, and theatres the like of which she had never before encountered, she observed the people, all happily communing. Each person contributed something to the city, whether it be trades of pottery, preparing meals, or clothing others; each person subsidized the whole. Just as her mind had settled into a place of comfort, readily dismissing the trickle of blood escaping her silk scarf, the ground shook beneath her feet. Innocent people ducked into their homes as if this upheaval was a frequent routine. Quiet moments passed. Quickly she scurried into a simple workshop, as a blacksmith continued his work, unphased by the looming fear that had shaken the rest of the town.

"Why don't you cower like the rest of the people?" Vega inched closer toward the hot coals of his forge, which highlighted the stoic features of his boorish face.

"The volcano erupts all of the time. This is nothing that hasn't happened before."

"What are you making?" she whispered.

"Not making; preserving. I am almost finished." He rubbed oil across the etchings of the now familiar metal plates. Trying to contain her anxiety, she spoke. "How did you come to possess those?"

Ignoring her question, he replied, "Come with me to the shrine of Apollo. There we will pay homage to the god of the sun, and his beloved goddess, Diana."

While he wrapped the plates in a heavy animal skin, Vega adjusted her scarf in an effort to conceal her injuries. He heaved the plates under his arm and motioned for her to follow. The silent streets seemed eerily familiar, as she dismissed any thoughts of where she might be, and what history had already reconciled. Instead, her eyes followed the quiet steps of the giant man toward a garden corridor

214

that opened up into a square. In the center, white marble stairs ascended to a platform flanked by dual pillars, representing the powerful duality of Apollo and Diana. A bronze statue of the sun god stood powerfully, in alignment with the goddess of the moon and the hunt, as if they were reaching out toward one another. Vega followed eagerly behind as he placed his metal plates onto the thick marble block in the center of the garden. Interrupting his clearly spiritual ritual, she asked, "Why?"

Annoyed, and yet amused by her lack of manners he answered, "The god Apollo came to me in a dream, and made me a promise. He said he would spare me from the volcano when it erupts, if I will protect these plates. I come here to show my work to soothe him so."

"Where did you find them?" she asked, skipping over the clearly more important question lurking in the background.

"This ring guided me to the plates, which spoke to me in dreams."

Vega contemplated his words, as the ground shook once again.

"There isn't much time. We need to leave now!" She looked up at the billowing smoke pouring out of the volcano, as the rest of the town resumed their festivities.

"Why is no one leaving?" she yelled as she scooped up the metal plates, and dragged him against his will through the streets and onto a small boat which was miraculously waiting in the harbor."

"Here in Pompeii, the volcano erupts regularly and nothing ever happens. This is no different! If it were serious we would know!" He pulled back as she leapt aboard the boat.

"Get on the boat! Now! There isn't much time! Remember when you were promised you would be saved from the volcano? Well, this is it! Get on the boat. Now!" She yanked his hand, pulling him onto the boat just as the sky burst with darkness.

Together they fled from the fire-consumed land and into the safety of the sea. Ash stained tears soaked his pale face as Vega attempted to lift his spirits. "You know, these plates that you've kept safe... they are going to change the world, thousands of years from now. That has to make you feel better, right?" she watched as the silent man wept, and gazed back at the darkness, where his heart remained.

"I'm sorry. I know this must be difficult for you. I want you to know that you may not see it now, but because you kept your word and fulfilled your promise, the world has a chance."

He turned his eyes away from the devastated shoreline for the first time in hours. "Why me?"

She looked into his eyes, which mirrored the countless times she had reassured Altair of his purpose. "Because it has to be you, and it has to be me."

"You say this as if we've done it all before..." He clasped the plates against the comfort of his broad chest.

She painfully smiled, remembering her journey. "We have done this so many times; we should have perfected it by now. Don't worry, it's smooth sailing from here on out." Her words rippled across the majesty of the Mediterranean as the sky collapsed into history; freezing an entire civilization in time.

Hours passed, as the darkness of night eased over the darkness of death. The stars were the only light to be seen for miles and miles. Vega watched her stoic companion who was seated upright with his back against the mast, slowly give in to sleep. She watched him disappear into his dreams, wondering where history might take him and the ring she knew would one day wind up around Altair's finger.

"I guess that I'm taking you right where you are meant to go," she whispered into his dreams, as he cuddled the plates like a teddy bear. Her eyes scanned the stars above, entertaining her ego as she whispered aloud the names of constellations above her, "Scorpio and Aquila." She took note of a star foreign to her knowledge, which cast an eerie glow around the boat. As they continued their journey, sailing through the green glass of the water a haunting voice rippled through the waves.

She stood at attention. "Who's there!?" she demanded. If she hadn't have been in that time period for so long, perhaps her senses would have been keener, but as it was, she became aware now that one, and maybe two people had now joined them.

"Who's there?" A mocking voice laughed as the fog rolled in, slowly exposing what looked to be the outline of a ghostly man at the edge of their ship. The dark, sunken features of the now familiar man revealed themselves, as the light of the moon illuminated the familiar face of Ben's companion, and the golden phoenix that he was twirling between his fingers.

Anger overtook her fear, and she stomped on the planks, forcing the dozing blacksmith to wake up.

"Where did you get that?" Vega focused on the simple object that had brought her peace of mind on so many occasions, but now evoked only rage each time it twirled through his slender fingers.

217

"You friend Altair had that very same question." The man laughed while disappearing into the fog, only to reappear at the other end of the boat. "To answer your first question, we have come to reclaim what is ours. Give me the plates, and we will be on our way."

"And what if we don't?" Vega challenged as the sea began to churn.

The man snickered as he looked down at the dark waters. "We will get them one way or another. Do you dare challenge us?"

While Vega searched the boat for the other being, the blacksmith rose to standing, drawing his dagger as he screamed, "The god Apollo is with us, and will defend us! These are his plates, and by my soul, I guard them!" As the ship began to succumb to the raging sea, Vega lunged at the quickly fading apparition, knocking the small figurine from what remained of his hands. The fog quickly collapsed into the sea, fueling the tidal wave conjuring up behind them.

"Hold my hand! We need to get out of here!" Vega demanded of the blacksmith as the plates and the golden figurine all slid across the deck in symphony to the now pitching sea.

"But the plates! I cannot leave them!"

"It is either them -- or us! We will find them again. Trust me!" She quickly began her song, as the rising wave pushed the front of boat up in the air, and sent them tumbling down, toward the back of the ship. The blacksmith quickly seized the golden phoenix before it could fly overboard, as if it were the only thing left that he could confidently save.

"I need to return to my time!" Vega yelled to the sea soaked man, knowing that the words meant little to him. "I'll send you wherever you wish to go!" She grabbed his hand and continued her humming. As the sea pelted the sinking boat from all directions, he yelled, "If you can send me anywhere, please, send me somewhere dry!" Thinking of the driest place she knew, she imagined Egypt, and they quickly disappeared from the turmoil of the storm. As their boat capsized into the crippling waves, a zip of blinding light collided with the darkness, illuminating the heroism of Melusine, coming to secure what they thought had been swallowed by the sea.

CHAPTER 15

Altair paternally paced the confines of their regal room, wondering what could be taking Vega so long to return. He stepped out onto the balcony to confront the setting sun as if it held the answer. "Where are you?" he nervously whispered, while reminding himself that they probably had stopped for dinner on the way home.

Before he could tear his eyes away from the courtyard below, his senses were assailed by the foul smell of smoke. Agitated, he leaned over the railing, and looked down to see the not so surprising site of Ben's leering friend. The skinny man paced intently around in the garden, flipping something between his wiry fingers. Curiosity caused him to inch further over the railing of the balcony, questioning his vision, if only for seconds. A small golden phoenix spun between his nervous fingers as he took another drag of his cigarette.

Altair ran from the room, tore down the hallway and burst into the now empty courtyard. The scent of a cigarette continued to haunt his senses, as he ran back into the lobby. "Excuse me, have you seen a man; lanky, dark hair, smells like smoke?" he asked with panicked breath as the front desk clerk chuckled in amusement.

"Sorry, no one of that description has passed through here," she said as the clearly fragrant smells of ash gathered in the lobby.

"Thanks." He walked back out into the garden, and stopped at the sight of the dark haired man, now sitting cross-legged atop a carved marble sphere, finishing his cigarette.

"Hello" he said as he hopped down.

"Hello," Altair answered, looking for any possible way that the man could have escaped the clearly confined garden.

He sneered. "You look...on edge. Care for a smoke?"

"Never cared for it," he replied while scouring the garden for any alternate exits.

"What has you so bothered, my man?" he exhaled a smooth ring of smoke up to the sky.

"Nothing. I just thought my friend would be back by now, that's all," he casually responded.

He reached inside the pocket of his perfectly pressed dress pants and pulled out the simple golden phoenix. "She might be a while."

Enraged, he leapt towards the man, who was nearly half his size, only to fall through a cloud of smoke and laughter. Confused and in a bit of pain from the fall, Altair picked himself up from the pavement while simultaneously looking between the garden statues for any sign of the now vanished mocking man.

"Your eyes can't move fast enough to see me." Altair could feel the man's stale breath on his neck as he swung at the seemingly empty air.

"Show yourself, you coward!" Altair paced the garden as the scent of the cigarette faded.

He quickly ran back inside, and through the hotel lobby to Stan's room, eagerly knocking on the door. After knocking for the seventh time, Stan finally opened the door in wide-eyed shock. "What's the matter Altair?"

"It's Vega," he struggled to catch his breath; "They've got her! Ben... those men... they're not human!"

Before Stan could get a word in, Altair insistently continued. "I was out on the balcony, looking for her, and down below -- in the garden, I saw Ben's friend. You know -- the skinny one with the dark hair and sunken eyes. He had something in his hands that reflected the sun as he kept spinning it through his fingers, and as I leaned over a bit more, I saw what it was... Vega's figurine! I raced to the garden to confront him, and when I asked where she was, he only replied that she would be a while! I attempted to tackle him, but he just.... Vanished!"

"Vanished? How?" Stan asked and despite the lack of an answer, guided Altair by his shoulders, toward the bedroom.

Altair replied, and restated the man's final words. "He said 'your eyes don't move fast enough to see me,' and then he just disappeared.

"I must say, I'm a bit confused." Stan creaked open his bedroom door, where Vega laid, sleeping.

221

"When did she come back?"

"It was the weirdest thing I've ever seen. Here I was ... just reading a book, and all of a sudden, a tornado of water and wind ripped through the bedroom like a hurricane and it spit her out there -- on the bed. I ran to her side. She was soaking wet, shivering, and barely moving. I wrapped her up in warm blankets and was able to get her to drink some water, but she's been sleeping right there, ever since."

"I've seen her in this condition before. She only looks like this after travelling through time. Something must have happened on her date with Ben ... and look there -- she has a huge cut on her forehead." Altair's eyes began to swell with tears as he growled, "he's a dead man."

Stan placed a cautionary hand over his racing heart. "We mustn't act impulsively. If they are affiliated with the constellations near to Hydra, then we have to be careful. Come, we have a lot of work to do."

They settled into the couches, surrounded by stacks of books, and poured themselves some ginger tea as they dove into the historical details of their future battles. Each took furious notes between sips of tea -- and sudden ah ha's, only pausing for a brief exchange of ideas. Hours passed and then suddenly, with an eye-straining gasp, Stan urged Altair to come close. Together they looked through tales of villainous legends, starting with the first of their enemies, Draco.

"See, it all begins with him...well, him and her." He drew a line across the page connecting Draco to Hydra.

"They are the equal counterparts; two snakes so to speak, twisting their powers together to form something bigger." He pointed to the mythological painting of a male and female side by side, with heads of humans and bodies of snakes.

222

"Is that them?" Altair scowled at the image.

Stan nodded while pressing his finger to the page. "See the symbol there -- of their bodies intertwined?"

"Now remember, when we examine the legends of the Goddess of the Sea, we find a similar creation tale, depicting two surges of energy coming from her hands, looking much like strands of DNA. Again, in the legend of Daedalus, he used his ring, infused with the energy of Apollo, to bring stone lions, and even the walls of the labyrinth; to life. So it seems that both our heroes and our enemies possess similar powers throughout time."

"I… have something to show you. Grab your books and follow me." Altair led the way to his room, where the three golden plates rested safely upon the bed.

"Good God! When did you get these?" Stan shoved his knuckle in his mouth, biting down instead of screaming out like a child on Christmas morning.

"Vega brought them back from … well … the future. She said there was a rare moment when she had to decide whether to grab all of the plates and run, or toss the vase that contained her green elixir to Deneb, who was in the well. She chose the elixir, and then, before she fled Lan's palace, she was able to grab just a few of the plates. It was all she could carry." He smiled at the thought of her mighty spirit.

"Why didn't you tell me any of this earlier?" Stan fearfully looked at the plates. "You aren't going to experiment with these are you?"

"We were going to tell you, but we kept getting sidetracked with other things. I want to know what they do." He possessively walked over to the plates, carefully looking over each image; the shield, the wine, and the egg.

223

"If you are going to try to bring any of these to life, you must be careful! Try something simple. As if any portion of the wheel of the year is simple!" Stan buried his head in his hands as Altair selected the wine.

"Do what you must," Stan murmured through his fingers, which were wrapped around his face. Not really knowing quite what to do, Altair pulled the ring off his finger, and looked at the simple etching of the lion, as he placed his other hand on the golden plate. Electricity surged through him, connecting his body and soul to the plate before him. The power of the lion invigorated his soul with each breath he took, and the world around him slowly began to reshape itself.

No longer did he feel like a human, or a man for that matter, but rather, a powerful force of primal energy that could shape or shift anything that his heart desired. For the sake of the test, he decided to shape the world based on the design of the plate in front of him. He studied the feeling of the wine, the grapes so supple and full of life, transformed into something that both altered the mind and spirit. He envisioned the joyful release of inhibitions that the wine brought, but was suddenly interrupted by Stan's rambling babble.

"Altair, this....this... right here is soooooooo weird!" he stumbled towards the couch with hands out, anticipating a fall.

His ferocious bond with the ring battled with his love for Stan, as his mind tore between thoughts of continuing -- or stopping for the sake of his friend. Stan laid on the couch and flailed a hand in the air. "Okay... you can sssssstop now!" he stammered.

"Stop!" Altair commanded, wondering just who -- or what -- he was telling to stop. He ran to get Stan some water, while apologetically detailing just what had happened. Silent moments passed as Stan returned to normal, and Altair waited for either a lashing or praise.

He finally spoke, in a shaky voice. "That... was simply the worst moment of my entire life."

"Stan, I'm so sorry. I had no idea what I was doing."

"Tell me exactly what you thought of while you did...whatever it was that you just did. It seems that you control the plates, so whatever you thought of, projected onto me. So...what was it?" Stan demanded of his assailant.

"At first I thought of the grape, and how wonderfully supple it is, and then I thought of the effects of wine," he shamefully admitted.

"It's okay Altair. Now, I want you to try it again, only this time I want you to think of the gifts of Yule, and tidings of Christmas. Think of only joy and peace as you try it again."

Altair quickly nodded in agreement. "And if for some reason you get drunk again, I'll stop right away!"

Stan snickered. "Thanks, I'd appreciate that."

This time, as he placed his hand to the plate, he kept the ring on his finger and focused his thought patterns on positive, uplifting images. Memories surfaced of his most joyous childhood moments at Christmas time, remembering the snow falling outside, and the warmth of family all around him. Tears crept into the corners of his eyes, as he recalled his mother, passed on long ago, and the last gift she had placed into his hands. He dove deeper into his memories, ignoring the results of his experiment for the time being. Vividly he saw his mother's face, illuminated by the white lights of the decorated hearth as she rocked in her favorite chair. Joy flooded his being as he looked over the room for someone to share it with, and he noticed Stan, peacefully rocking in the wooden chair in the living room.

225

"Stop," he calmly said, as Stan ceased his rocking.

Stan slowly wiped a tear from the corner of his eye. "Altair, that was the most beautiful thing I've ever experienced. It was as if I was inside a snow globe of your fondest memories. Not only did I feel the love that you felt for your mother, but I felt her love for you as well."

"Do you see what this means? I don't need the crystal to travel, nor do I need Vega's song!" A hint of arrogance strengthened his voice.

"It also means that the power of the plates resides with the intentions of their holder, and those affected can feel you too." Stan grounded their conversation.

Protectively, Altair stood beside the bed. "These must never fall into the hands of Hydra. Come on -- let's check on Vega and see how she's doing."

Immediately, thoughts about the whereabouts of the other five plates triggered him to collect the three that were in his possession, which he carefully shoved into the only safe place he knew -- Vega's backpack.

As they made their way back to the room where she continued to soundly sleep, Altair asked, "Stan, how many people can each plate control? I mean, I was able to control your mind so easily, almost without effort. Was it because you were right next to me, or do you think that for that moment in time, everyone on the planet also felt some sort of joy?"

"I'm not sure Altair, but it wouldn't hurt to go have a look around the hotel, you know ... see if anyone else is talking about having a weird experience. Tell you what, you go check on Vega and I'll take a lap around the lobby."

As Stan stepped onto the elevator, Altair called out one more question. "Stan, is this the gold that we're expected to

226

trade?" The sadness on Stan's face clashed with the impulsive foot that he jammed in the closing elevator door. "We'll find another way."

Altair softly stepped into the room, startled by the vision of Vega now sitting upright on the couch. In a soft, somewhat robotic voice she whispered, "What are you doing with my bag?"

"I wanted to put all of your important things in here; right where you are." He sat down beside her, and opened the top of the bag to reveal the plates inside.

"Thank you." She wept into her hands, ignoring the wound on her forehead, as it broke open once again.

"Oh my, hold on, you're bleeding..." He rushed into the bathroom and grabbed a towel. His hands began to shake with fury as he tended to the wounds of his fractured friend, who he never thought could break. "He's going to pay for what he's done to you. I swear to you."

She tried her best to collect her thoughts as she wiped the blood soaked tears from her face. "It is so much more than we thought Altair. Ben... is...Lan."

"What? How?"

"He must have come back when Hydra came back, since they are tied to one another. He cannot be without her, and she cannot be without him. He changes appearance every lifetime, which for him, is every five hundred years. I should have known immediately, when I felt so drawn to him, but didn't know why."

"Oh no. Don't you go blaming yourself for this. He is evil Vega...all of them... they are all evil."

"They? How do you know about the others?" she whispered while pressing the towel back onto her forehead.

"I saw the skinny, shifty one down in the garden and he had your figurine in his hands. I ran down, to confront him and it was as if he just evaporated when I lunged at him. I swear Vega; I have never seen anything like it in my life. He just vaporized into smoke, and said something about my eyes not moving fast enough to see him."

"He manifested on the ship with me and the blacksmith as well, right before the boat capsized into the waves."

"Blacksmith? Wait, what happened to you?" He stopped his pacing as the door flew open.

"Oh good! Vega, you are awake! How are you?" Stan rushed to her side, putting a hold on his findings.

"I'm..." she paused to rub her aching head. "I am okay, but I'm scared that he is still out there. Ben... he and Lan are one and the same." She looked at Stan with injured eyes.

"Oh why didn't I see this coming," he scolded himself. "Tell us what happened, and how you got that gash on your face."

"We were hiking and when we got to the top of this overlook, there was a bridge we had to cross, and as he leaned in to kiss me, I noticed the scar on his face. He said someone long ago gave it to him, and for a moment, I remembered how the spear nicked Lan's face, but I ignored that memory, for the moment. He leaned in once more, and I swear, I felt his soul as we kissed." She paused to reflect on her error, and then continued. "I asked him, just after he pulled away, to tell me about his most interesting find and then ... he pulled out the watch." Noticing their blank stares, she continued. "OK ... when I was in the future and grabbed the vase that contained my green elixir, the watch fell off of my wrist. I didn't have time to retrieve it and so, you can imagine how shocked I was when he showed it to me. I tried to run away and tripped backwards, falling off the side of the bridge. I begged him to pull me up but he insisted I join them. I dangled there above the rocks for what seemed like eternity, and then he just... let me go."

"Oh Vega!" Altair wrapped his arms around her as she sobbed into his chest. Stan, more inclined to assess their enemy, pressed on.

"I'm assuming that you got that nasty cut from the fall? It is a miracle that you're still..." He stopped, realizing for the first time that perhaps she too was an immortal creature.

She excitedly wiped her tears, resuming the story. "But *then* the most incredible thing happened! Deneb saved me!"

"What?"

"How?"

"She said that she made a trade with a pirate long ago and traded all of the gold that she had collected over the years for just one hour with her crystal. Altair, remember when we read in her journal that she had dreamt of being a mermaid, speaking with a pirate? Well, I think that actually happened! I think that she dreamt of an interaction that took place long ago. If she was not in that weird form that she is in, I really don't know where I would be. Speaking of ... you are not going to believe where she dropped me! It wasn't back here in present time! Oh no, that would have been too easy!" she laughed.

"So ... interesting ... She borrowed her own crystal to travel? Why didn't she just use the plates and the portals of time?" Stan asked.

"Because I had them, well, let me rephrase that. A blacksmith in Pompeii had them and she dropped me *there* to save him, right before the volcano erupted. I have never seen a place as beautiful as Pompeii. The streets glistened with white marble; the shops overflowed with aromatic foods and handmade goods, and the people... every single person seemed to contribute to a joyous, functioning city. It was lavish, and yet simple. Anyway, I followed Deneb's instructions, which were to find the blacksmith, and leave. This man had all of the plates -- which he said he was safeguarding for Apollo," she laughed. "Go figure! He said that he had made a deal to preserve the plates in exchange for his life to be saved when the volcano erupts. I suppose I was part of that master plan, because as we set sail, the volcano blew. Get this! When I asked him where he had found the plates, he said that the ring guided him to them. Altair, he was wearing your ring!"

"Whoa! Wait a second. You mean to tell me that you not only roamed the streets of Pompeii, but you saw the moment when Mt. Vesuvius blew?" Stan wheezed, trying to fathom the sights.

"Yes, and just let me say… that if it weren't for me being there, that man would have been a goner."

"What was the blacksmith like?" Altair's interest was flamed.

She laughed somewhat to herself. "Just like you, only ancient."

"Okay, so let's get back to Pompeii for a moment. You left on a boat, with the plates, and then where did you go?"

"We sailed for what seemed like days, and I could feel my soul rapidly aging. Then something came out from the fog that was rolling over the sea. At first it appeared like an eerie, greenish light on the water that shone through the mist. I paced up and down the boat as the blacksmith slept, searching for who or what might be waiting for me; and then, Ben's skinny, dark haired friend appeared through the fog. He blithely tossed my figurine between his slippery fingers as he offered his casual list of demands."

"Wait! He had your figurine when you saw him?" Altair ran through his memory trying to organize the sequence of events.

"Don't bother." Vega preemptively halted his thoughts. "It seems that time is operating under different rules than we're used to. He must have gotten the figurine from Ben, I mean Lan, and then decided to pay you a visit, and then me. Obviously he's not human, so what the heck is he?"

All eyes turned towards Stan, who seemed remote and silent. Before he could provide his assessment of the situation, Vega added to her story. "I guess I should have said, who are *they?*"

"They?" Stan lifted his eyes, from the book in his lap.

"There was someone else there; something dark, contained within the water. Every time I challenged the dark haired man who had come from the fog, the sea grew angrier, until it stretched far above the boat in a rising tidal wave. If it weren't for my song, both the blacksmith and I would have perished when the wave capsized the boat."

"Vega, it is clear that you used your song to return to present day, but what became of the blacksmith?"

"Right. Well, he demanded that I send him to somewhere dry so I sent him and my figurine to the driest place I could think of, Egypt. Who knows what time period he landed in," she cringed.

"Do you want to hear my theory on who it is that we're up against?" Stan swiveled around the book on his lap so that it faced them. "The Northern Crown is part of a family of constellations within Ursa Major; which includes Draco, Lynx, Bootes, and Coma Berenices. Now, each of these constellations consists of primal power that dates back to… well… the beginning of creation. The beings that we are dealing with are not only powerful, but also wise beyond

231

belief. They have each evolved over millions of years, to become what they are today. It is time for us to familiarize ourselves with the origins of Lynx, Bootes, Draco, and the Scorpion.

"Wait! There isn't a scorpion in Ursa Major." Vega scanned the list of villains on the page.

"You are correct. However, remember when we visited Villa Farnesina and studied the painting on the ceiling? Do you recall the beautiful woman with two strands of DNA over her head and the scorpion behind her back?" Nodding heads acknowledged him as he continued. "I believe that the woman was Hydra, and that the powerful secret behind her back is Scorpio."

Vega shuddered, picturing pinching claws and a painful sting, as Stan attempted to ease her mind.

"The Scorpion that I'm sure you are conceptualizing is far different than the Scorpio of which I speak. Of all the water signs, Scorpio is essentially a part of the ocean's fury, easily aroused, and of enormous force. Now, something to note… it appears that this particular character should *not* be part of Hydra's entourage of heathens. So, it might be worth exploring the idea that perhaps he, too, is indebted to her in some fashion. Let's move to the first, and perhaps the most powerful of her clan; Lynx." Stan flipped the page as Altair pulled out Deneb's journal.

"Good idea." Stan tossed him a pen.

Altair marked a firm dot on the page labeled Lynx, and then returned his attention to his teacher.

"The astronomer Hevelius named this constellation, which resides near Auriga the Charioteer, and stated that because it was such a faint constellation, it would take the eyesight of a Lynx to see it. Few people have seen Lynx with their naked eye, but one who *has* seen him was the well-known

Greek hero Jason, who went on a lifelong quest to reclaim the Golden Fleece... a mythological blanket of power, woven of golden hair. Many interpretations have been given for the Golden Fleece, most tying it to a magical force that was able to sway the masses. Can you think of anything similar?" He looked at Altair. "Remind me to tell you both the results from the experiment that we conducted earlier today. Now... where was I? Ah, right, the ancient Etruscans believed that the Golden Fleece was much more than a material object; that it was rather, a symbol of prophecy and prosperity. In many tales, golden fleeces were hung to resemble the renewal of royal power, or the relinquishment of same. Why golden, woven hair? Well, let's move on, to the next member of this tribe; Berenice."

"Berenice, dating back to the Ptolemaic dynasty, was an Egyptian Queen; magnificent and dignified. She was an equestrian, and is said to have participated in the Olympic Games between 245 and 241 BC. She put her soul on the line for those she loved, and was often seen on horseback alongside common soldiers, in times of battle."

"She sounds amazing," Vega whispered, picturing the heroine. "How could someone like that oppose us?"

"Let me continue with the story of Queen Berenice. It is said that her lover went off to battle, and being a woman of intuition and sacrifice, she cut off a lock of her golden hair and placed it upon the altar of the Goddess of Creation, Aphrodite, the beloved wife of Hephaestus. Of all the symbols associated with this goddess, the swan and the rose are the most influential. When her lover returned from battle, the lock of golden hair was found to have gone missing, and therefore, the people claimed that the gods had tossed it into the sky, thus sealing her legend into the stars. BUT what I think, is a bit different," Stan raised his eyes to ensure they were still closely following.

"Hold on, so this queen cut off her hair and laid it down on the altar of creation to ensure that her true love would come home from war? Is that right? It seems like she *could* have battled alongside him, but for some reason, she decided there was more power in her golden hair than in her...actions?" Vega asked.

"That is why I suggest to you that we look at this from a different angle. I do not believe that the gold she laid down on the altar of Aphrodite was mere hair from her head. How many Egyptian queens do you know of who had blonde hair? I believe that Queen Berenice discovered the plates, learned of their power, and someone or something convinced her that her true love would safely return from battle if she agreed to a trade."

"So she was tricked?" Altair marked another star on the page, circling Berenice's name.

"Well, we know that Hydra is manipulative and thrives on collecting things that she can control. I'd say that most definitely the great queen was tricked into serving Hydra, and gave up the golden plates in her possession," Stan said as Altair continued to write in the journal.

"Hey, how many plates are there again?" Vega began to formulate a new theory.

"Eight," Altair drew a figure eight on the page.

"And how many villains are there in her gang?

Stan recited them aloud. "Draco, Hydra, Scorpio, Lynx, Bootes, Berenice, and Lan; that's only seven."

"What in the world did Hydra promise these people? Do you think she promised them each a golden plate, and if so, why only seven of the eight?" Vega said.

"If they each were promised a portion of the wheel of time that they could control and revisit eternally, then perhaps they went for it. Hydra is a manipulative beast, and I think it safe to say that she could have found a way to make it happen. What's important *now* is that we find the remaining golden plates, and find a way to trade them for Deneb."

"We aren't actually going to give her the plates, are we?" Vega erupted.

"Of course we aren't. However, as things stand now, we only have three plates to trade, which means that at this moment, she has a portion of the wheel... a segment of the universe, under her control. Furthermore, if she is using the plates the way I think she is, then *many* people are in trouble."

"Stan?" Vega said with chagrin, "There is something else that you both need to know. When I was with Ben... I swear I saw him wipe the rim of my coffee cup, as if he was collecting a sample or something. Why would he do that?"

Her whisper stretched to stark silence as they pondered the many ways that her DNA could be replicated; and why. Stan's lip quivered as he responded to her thoughts. "Are you sure that you actually saw him wipe the rim of that cup after you drank?"

She nodded in affirmation, as Altair added another layer to the story. "When I travelled back to Chartres Cathedral and transformed the plates from metal to gold, Hydra wasn't far behind me. She appeared to me in the forest after the others had escaped with the plates. I thought that I was a goner for sure, but she said there was something else that she wanted; a student."

"Wait a second. You changed the plates from metal to gold?" Vega shrieked.

"Remember when we both jumped through the well, and you went to the future? Well, it seems that I went far back,

235

into the past. I emerged in a dark, somewhat stagnant place, beneath a grand palace where all the local artisans lived and worked, together. They were a sort of commune of artists, mathematicians, poets, and scholars, that the king saw fit to house in an area beneath his palace."

"Oh my goodness, Altair! Now it all makes sense to me! Why didn't I see this before? The Louvre was once said to house some of the most famous artisans of all time. The king was somewhat of a collector; some say he was obsessed with the arts; and so he opened his doors for his favorites, allowing them a permanent residence at the Louvre. The Louvre is said to have gotten its name from the French word *rouvre*, meaning "oak tree," and the word oak equates to the word 'duir' which means doorway. You went through tunnels -- correct?" Stan said.

"We walked for what seemed like miles and miles, through these tunnels until we came to a symbol on the wall. It was a double axe. At this point, we exited the tunnels via a secret door and came out in the forest, near the cathedral."

"Hold on..." Vega interrupted. "So you're saying you went back in time to the Louvre, where you met some of the most prestigious artists of that time period, and then you transformed the plates to gold... when?"

"They had metal plates with them, and they had taken them to the well many times before. When we got there, we rubbed some kind of oil on our feet and walked in a kind of maze-like pattern, until we arrived at the well inside. That is where I saw Deneb -- I mean Melusine. She was so beautiful that I sobbed. Then, it was as if something triggered a reaction within the plates, so I ran outside and put them into a basin of water, and somehow used my ring to change the plates from metal into gold. I know it sounds crazy, but that's what happened."

236

"Remember when I mentioned my theory about the tears really being pearls? I believe that both of you simultaneously cried into the wells.... and re-awakened the plates of Apollo. You are both from the fire sign, Leo? Correct?"

They nodded in unison. "I think it safe to say that my theory proves correct, which is why the plates are now golden, and very much alive. I also believe that using your ring, you possess the power to control these plates, but something seems to be missing. Why would Hydra want Vega to become a student of hers so badly?"

"Well, if one of the plates is affiliated with me... and the Lyre, perhaps it is somehow unobtainable by her without assistance? Maybe she needs me. That might be why only seven of the eight were promised. Lan told me that once, long ago, Hydra had captured me and it was at that time that he bartered his servitude, for my existence. I've never been able to pinpoint the exact place in time when I was captured by her, so perhaps it was the plate that bears my namesake that she came to possess, and not me physically."

Altair cringed. "Hydra did allude to something when she said that Vega would end up joining them, one way or another."

"Which brings me back to my original question. Why did Ben wipe the rim of my coffee cup? Was he trying to steal some part of my genetics? Part of me?" Out of habit she scanned her body for her figurine, and became even more dismayed that it too, was gone.

"Your genetics are primal, and have been recycled since the beginning of time, to evolve into the...person, that you are today. Your genetic makeup, in essence, is linked to Lyra, one of the most powerful constellations in the entire universe. If they did find a way to replicate your genes, then

237

maybe they also found a way to utilize the eighth plate, and open the portals of time." Stan rubbed his tired eyes as he tried to comprehend such a thing. "We're going to need to find a way to sever the bonds between Hydra and her faithful servants.

"That's right! The dagger!" She bounced up in a spasm of hope. "In my dream, Lan said that I needed to use the dagger to sever the bonds! Maybe the dagger can cut the ties between Hydra and those bound to her. Now... where is it?"

"You dropped it." Altair reminded her.

"Oh. Right. So... do you think that if we go back to the fountain, we will find it buried there?"

"I beat you to it." He winked as he pulled it from his jacket.

Relieved sighs paved the way to the next idea. "We need a plan. The plates that we possess depict the shield, wine, and an egg. Now, judging by our little experiment, it seems we are able to use your ring, in conjunction with the plates, to control the emotions and experiences of those around us. We know the effects of the wine. What about the others?"

They stared in silence at the egg and shield as Altair excitedly reminded the group, "In the story of Daedalus, he used wax from the bees along with the plate depicting the shield, to safely escape from King Minos! The shield must offer some form of actual protection to those who possess it!"

"Okay. So what about the egg?" Vega scanned her memory trying to recall images of it. "Oh! Remember when we were at the Villa Farnesina, and the fountain turned into a doorway when you put the egg near the water?"

"Interesting. So maybe the egg is some kind of creation catalyst, and can open doorways hidden within the water.

238

Knowing that Hydra already has five plates in her possession, we will need to be extremely careful. She will want to arrange a trade for the other three plates, in order to gain control of the wheel. And knowing her, there is surely some sort of trap involved."

Altair scoured his memory once more, as another alarming thought jarred him. "In one of my dreams, I saw a doorway between the Louvre and a citadel, where words were painted in a circle up on the ceiling. It was only when I spoke the words, that Deneb was freed. I still don't know what citadel that could possibly be."

Stan shamefully spoke his almost certain to be regrettable response. "I think we should conduct a test."

Alarmed eyebrows raised in unison. "What kind of test?"

"I want to see how all three plates work, and of even more importance, if one or both of you can use them. I would like for each of you to take a plate. Vega you take the egg and Altair the shield. Travel to another city, say Barcelona, and use them in some fashion."

"Why can't we just do it from here?" Vega whined.

"Right now Ben thinks that you are dead, and so do his friends. If we use the plates here, every person around us for miles will feel the impact of them. Just by using the wine plate for a moment, the entire hotel staff became so drunk that they are still passed out in the lobby! We cannot risk you using them here."

"Fine, but this is a quick experiment and we return immediately." Altair firmly stated.

Vega nodded in agreement. "It has to be fast, if I am to have any energy remaining for our battle with Hydra... and who knows who else may show up."

Together they heaved the plates into the isolation of their possession, as Vega began to hum. Their eyes locked as Vega whispered, "see you in Barcelona."

Together they landed on a grassy hill, as doves scattered through the treetops of the forest. A beautiful mosaic, gingerbread style house stood silently before them. They shielded their eyes from the morning sun, getting a better look at the steeple of the house; adorned with what looked like broken pieces of white coffee cups. "What is this place? It looks like a trippy version of something from Hansel and Gretel." Vega looked over the oddly amazing gem of a home. Every one of the brightly colored pieces of broken glass that covered the exterior of the castle-like home shimmered in the sunshine as she neared.

"I don't know, but I think we should get on with our experiment and get out of here. Look, there is a fountain in the garden! Hurry! Hold the egg over the water and try to conjure a doorway," Altair anxiously demanded.

She calmly laughed. "Oh okay, a doorway to where exactly?" She eyed the ominous face of the dragon spitting water into the fountain. "How about I work on that while you try to create a shield of sorts? Actually, you know what would be kind of cool, since we are both here and all, and can experiment? Why don't you try to use that ring of yours to bring one of the stone figurines to life... like Daedalus did?" She smirked as she extended her plate over the trickling water.

He sized up the dragon, "maybe another time."

Water began to swirl within the fountain, occupying their attention from the ash and smoke rising from the grass behind them. Vega hummed louder, speeding up the water of the quickly forming vortex. Thick gusts of smoke wafted over her hands, breaking her concentration, as she screamed, "Altair! Look!" She spun around in panic, watching as the world around her began to decinagrate.

"What's happening?" Altair shouted, as the sticky smoke of Lynx's soul began to take form.

"You must be wondering what is happening to this once beautiful city." His voice drifted through the smoke as the trees began to burn, and the artistic soul of the city collapsed around them. "Barcelona exists no longer; destroyed by a fire that not even the great lion could extinguish."

In a moment of fury, Altair screamed and hoisted the heavy plate above his head; casting a protective blanket of light around himself. Blinded by the electric glare coming from his shield, Vega closed her eyes and continued her song. With blind faith, she extended the egg over the water, and felt the vortex of the spinning doorway opening before her. Indecisively, Altair paused for a fraction of a second, to see what she would do as the shadowy clouds overtook her, and sent her crashing through the rapidly closing tunnel of stormy water.

He watched in dismay as the precious golden egg fell to the ground, breaking the protective shield he held with his consciousness. He looked into the deceptive, now quiet waters, realizing only in that moment that there were *two* women he longed to save, hidden within the confines of time. "I'm coming."

Quickly, he conjured the portal, and jumped through time, unsure of where his intentions would take him, to the location of Vega or Deneb. He landed with a thud on the dirt floor of a barely visible, fog-covered place as the towering walls of the colosseum came into focus. "No way,"

241

he whispered to himself, wondering if somehow the fog was listening, absorbing his fears.

"Vega?" he thought to himself, just as she answered with a timely scream.

"Altair?" the power of her voice sounded strong, despite the chains that bound her to the center of the colosseum floor. He blinked a few times, adjusting to the vision taking form in the distance. The outline of a noble woman, with scythe in hand, sat silently upon her horse, high up in the stands, as if she were one of the many lion statues standing around the upper terrace.

"Altair!" Be careful. It's a trap!" Vega cried while clattering her chains.

With a watchful eye, Altair rotated in a slow circle, scanning the vacant seats, which had once held the attentive audience, blindly captivated by the sacrifice that took place within. The sound of heavy hooves echoed around him, as the eerie equestrian raised her scythe, as if calling to a hidden army beneath the fog.

"Altair!" Vega again cried from the center of the ring, as he made his way to her. Between quick breaths she whispered, "That woman on the horse is Queen Berenice, and she's been promised the most important part of the wheel; Litha. Bootes is a giant of a man, and is said to have won countless battles here in the colosseum, and he is poised to battle you -- here... today. And Lynx, the one whose essence is formed from darkness and deception, has brought me here... for all to see."

"How do you know all of this?" he hastily whispered.

"I've been chained here for months, waiting for you. We all have." She looked around the vacant amphitheater searching for any trace of her captors.

242

"Months?" he jumped back as a cage shot up from the tunnels below and onto the main center stage. The bars of the ancient wooden cage opened slowly, releasing no more than a gust of cold winter air. "Altair, something is here," she staggered into a defensive stance, guarding herself with what little she had.

"I see nothing," he whispered in response as another cage erupted from the ground, releasing a giant, venomous lizard. As the third cage catapulted up from the tunnels, a thunderous laugh shook the ground where they stood. Flickering green eyes glowed through the heavy fog, suffocating their thoughts while heavy footsteps heaved toward them. "Ummm ... Altair, I think that's the giant.... I think that's Bootes!" Vega yelled while quickly rolling a few feet away on the ground as a giant fist slammed down on the space she had just vacated. "Can you see him?" Vega screamed to her perplexed friend who seemed lost in the fog.

"I can hardly see anything!" he yelled, as the shadow of the giant's fist raised once again.

"You move when I say move! Now!" she demanded as Altair dove out of the way. A choir of evil laughs echoed through the fog as the ghostly silhouettes of spectators began to fill the stadium seats.

"Don't look now but I think we have *more* company!" Altair yelled as the giant came into focus. "Who *are* all of these people?" He scanned the pale, ghastly faces of the crowd, with their sunken eyes, and observed the unusual patterns on their skin, made by red ink.

"These people are all part of her tribe! They're not from here, but have come from far away to witness her triumph, i.e., us -- dying!"

Defensively, they stood back to back, and moved in a slow circle, keeping a close eye on the lizard, the giant, and the

243

undulating clouds of fog, now beginning to take on human form. Altair twisted his ring, changing the once binding chains around Vega's ankles, into two slithering snakes, who now quietly moved in on the lizard.

"Watch out!" Vega screamed just seconds before a silver spear flew by, just missing her face. "Ummm Altair, I think we've got company!" The pointed tip of Ma Qiang's golden helmet sparkled in the sliver of sunlight that began to unwind from the round sundial overhead. "I've seen a similar ceiling, when I went to Lan's temple in the future; just above the well where I saw Deneb. There was a circular ceiling which revolved and opened to let in the light during the equinox!"

The spear-carrying warrior lowered his weapon, and slowly bowed toward his enemies as if acknowledging the great battle about to take place. Secretly, Altair twisted his ring, breathing life into the stone lions that circled the theatre, and watching as the confines of time crumbled from the mighty beasts. As if mentally controlling their primal instincts, Altair smiled as they slid through the aisles, unseen, joining the hunt. Hearing the subtle growls of the ancient kings, Vega smiled in disbelief, "I think we have everyone marked, right?"

With his attention solemnly locked on Vega, a second spear slipped through the fog, and glanced off his shoulder. He winced in pain, fueling her rage. Her racing heart, coupled with the footsteps of the giant who ran toward them, shifted her focus to the blood-covered spear. With a deep intake of breath, she lifted it from the ground, and exhaled as she thrust it forcefully, into the giant. As the silver spear sunk deep into its chest, the lions lunged at the collective darkness of what once was Lynx, removing two of the universe's deadliest creations.

Heavy drops of rain replaced the fog, washing the stains of their enemies into the colosseum floors, where they joined thousands of others before them. As the rain grew heavier, pummeling their skin like pebbles, a panicked, yet familiar voice screamed, "NO!"

Vega pressed her back against Altair, as if returning to home base, and gathered her thoughts and her energy.

"Altair, something is off. I have never done that before. It's as if I absorbed a gift that wasn't mine. My breath or maybe it was my intention, sent that spear into Bootes. I don't feel right," she looked up towards him with panicked eyes.

"You did what you needed to do. Don't worry, I'll never leave you."

"Speaking of... I don't think everyone is here. Draco and Lan seem to be missing." As she wrapped her arms around him, a voice echoed through the rain.

"I see you've brought my gold."

Altair squinted through the heavy sheets of rain, only to behold the familiar, yet dreaded apparition taking shape directly in front of them. Watery serpents spilled from the crown of her head, and raced into swirling puddles encircling them. The heavy hooves of Berenice, now silenced by the rain, closed in on the duo as Hydra screamed her demands.

"You have two choices! Give me the remaining plates and I give you your precious Deneb, returned to human form." She openly cringed at the thought of humanity, before continuing with her second demand. "Or.... If it is a battle that you prefer, then a battle you shall have. Either way, we will take what is rightfully ours. The question is.... will you be a part of the world we control, or will you simply return to your rightful place among the silent stars?"

Vega instinctively whispered. "She will not hand us Deneb. We both know that the only way she can be freed is by speaking the words on the citadel ceiling, right?"

He silently nodded. "If my dreams are as accurate as yours... then, yes."

"Then we answer her call to war, and we sever the bonds that bind those closest to her."

"We hereby accept your challenge!" Altair called out, as snakelike heads emerged from the slithering puddles around them. An eerie smile glazed upon her face as she turned to the pale crowd, who was now drenched in her essence.

"Let the show begin!"

A chorus of groans erupted from the stands as another silver spear whisked past Vega's face, barely missing her. "Don't worry Altair. I can hear his vibration; it is what makes his aim so precise. If I hum a tune opposite to his, he will be reduced to uselessness." She smirked while confidently striding up to the man she somehow both respected and loathed. He drew another breath, and pulled another spear from his belt as Vega began to hum, immediately freezing his weapon in mid-air. For moments that seemed to last forever, she locked eyes with the man who seemed more loyal to Lan than Hydra, and wondered if he too was but a slave to her lies, and if so, could he also be saved? The sound of rapidly approaching hooves shook her from the introspective moment, which sent the spear crashing to the ground.

"Vega! Look out!" Altair screamed while whisking a shield of light around them, deflecting new blows from the savage equestrian warrior. Each attempted hit sounded like heavy stones hitting a gelatinous wall, vibrating out in slow waves as Berenice tried repeatedly, to strike them. Vega wrapped a brotherly arm around Altair as she caught her breath. "Can they hear us in here?"

"Beats me." He wiped sweat from his face, and assessed the slow moving battle scene surrounding them. "Everything is going so slow out there. Did I just stop time?"

She laughed, "I don't know what you did, but I appreciate the break."

"We still don't know where Deneb is, and I don't...." his words froze in his chest as the colosseum began to fill with water, surrounding their protective shield with quickly rising waves. As the top of their bubble submerged beneath the dark waters, Altair grabbed Vega's hand in a panic, pulling her close to his lips. "Vega, I... I need to tell you something..."

"What is it?" In a moment out of space and time, she found herself lost in his energy. "I think I know exactly what you're about to say," she lifted her chin towards his lips.

As he leaned in to softly brush the knotted red hair from her face, something crashed against the side of their bubble, and pressed its hands firmly on each side. Two gleaming eyes longingly looked in at them, as if calling to his soul. "It's Deneb!" he screamed, as he tossed Vega aside. Feeling a bit scattered, Vega averted her eyes from Deneb's, instead looking for a way out of the only safe place she knew.

"She's trying to say something!" Altair pressed his hands towards hers, attempting to read her screaming lips. "Warp? Scorp?" he continued frantically guessing.

"Oh no." Vega stepped backwards into the center of the bubble, yanking Altair's sleeve to turn around.

"Wait! I think I know what she's saying!" His eyes remained locked on Deneb's, which were now looking past his shoulder, and at the giant face emerging through the water on the other side of the bubble.

"Scorpio!" Vega screamed as the enormous watery mouth opened, sending them soaring through the turbulent waves.

"Altair! I have a plan!" Vega struggled to stand, as they tumbled and swirled around the colosseum like a penny in a spiral wishing well.

"You still have the egg, right?" She attempted to secure her hands and feet to the sides of the bubble to keep from falling.

"I do." He followed suit, pressing his hands and feet to the sides, leaving mere inches between their faces.

"Good! I think we can use it to create a new doorway in the water to get out of here! But before we do that, we need to find Hydra, and use the dagger. You do still have the dagger, right?"

He quickly nodded, removing one hand from the bubble to pull it from his pocket.

"Good! Okay, hand it to me and on the count of three, drop your shield and swim to the surface. Hydra will see you struggling and show herself. I know she will. Now, this is important. Once the portal door is open, you *must* grab Deneb and pull her through to wherever that citadel is. Once you speak the words written on the ceiling, she will hopefully return to her human form. I'll work on the rest."

"What do you mean, you'll work on the rest?" he questioned as he inched his hand along the walls of the shield towards Deneb's pale fingers, stuck to the outside.

"One of us has to stay behind and sever the bonds. We still have Hydra and Draco to face."

"What about Berenice, Scorpio, Ma Qiang, and Lan?" He squinted as the blazing sun, now directly overhead, illuminated the water, nearly blinding him.

"If I'm right, we won't need to worry about them."

"And if you're wrong?" he demanded, as he again inched his hands back along the walls to Vega.

"I'll take care of it." She firmly yanked her hands from his, resuming her focus on the golden egg. "Ready when you are."

CHAPTER 16

With a mighty thud, Altair crashed onto the dirt floor of the cave-like structure, flailing his arms to clear away the dust that now surrounded him. He searched the near empty fortress, devoid of any windows, and realized that he was alone in the citadel. With a swift push, he thrust open the wooden door, and stepped out into the forest. "What the..." he whispered to himself as shimmering specks fluttered around his head. "Go away!" he growled at the annoying flickers of light as they dispersed, and joined the golden leaves of autumn raining around him.

"This way... there isn't much time...." whispered through the breeze. Hurriedly, he followed the golden lights, which moved like a swarm of bees into the forest.

"Her golden hair has fallen down; another trapped within the crown. A slave of soul she'll always be, forever trapped, and never free," the collective swarm of lights sang out.

"What?" He tilted his head to one side as he approached the crystal lake, and watched in disbelief as the reflection of golden fairies lit a pathway across the water, to the fallen creature who lay on the other side.

"Deneb!" he screamed, and watched in panic, as Berenice emerged from the woods behind her, with scythe in hand. She moved like a beaten dog as she neared the fallen

250

heroine, lowering her weapon as if to admire the resemblance to the powerful being she once was.

"Berenice!" Altair screamed across the water. "You will not find a fight from her! Are you but a coward!? See your skills challenged by me, not by a dying creature!"

With a mighty shudder, she gripped her scythe once more, as the ground began to vibrate violently, shaking the trees, which now dripped with honey. She arrogantly raised her frail arms above her head, and conjured the swarms that awaited her command.

Without thinking, he dove into the water, beneath the thick, dark clouds of buzzing bees. As he pushed himself through the water, he cast a silvery beam of light in the direction where he knew Deneb lay dormant, and pulled her into the water to join him. Her heavy eyes struggled to stay open, as he pressed his lips to hers, hoping that somehow his breath would become hers. The shadowy ceiling of bees shook in tiny waves around them, and triggered her memory.

"Are we returning to the garden? I remember the water feeling like this on the way in. Where is Cygnus?" she looked around in puzzled wonderment.

"He…. he's not here right now Deneb. I need you to stay with me. It's me… Altair."

"Oh yes, the bright star… over there … I like that one," she pointed overhead through the ceiling of water.

"You're going to need to stay right here, okay? But it's just for now." He looked intensely into her eyes moments before he pressed his lips to hers once more. "I feel like we've done this before."

"I'd remember if we had," she whispered, as a glimmer of light returned to her brilliant, blue eyes. "Altair, I've waited so long for you. Please, be careful. She possesses great power. They all do."

"So do I," he assured her, as he propelled himself to the surface where thousands of bees awaited him.

"Berenice!" He called through the cloud at the demented woman, who was slowly running her fingers through her hair of golden honey. "You don't have to do this! You were not always a bad person! You were tricked by Hydra!"

The bee-covered silhouette of the woman paused, tilting her head to the side as they flew from her ancient, scarred face. "I hate and I love. Why do I do this, perhaps you ask? I know not, but I feel it happen and am tormented."

"You are tormented because you were promised something... the return of your love, and you were tricked! You are tormented because the things that consume you are power and greed, and you remain hollow and empty because of the promises broken! You do not need to hold on to that promise anymore. Let it go Berenice. Please... there is still time."

"Time..." She wiped the honey from her lips. "Isn't that a funny notion?"

CHAPTER 17

Carefully, she held the dagger between her teeth, and freed her hands so she could climb up the sides of the colosseum walls. She moved in harmony with the collective pack of lions, who closed in on Hydra from behind. She listened from the shadows as Hydra called out to the fast moving water in frustration. "Scorpio! Be Calm!!!!"

As her screams echoed from all sides of the stadium walls, Vega pulled herself up to get a good look at her enemy, shocked at the sight before her. The familiar dress blew in the breeze, as she adjusted the emerald headdress that now lay flat on her forehead. "Why didn't I recognize that dress when I saw her before?" Vega mentally scolded herself, as the dagger slipped from her teeth, clanking on the marble seats as it fell. She winced, and felt the attention of seven sets of eyes, as the lions slid back into the shadows, awaiting her next move. Quickly she shimmied down the stairs, and slid the dagger into the secrecy of her jacket before stepping out into the moment she had waited lifetimes to experience.

"Ahhh, Vega, child of Lyra," Hydra hissed as the turmoil of water spun below them. "I see you've not dressed for the occasion … as usual." She lifted a judgmental eyebrow at Vega's boyish outfit. "Nonetheless, happy to see you've come to join me. Did you know… that because of your precious tears, I now have access to powers I never dreamt possible? Speaking of dreams, how are you sleeping?" Her eyes flickered in excitement, "Oh! Here is our first lesson together! How exciting! Did you know that the plate of Samhain allows me to communicate with my long forgotten brothers? Able to conjure and connect with the great warriors of my species who were slain millions of years ago?" she said with an elegant, yet motherly smile.

Vega scanned the vacant seats searching for the remnants of the ghastly audience. "Don't worry, they're always watching us. I have so much to teach you! I cannot place why I feel so drawn to you… in a way that I have to say, surprises even me. Your rage or maybe it's your ancient, dark soul… sparks a fire within me… calls to me in a way."

"Oh really?" Vega humored her demented views.

"Did you know that your song has been used for millions of years to cause destruction, and rip apart civilizations that have stood together for thousands of years?"

"I watched Barcelona fall to ash with my own eyes, because of Lynx. My song took no part in that."

Hydra laughed at the acute understanding of her chaos. "Oh Vega, you think that Barcelona is the only city that we destroyed using your song?"

"Not possible, you don't know my song. You need me to control the eighth plate…"

With an excited eye roll, she huffed, interrupting Vega's justification. "True I don't possess your song, but you see, I possess the plate of creation… the plate of life itself. Just a molecule of your DNA allowed me to mimic the very essence of your being, and wasn't it magnificent?" She beamed at the thought of her own triumph. "See Vega, you are as much a part of the chaos, as you are the cure. You are drawn to the darkness because you helped to create it!" She laughed as she whisked the dress around her body with a childlike twirl.

Flickers of yellow obedient eyes met with Vega's, spawning a new idea.

"If I am one of you, then I'd like to take my place next to my soulmate." She calmly looked into the pit of Hydra's eyes.

"I'm afraid that's not possible my dear, as I'm almost certain Queen Berenice has had her way with Altair by now."

She paused, awaiting Vega's more than certain, anger driven response. Seeing none, she hissed in excitement, "You could be so happy here with me. Trust me; you deserve so much more than being the third wheel in a love story that shouldn't even involve you."

She paused, and reflected on the trouble she had brought to both of their lives. "What would happen if I stay?"

As the tumult of water spun faster inside the portal below, Vega slid the dagger from the cuff of her jacket, calmly approaching the deceptive beast.

"We'd overturn the wheel, together, and reshape history... in our favor."

In a decisive attack, the lions sprang from the shadows, and pinned each of her heads with their giant paws as Vega drew her dagger.

"I'd rather be a third wheel than a monster."

With her last breath, Hydra laughed. "You're already both."

CHAPTER 18

Triumphantly, Vega stood alongside the lions, looking down at the severed heads of the rapidly decaying beast. She wiped the blood from the blade, as she stepped over the trails of venom with her worn leather boots. The lions kept a watchful eye on their leader while she gazed out towards the ghastly tribe of obedient, dark eyed onlookers.

"Your bonds have been severed! You are indebted to her no more!" She thrust the dagger up to the sky, as celebratory roars from the lions echoed through the stark silence of the colosseum.

She scanned the crowd, searching for any sign of Lan as the sun passed over the top of the dome. Dark, watchful eyes dripped down the faces of the former servants, as their translucent bodies began to melt and slide down the steps into the stagnant water below. Each fallen star, now swirled into the dark waters of Scorpio. In an attempt to reach yet another one of Hydra's former servants, Vega shouted "Scorpio! The bonds are severed! You are indebted to her no longer! Rise up! Show yourself to me!"

The waves began to churn, and gathered themselves into a rising mass, which quickly covered the stadium seats. "Go!" Vega commanded her lions as they climbed to the top of the colosseum, looking in at the storm. She yanked the emerald headdress from atop the pile of leathery soot as a thunderous voice came from the water. "Daughter of Lyra, host of the stars. There are bonds that even time cannot sever. Though our queen has fallen, the wheel has turned."

She teetered on the edge, looking back to the fallen city now behind her, enclosed in smoke and dust, just as a glimmer of flashing light drew her attention back to the water.

A familiar voice coursed through her body in chilling waves as she heard Lan speak. "Vega, I am your only way out. See the light; not the darkness, and come down the stairs."

As she quickly searched the now-submerged colosseum for any remaining steps, a glowing staircase of elongated, white light emerged directly in front of her, splitting the dark water to either side. Fearlessly she walked, with the lions following right behind her, down the glowing staircase of watery light, and disappeared into the abyss of time.

She stepped out of the water, and up into the familiar, yet thoroughly changed Chinese Palace of Lan. The once bare, metallic walls of the balconies were now covered in fragrant layers of jasmine and rose. She looked up to the hexagon shaped opening of the pagoda, and counted the additional balconies he had added since her last time there. She walked up to the shelf that had once held her copper vase, and admired its vacant spot, before returning to the trickling fountain she had just stepped from moments earlier.

"Vega," a loving voice echoed from above.

"Lan!" she ran up the familiar steps, towards the rooftop towards his voice. She paused at the top, the icy wind constricting her breath, and gazed at the cloaked man, obscured in the darkness of a black silk cloak.

"I have waited for you, so long," the hidden man called from a distance.

"Why are you covered? Show me your face." She demanded as gusts of snow blew over the balcony, collecting on the lion's fur.

"There are some things that time bid me not pursue, for a trade has been made. Take the plates and close the Serpent

Window." He pulled his cloak aside slightly, revealing the silk wrapped plates, draped in scarlet.

"What do you mean a trade has been made? What have you done?" she cried. "I've traveled to the end of time, and I am not leaving here without you!" she screamed while running toward him, causing him to suddenly collapse, and melt into a pool of icy water.

"I am here, but changed." His final words rippled upon the puddle as she wept over the instantly freezing water. Flakes of snow fell gracefully around her reflection, as the lions moved to position on each side of her. Feeling simultaneous confusion, betrayal, and heartbreak, she gazed into the icy mirror one last time, before rising to her feet.

"The plates are now ours to protect, and together we will find Altair, and free Deneb. Come!" she wrapped herself in the black silk cloak, now piled on the ground next to what was now only a memory.

"Look! Who is that?" echoed from below. She froze, looking down towards the hordes of freezing civilians just outside the palace gates. She squinted at the frail women and children, as she lowered her hood revealing the golden headdress. "It is I, your queen! Come and take refuge within the walls of the palace!"

An outcry of pure joy rose from below as she ordered the gates of the palace to be opened, allowing swarms of people to take shelter within. She walked through the company of happy families, and beamed with delight as she thought about how much good she could accomplish as a ruler... in any time, or place. In that moment, love filled her heart, and she thought not of Lan, but of Altair. Fright directed her footsteps as she hastily fled the common area and returned to the safety and comfort of the fountain. This time, as another tear fell into the water, she wept not for her missing friend, but for the betrayal that now lay heavy on her heart.

CHAPTER 19

"There isn't much time! Take this, if you wish to fly once more." Queen Berenice placed the honey-covered plate at his feet as he realized what must have transpired to sever her allegiance to Hydra.

"You are a long way from Egypt, my Queen. Will you join me on my voyage? I promise to return you to your land, once our quest is complete."

She nodded with certainty, while her eyes remained locked on the creature, who was swimming just beneath the surface. "And what of her?"

He sighed, "I... I do not know. Until I say what needs to be said, she will remain trapped in this form forever."

"Where are these words written?"

"Painted upon the ceiling of the citadel." He wavered, unsure of the direction to take.

She looked to the forest, then back at Altair. "Come! Lift her from the water!" With a tribal hymn, she called to the trees, and was answered by the sound of galloping hooves and a gust of golden wings, which fluttered down from the branches. They mounted her horse, and rode with the fairies of the forest towards the grass-covered dome. Together they carried Deneb's slippery body into the stale darkness of the citadel. Altair quickly removed his shirt, tossing it onto the ground for her to lay upon. He squinted up at the ceiling, and cried, "I can't see a thing in here!"

As a tear fell from his eye, to the thirsty skin of his lover, a speck of gold was reflected onto the ceiling. One by one, the golden fairies flew to the ceiling, illuminating the symbols that had long been masked from common sight.

He quickly stood, attempting to decipher the images, now glowing above. "They're familiar, yet foreign, but I think maybe I can read them!" He called out just as the golden lights burned even brighter, this time shining directly upon his ring. He began to twist the ring as the symbols began rotating, spinning faster as he continued to turn the band. The earthen ceiling, now transformed into a golden timepiece, rotated its gears as the symbols of the wheel shone brightly. He announced their names one by one, beginning with Imbolc and ending with Yule, as the wheel began to slow to a stop. Fear began to oppress his heart as the last symbol faded back into the dust of the ceiling, and Deneb struggled to raise her head. He pulled the ring from his finger, illuminating the face of the lion within, as he cried out more name, Apollo.

A blinding light shot through the cavern, and the symbols lit up once more, quickly spinning a vibrant tunnel of gold around them. He knelt down, shielding Deneb from the whirlwind of dust and light, as Berenice knelt in humble admiration toward the pixelated face now emerging from the sands of time.

"Apollo?" he whispered, as a radiant force pulled them through time, and spit them out on the cold marble floor of the Louvre. He rubbed his head, attempting to put the elaborately painted ceiling into focus as he blinked. A puzzled smile crept across his face, as he took in the familiar grand gallery of Apollo.

"Altair?" Deneb's voice echoed through the hall as he ran to her in relief. "Where is your shirt?" she laughed as if it were the only irregularity.

He smiled. "My shirt, huh? That is all that's different here? How about... where are your fins?"

Her legs, still sticky with some kind of gooey substance, shook as she attempted to stand. "I'll need some help until I regain my strength," she whispered, wrapping her arms around him.

A powerful voice reverberated through the galley, "C'est la porte magnifique portail!"

Altair smiled at the sound of her new, yet familiar dialect, "You adapt well I see. Deneb, this is Queen Berenice, one of Egypt's greatest queens. She once held the plate of Litha; the plate of the Bee, and assisted in your rescue."

Deneb humbly bowed to the queen. "Throughout the course of history, I've guarded the plates; watched as they passed through sacred wells and sacred hands, and I've also seen the chaos that arose because of them. I'm sorry that you were promised love that never returned."

Altair silently pondered her words as Berenice turned to him. "There is another? Yes?"

His mind spiraled down guilt-led paths as he thought of Vega. "Vega?" he replied while averting eye contact. "She stayed in... well, I don't know what time period we were in, but the city was Rome."

"Was?" Deneb asked.

"Several cities were destroyed by Hydra; at least one that I know of."

Her head sunk as she exhaled, "I knew something like this might happen. I had a vision of a man taking my place in

262

exchange for the return of civilization. Did that not happen? We must go to China."

"How?" he looked to the gallery walls, richly covered in paintings, as if they held the answers.

Berenice interrupted his pensive stare, "The golden bee of Litha has long been used by great warriors at times when flight was the only method of escape. Legends of Daedalus tell of the blacksmith evoking powerful wings, soaring from the towers of King Minos. May you fly once more."

Puzzled, he gripped the golden plate, sticky with honey, as she walked enchantingly up to an old lamp, framed within a case. "This lamp. It is Egyptian. I feel as if I've seen it before?" she whispered, pressing her sticky hands to the glass.

"Hurry, we must go now. The earth is shifting!" she commanded as the ground began to shake, causing the heavy chandeliers above to shake and sway. Altair flipped through historical memories, trying to recall any great earthquakes in this location as the chandelier fell from the ceiling. The sound of their hurried footsteps was drowned by breaking glass as they took shelter beneath a neighboring exhibit. Altair held Deneb close to his side as a case crashed to the floor, breaking the glass around the old oil lamp. Attempting to occupy her mind, if only for moments, Deneb read from its information card.

"Work: Frog, oil lamp. Department of Egyptian Antiquities: Roman. Egypt (30 BC – AD 392) "The ovaloid shape may symbolize a creation myth developed at Hermopolis: from the broken shell of the mysterious primordial egg which burst forth the new-born sun, prelude to the creation. The sun embodies light, which here takes material form in the illuminated wick, which annihilates the evil forces of darkness. With its ability to purify and to ward off evil, illumination played an essential part in the divine, funerary, and domestic cults of the Greek and Egyptian

263

religions.

The frog, a symbol of rebirth, appeared in amulet form as early as the Pre-dynastic Period. During the Dynastic Period it was identified with Heket, goddess of birth and fertility. The hieroglyph "frog" formed part of this goddess's name. Associated with the god Khnum, Heket was worshipped in the city of Antinoe, near Hermopolis.

In funerary iconography, the vine branch or foliated scroll, was an image of rebirth. For this reason, frogs and vine fronds appeared on Christian lamps, along with the "ankh" sign (signifying "life"), and sometimes the inscription "ego eimi anastasis formula," "I am the resurrection."

As numerous other precious objects crumbled around them, Altair took hold of the lamp, placing his other hand on the bee. "Hurry! Grab onto me! We must fly!" he demanded as Berenice slid across the floor, and ducked under the table as the vibration of Litha swarmed around them. Deneb nuzzled beneath his shoulder, wrapping her frightened arms tight around his waist as the light from his ring fused with the archaic lamp. Bursts of heat pulsed from his ring, creating a protective shield of light around them as time seemed to slow once more. All eyes turned to look at the simple oil lamp, now glowing bright with silver light. His eyes locked with Berenice, and in that moment, it was as if he could read her thoughts, 'your intentions steer the ship.'

A powerful flash radiated from the lamp, shaking the ground as it expanded to surround them in an extravagant metallic balloon, which lifted them through the now open ceiling of the Louvre. Deneb gripped the cold sides of the flight machine, wondering how something so old could transform into something so... astoundingly futuristic. Gears spun overhead as Altair took hold of two leather handles, which dangled from above, and took command of the ship, following his internal compass in the direction of China.

As they vanished into an ocean of clouds, Deneb recounted memories of the well, and the versions of Lan she had seen staring back at her throughout time. "What time period was Vega left in?"

"I... I don't know where she is, but somehow it's like I can feel the vibration of her song... like it's guiding me back to her."

A hint of jealousy posed her next question. "Is this new to you, or have you always been able to feel her?"

Feeling the heaviness in both women's eyes, he fumbled for a reasonable answer, if there was one. "It's new, but I think it's because we've travelled together so many times."

"You've travelled together?" She winced once more, feeling the strength of their bond lesson.

"We had to! Everything we did was in an effort to get you back! Don't you see that?" He looked into her injured eyes, which now gazed out at the horizon. A soft breeze blew across her face as she exhaled, savoring the bittersweet moment of becoming a human again.

"When I was in the form of Melusine, somehow my soul was completely empty of human emotions and instincts; reacting only in behaviors of survival and obedience." She exhaled again, "I think that I'm still adjusting. I appreciate all that you did to bring me back... all of you." She smiled at Berenice, whose gaze remained fixed upon the crown of the temple protruding through the clouds below.

"We've arrived," she said, pulling an odd pair of goggles from the dangling leather straps and handed them to Altair.

"What are those?" Deneb smiled as he held them up to the light, wiping the dust from the lenses.

"I... I don't know," he answered, placing them atop his head. "Are we ready?" He looked to both women, and received nods of affirmation.

As they dipped through the clouds, and circled the peak of the temple mount, something caught Deneb's eye. "There! Look! The lake is rising!" As they rotated around to the other side of the temple, they got a better look at the familiar waves of Scorpio, as another vision caught their eye. A stoic figure stood proudly on the rooftop, cloaked in ripples of silk, with three lions at their side.

"Who is that? It has to be Lan!" Deneb recalled visions of his youth.

"If Scorpio is here, then all bonds were not severed with the dagger. How do we know Lan is one of us?" Altair called while steering the balloon into the privacy of the clouds.

Berenice gripped the sides of the ship, watching in fear as the tidal wave rose to meet the height of the temple, and then paused, as if awaiting a response.

"Something is wrong!" Berenice screamed, as a silver spear struck one of the lions. Altair winced in crippling pain, as Deneb grabbed hold of the reins, in order to steer them closer to the cloaked figure. A strand of red hair waved from beneath the black hood as Deneb yelled, "its Vega!" She pulled the balloon hard to the right, racing alongside the balcony as the tidal wave moved in on the temple.

Vega dropped her hood in bewildered shock. "We need to get out of here!" she screamed as another spear sped past her face. Angered, she turned, looking for the lions who should have been by her side, just as Ma Qiang approached. A blinding light flashed as she reached for the plate depicting the Lyre, freezing the world around her as it fused to her palms. Taking advantage of her solitary moment in time, she looked around, admiring the vision before her; lions frozen mid-air attacking Ma Qiang from

266

behind and the futuristic metallic balloon, arriving just in time to aid in her escape. Deneb's face, though refreshing to see, seemed different somehow. As she studied her long lost friend, something else caught her eye, Altair. Their body language told a deep and tragic story that she feared she had somehow written. She turned away from the scene and headed back to the puddle of her lover.

"Why did you leave me?" she screamed at the shallow puddle, as the slow ripples of her breath extended what looked like a staircase of light upon the water.

A deep yet refreshing voice answered through the breeze, "I will never leave you, Vega of Lyra. All that I ever was, and all that I ever will be, is because of you. Ten staircases lead to me, and you will always have a choice." His voice faded as she looked back at Altair's love struck eyes, filled with guilt and passion. Behind them, the tidal wave rose, ready to strike the temple. She called out, "Scorpio! The innocent people inside the temple are not what you seek; I will battle you, but not in this place!"

The sound of creaking wood reverberated from the water as he leaned in over the temple walls. "While my destruction has no limits, my energy is not worth wasting on peasants. I am around you, and I am within you... and I will never stop."

The haunting mist of his words stuck to her skin, as the tidal wave decisively retreated to the stillness of the lake, flooding the outskirts of the land as he fell. Slowly, she pulled her hands from the plate of Lyra, reawakening the world around her in electric musical tones. She sprinted across the palace rooftop, attempting to catch up to the quickly moving balloon, which was racing through the clouds. Altair threw a rope over the side as Deneb steered close enough for her to take hold. She looked through the fog-covered scene below as the wind whipped the dangling rope side to side, she turned one final time to look at the palace, watching the shadows of her pride rip apart what remained of Ma Qiang. The two lions, red with stains of victory, took their seats at the entrance of the palace with eyes towards the sky, as they returned to stone.

A familiar hand reached out for hers, pulling her and the golden plates into the safety of the balloon, as the sun peeked through the clouds, highlighting his face.

"Man, am I glad to see you!" She pulled away from the hug she so desperately longed for, and turned towards Deneb. "I... I can't believe you're really here." She dropped her chin over Deneb's shoulder, closing her eyes as she silently wept.

"It's okay, I'm here now!" She happily released herself from Vega's hug.

With heavy eyes, Vega addressed the present. "You are, aren't you?" She placed a smile upon her face. "What an adjustment this has got to be, going from the depths of the sea, to a crazy hot air balloon. I am so glad you are back. Man... I bet you'll never dive again." She looked with saddened eyes towards her long lost friend.

Deneb smiled, "When I was really little I made a promise to someone special that no matter what happened in my life, I would never let fear keep me from something I love. I will always be a diver. Nothing can keep me from that."

A look of relief spread across Vega's face as she returned to the task at hand. "Now that we have that settled," she smiled, "we need to go to a place that Lan told me about; a place called the Serpent Window."

"And just where is that?" Berenice intervened as all eyes turned towards Deneb.

"The Temple of the Sun rests high within the mountains, hidden among a system of complex waterways and mystical pools. It is a labyrinth of universal portals, a fortress of protection, and a vortex of peace. When the light shines its brightest, the portals open for all who stand at the gates of the universe."

"The portals... what causes them to open?" Vega asked, envisioning her next escape.

Deneb looked at the brilliant colors of the setting sun; a vision she had waited so long to see. "When the sun rests in the chalice of the mountaintop, the solstice door illuminates. When the sun rises above the fortress, packed with food for winter, another opens. Each door opens according to the timing of the universe, which only those in tune can see." She admirably smiled at Vega.

"What about the Serpent Window?" Vega said.

"At the highest point, a single boulder aligns with four mountains that surround it to the north, south, west and east. I don't know what opens that gate, as I've never seen it done."

"In my last moments with Lan, he told me to close the Serpent window... or was it door? I can't remember, but I know he told me to close it." Feeling emotions bubbling up, she blurted out random thoughts, "Do you think that anyone can even see us up here in this crazy metallic balloon? I mean we must look like a giant mirror of the sunset -- just floating through the clouds. How cool is that?"

Without Stan there to halt her rambling, Altair stepped in, "Vega?"

"What?" she carefully raised the oversized black hood, to conceal the tears threatening to fall from her eyes.

"What happened down there?" He moved beside her, as the tears spilled.

"I.…I don't want to talk about it right now. We have more important things to figure out." Her envious eyes settled on Berenice, rigidly devoid of emotion, gripping her scythe as if it were an extension of her being.

"Talk." Her tone shot shivers down Vega's spine.

"When I jumped through the portal, I went back to Lan's palace, although this time, the once stale metallic balconies overflowed with life and richness. Music played, and food was plentiful. The people were happy, and praised their leader… me."

"Wait, what?"

"After I killed Hydra," she proudly smirked at Deneb, "I pulled the golden headdress from the leathery ash of her remains, and took my place along the balcony. I looked down at the people, shivering outside the palace gates, and let them in. I… was their queen." Her stoic eyes locked on the last sliver of the sun as she exhaled. "When I saw Lan, he was wearing this." She lifted the long sleeves of the black silk cloak, dropping them in disgust. "I couldn't see his face."

"Then how do you know it was him?" Berenice calmly demanded, stirring Vega's thoughts.

"Even in the darkest room, I could see him."

"If he loves you so much, why isn't he here with you now?" Deneb wrapped her arms around Altair.

"It wasn't my choice… a trade was made," she tilted her head back, staring at the distorted reflection of herself in the silver balloon.

"What sort of trade?" Altair draped an arm over Deneb while stepping towards Vega.

"A trade that turned him into water." Tears continued to stream as she stared at Deneb.

"For every action, there is an equal and opposite reaction. Everything I gave was not without receipt. The trade that was made happened long ago, Vega. This trade occurred long before you…"

"I what? I ever knew him? Like all of the times I travelled with you, or with Altair, somehow don't even count or matter? I've known him for lifetimes, dream or reality… all the same to me."

"Vega, I know that you are upset that this trade was made without you, but this is reality now."

Her eyes bounced around the balloon like a nightmarish mirror house reflecting her thoughts back to her, as she adjusted the headdress once more, "But I've always been able to change that."

As the sun gave way to the moon, moments of darkness crept into Altair's mind as he looked at both women; the one who he'd promised to marry, and the other, an abnormally beautiful girl he had grown to love, dare he think it. Was he confused, or perhaps, could he love both?

"Altair?" both women said in unison.

Flustered, he looked to the stars for his answer. "I think we need to get some sleep."

"He's right. According to the compass star, we will arrive at Machu Picchu near midnight, and we'll need to be rested for the journey ahead," Deneb said as Vega moved over to the opposite end of the basket, pulling her hood over her head while sliding into the corner.

"Goodnight," she murmured, giving in to exhaustion.

CHAPTER 20

They drifted through the darkness of a foggy canyon toward the ancient city nestled high within the mountains. Altair carefully steered the ship, while the others continued to sleep. All except one, who stood by his side, whispering as they slept.

"This is unlike anything I've ever seen." She leaned over the edge of the balloon, gazing up to the majesty surrounding them.

"Never seen mountains like this before?" He took his eyes away from their path momentarily to admire her wide-eyed expression.

"Not the mountains -- the stars. I have never seen the sky this clearly in all of my life. I feel like this is what it must have looked like thousands of years ago. No wonder so many myths involve constellations and stars."

He looked back at the sleeping women, ensuring that there were no listeners. "How did you do it?"

"Do what?"

"Kill Hydra." He eagerly awaited her answer.

She pulled the stained dagger from her cloak, placing it back in his hands. "The way I said I would." She added her own question. "How did you save Deneb?"

He gazed straight ahead. "When I jumped through time, I landed in the citadel, and somehow I was surrounded by golden fairies who lit up the ceiling, revealing symbols affiliated with the wheel of time. I spoke each name aloud, and just when I thought I had failed her, I said one more."

Before they could speak another word, three golden specks of light flew from the balloon, illuminating the outline of the city carved into the mountainside. "Golden fairies, huh?" Vega laughed.

Moments of silence followed, as they contemplated just what they had brought back with them. Vega laughed, "So, I guess we have to figure that out at some point."

He cringed, "I... I really don't even know where they came from. I mean, I guess if I think about it, they had to have come from the citadel, and were somehow pulled through time when we left there. I don't know. What a mess."

Hoping to relieve his troubled mind she switched the subject, "So, how did you know where to find me?"

He paused before revealing the truth. "It was like I could feel where you were, like an internal compass of some kind."

"Really?" she smiled. "That's kind of cool, but weird at the same time."

"Well, that... and Deneb suggested we go to China to find Lan. She told of a trade being made... someone to take her place to save humanity from crumbling. When we told her about Barcelona burning, she knew something had gone wrong."

"Wait. So the only reason that you guys found me, was because you were trying to find Lan?"

"No," he quickly assured her. "The reason we found you is because I could feel you... I could sense exactly where you were."

"What else can you sense?" she awkwardly laughed.

"It's weird... the best way to describe it is like a vibration, or some kind of sonar that only I can hear."

"What does it sound like right now?" she raised an eyebrow.

"Peace."

A groggy yawn interrupted the silence, as Queen Berenice rose to her feet. "Is that it?" She nodded toward the giant step-like terraces protruding from the mountainside. Refreshing mist settled on their cheeks as he steered the ship to land in a grassy area surrounded by brilliantly chiseled stone walls. The sound of trickling water welcomed them, as they disembarked from their ship and made their way through the unnaturally quiet sanctuary. As if captivated by the sounds of the tranquil waters themselves,

Vega followed the pathways of streams and quickly lost sight and sound of the others.

She dipped a playful finger into the icy water, before taking a well-deserved drink. In that moment, while the water nourished her, she thought of Lan, and then of Scorpio. She took another drink, swishing the water around her mouth as if picturing the dark and light fighting a battle within her. She leaned in once more, this time seeing her own reflection in the water. Memories quickly returned of all the people she had helped while in her short-lived time as queen, and then of Hydra. Words echoed in her mind. "You are as much the cure as you are the chaos."

"There you are!" Deneb called from atop a large boulder, smiling down at her friend. "Come up here! You're going to want to see this!"

She rapidly ran through the tight, stone cut paths until she reached the platform where the others stood, collectively looking at two pools of water. The stars of the sky illuminated the surface of the water, as Berenice spoke. "The constellation here is Pleiades. Known as the seven sisters, they are always watching over us. The water glows with their light."

Deneb's thoughts sent her eyes dancing up the mountainside, toward the grassy landing where she knew the Serpent Window awaited. "There are many doors here; one illuminated according to Litha; one according to the shield and the other... at the highest peak, is the Serpent Window. Berenice, I think it best that you stand in the doorway of Litha, as you were promised the plate of the bee. When the sun rises in the east, it will shine like gold through the doorway of stone, filling the circular terrace with sunlight. Altair, since you hold the shield, I find it only fitting that you stand in the place where food was hidden away and kept safe. Vega, I would like for you to command the Serpent rock."

"Why not you? After all, you were the Serpent Goddess. Also, you have more experience with passing things through portals. I'd just mess it up."

Shock mirrored on the faces of Altair and Deneb as they witnessed the first moment of self-doubt ever to occur in Vega.

"She does make a point. Deneb, you were the Serpent Goddess, and you've passed the plates through the gates of time for ages." Berenice said with eyes lovingly locked on the glowing reflections.

"Fine, but we will need to take the balloon to get to the top of the mountain. It is too far for us to climb up on our own. Vega, will you fly the ship?"

She laughed for the first time in weeks. "Sure, but only if I can wear those weird goggles that come with it."

Concealing his smile, he removed the goggles from around his neck and handed them over. "Knock yourself out. Oh! And I think this belongs to you." Altair turned to Deneb and handed her the crystal. She looked like a child on Christmas morning; beaming with joy as she quickly tucked it away.

Berenice spontaneously joined hands with the others, forming a circle surrounding the small pool below. Silence settled over the group, as they looked to the light for strength, wisdom, and protection. "In the light we find ourselves, and the doorway to the sun. May we tether the plates to their rightful positions."

All nodded in agreement, as they set out for their outposts. Berenice, with scythe proudly clasped in hand, took her place in the circular terrace, which resembled the remnants of a castle's tower. Altair slowly walked beneath the shadow of the balloon, climbing slowly up the mountainside, while both women watched from above.

276

Ending the silence between them, Vega spoke. "I love it when the sky brightens just before sunrise. It's incredible to think that something so far away could be so powerful that it changes the entire color of our sky." Both girls lovingly looked toward the place where the sun would soon rise.

"It's astounding, if you think about it. So much revolves around one single thing in our universe..." Deneb said as she narrowed her focus on Altair.

Vega watched as his shadow dipped into the storage house below. "And if it were removed, the world would just fall into darkness. There is just so much we take for granted, ya know?"

Somewhat puzzled by her response, Deneb turned a quick eye to her before hopping over the side of the basket, "Everything is going to be okay."

"So... I just stand here and wait huh?"

She extended her hands, waiting for Vega to hand her the plates, "Yup. You're the most important part."

"How so?" Vega nervously called from the basket as Deneb walked up to the cross shaped boulder protruding from the grass. The wind ceased as the first sliver of sunlight announced itself, while Vega paced the confines of her metallic container, nervously waiting for some kind of a doorway to appear. Deneb, calm in her faith, knelt before the cross-shaped stone, placing the golden plates on the grass before it. She bowed her head, silently waiting as the sun cast the first rays of morning light across the sky.

The ground shook beneath them as the sun passed over the doorway of Litha, where Berenice stood, engulfed in the subtle vibration awakening a great presence around her. Hours moved like seconds as the sun aligned with the next place, shining through the thatched roof of Altair's hideaway. His calloused fingers gripped his ring, and cast a reflective orb of light around him as the sun passed over Deneb, whose head remained bowed, forehead pressed to the cold stack of plates. Moments passed in awkward stillness as Vega ceased her pacing, and looked at the stagnant scene in annoyance. In an intuitive moment of decisiveness, she pressed the old goggles to her face, gasping at the spectacle before her. Seven doorways of misty morning light revealed themselves through the clouds, circling around where Deneb knelt. Quickly she jumped over the side of the basket, tethering the rope to the mountain, and ran over to Deneb. She placed a careful hand on her shoulder, and whispered, "Do you see what I see?"

Deneb slowly lifted her chin, shaking her head in disappointment. Silently, Vega grabbed the plates, placing each according to the wheel of time in front of its matching doorway, while hanging onto the eight plate; her own. Behind the vibrant golden light of each doorway, seven female apparitions appeared, slowly moving to their rightful symbol. Soft angelic words came from within as they collectively spoke. "We are the seven sisters, and we have come to tether the wheel to the sun. No longer will copies be made with the serpent's energy. What words do you wish to speak? We shall hear your command."

Tears melted down her face, enthralled by the primal beauty before her as she answered. "I wish to find love." The glowing apparitions nodded in unison, before pulling their shadowy hoods up over their heads. Following suit, Vega did the same.

"It is done. In all times, in all dimensions, in all places, Child of Lyra, love you shall find. Careful now, the water is rising." A radiant burst of light flashed across the canvas of the sky, shaking the mountain as the sisters reclaimed their plates.

"What just happened?" Deneb madly searched for the plates that had just vanished into thin air.

"The goggles… they were the key to seeing the portals! There isn't much time, we have to go!" She motioned to the balloon as the earth continued to tremble and shake.

"What do you mean?" Deneb called after her reinvigorated friend as she hurdled over the side of the basket.

"They said that the water was rising! I know what that means. Scorpio is not far behind! Hurry. Untie us and get in!" She reached her hand over the edge, pulling Deneb inside as they flew down the mountainside searching for signs of Altair and Berenice.

The outline of a woman, waving a scythe back in forth in acute distress erupted giggles from the girls, as they dipped down towards the ancient queen. "I mean, why can't she just drop the weapon?" Vega laughed.

"Right? Like, okay, we get it, you are ancient and used that to kill a bunch of people, but you don't even need it anymore." She laughed as she steered the balloon closer, allowing Vega to pull the rigid queen aboard. Silence took over the group, as they hid their laughter behind bitten lips.

"We are missing one," she stated, as both girls quickly nodded.

"There!" Vega pointed at the thatched hut, encapsulated by a glowing bubble of light.

"Altair!" Deneb screamed.

He waved his hands, motioning to the surrounding river, screaming inaudible words as he ran to the edge of the terrace. Vega pulled the balloon hard to the right, screaming for Deneb to reach out for him as she approached.

"I... I'm not strong enough to pull him up!" She frantically pulled her arms back in, capturing the fear in his eyes as she moved away.

"Switch places with me!" Vega ordered. Her eyes locked with his as she thrust herself over the edge, ensuring her balance with her song as they locked hands. "I've got him!" she screamed as the river quickly flooded the canyons, and churned toward them just as she pulled him to safety.

With a mighty thud, he landed on the floor of the basket. "I..." he attempted to speak between quick breaths, "I didn't know if you were going to get to me in time." He closed his eyes and placed one hand to his chest, feeling the rise and fall of his breath as a tear of joy escaped from his masculine façade. "Thank you."

"Vega, will you take over?" Deneb instructed as she took her rightful place beside him, cradling him in her arms as the mountains continued to quiver.

"Um... guys... I don't think we're alone here," Vega looked through the abyss at the abnormally high, rising water below. "We've got company!"

A weathered voice shook through the air as they sailed through the impending raindrops, "I FOUND YOU."

"We need to get out of here!" Vega screamed, steering the balloon toward a glowing light, hundreds of feet below.

"Vega! What are you doing! You're taking us right into the river!" Deneb cried as she ducked beside Altair.

"Trust me! There is a doorway of light down there! Don't you see it!?"

"I trust you!" Deneb screamed, covering her head as they plunged into the water.

CHAPTER 21

Between painful blinks, Vega opened her eyes as the unfamiliar bedroom ceiling slowly came into focus. "Hello?" she groaned, turning her head to the pool of dried blood, stuck to the pillow. The freshly healed cut on her forehead pulsed as if it had its own heartbeat. She cringed, and pulled at her once elegant headdress, untangling it from the knots of her hair, as panic set in. Her hands scrambled across her body and then the scattered sheets of the stranger's bed, madly searching for the goggles. Not certain what she should tend to first; the goggles or determining her location; she made her way to the wooden door, and gazed down the hallway of the old home. The smell of the wood burning fireplace awakened her senses as she creaked along the floorboards and down the stairs where voices were heard along with soft music and crackling wood.

The voices paused, as they sensed her presence on the staircase. "Vega?" Stan called from the living room as she ran into his open arms. Between unexpected sobs, she rattled off quick fragmented thoughts. "I didn't think I'd see you again, but we saved Deneb, and there was a balloon and goggles, and now we're all here... where exactly is here?" she looked around the simple living room as she caught her breath.

"We're in Altair's home, in France. Honestly, I was quite worried you were not coming back. After all, Altair and

Deneb arrived several days before you. We tended to the wound on your head, and thought it best that you rest."

"We all made it?" she asked aloud, while internally questioning why some part of her was not pleased.

Altair solemnly nodded. "Deneb is still sleeping."

Vega began pacing, despite her growing headache. "I wonder what happened to Berenice."

"The Egyptian Queen?" Stan's eyes widened in shock.

"It's quite a long story Stan," Altair intervened. "Perhaps one I can tell another time. Vega, how are you feeling? Would you like something to eat? Stew?" He hurried to the kitchen anticipating her answer as she took her seat on the floor in front of the fire. Stan wrapped a blanket around her shoulders as he knelt beside her.

"I know you've been through an awful lot, but I must say I'm dying to know what happened to you. Tomorrow, over breakfast?" he raised a hopeful eyebrow.

She smiled. "You got it."

"Just tell me one thing… did you do it?" He waited in silent anticipation.

"I did more than I ever thought I could do," she smiled. "But if you're referring to killing Hydra, yes."

Together their eyes settled into the calmness of the fire, as Altair returned with the steaming bowl of stew. Joining them in the comfort of silence, Altair took his place on the other side Vega, and wrapped a comforting arm around his faithful companion.

She quickly devoured the soup, licking the last drops from her satisfied lips. "I'm exhausted. Is it okay if I return to the room I was just in?"

"Sleep as long as you'd like."

She rose to her feet, with the heavy blanket still draped around her shoulders like a cape. Her face wrinkled with troubled thoughts. "Something's wrong."

"What is it?" Both men gave her their full attention.

"Seven beings appeared to me as I tethered the plates to the sun, and their words... I will never forget them... no longer will copies be made with the serpent's energy."

They silently waited for more to follow, although nothing did.

"Why do these words frighten you?" Stan looked at the pale resemblance of a queen, lethargically standing on the steps.

"What was copied?"

Neither man answered as she silently made her way back upstairs to the comfort of the bed. She tucked herself back into the layers of blankets, as her heavy heart buried her with guilt. Though she'd never admit it, some part of her wished she were alone with Altair, while another part of her longed for Lan, a man who by her own design, would never be faithful to her. Her heart ached for someone who could never love her completely... in both cases.

She stared at the ceiling as her inner demons raged on, 'How could she be upset with Lan for turning on her, when it was her time travel that had resulted in the forfeit of his existence. Because of her he ended up serving Hydra, and because of her, he was now even worse off. Whatever betrayal he had inflicted she surely deserved. As her mind continued down the self-destructing paths, she began to wonder if she was the cause for all of their chaos. Would the history of the world change for the better if she never existed? Her eyes grew heavy, as she tried to get to a safe place in her mind, as she reassured herself, 'God doesn't make mistakes, I exist for a reason, and I serve the light. The world is a better place because of me.'

"Vega?" A voice called through her dreams, pulling her feet from the warmth of the bed, to the cold wooden floor. As if in a trance, she followed three golden glowing lights down the stairs, past the place on the floor where Altair laid wrapped in blankets in front of the now extinguished fire. Her eyes flicked open, though still masked in slumber, as she walked over to the cellar doors. She paused only for a second, looking back at Altair before disappearing, step by step, down into the pool of water now flooding the basement.

"Vega," a voice echoed as she stepped into the water.

"I'm here," she whispered the golden specks illuminated a staircase of light upon the surface.

"You have been promised love, but you will not find it if you stay. Join us in the Atrium. Step down into the water."

Perplexed emotions nearly woke her as she thought of Altair, and then of Lan. As the chilly water reached her chest, the light became brighter, beckoning her. As she disappeared beneath the water, Altair sprang from his own nightmare, and quickly ran up the stairs to her vacant room.

"Vega?!" He tore the covers from the bed, and ran down the hall to wake Stan.

"She... she's... gone!" Tears drenched his face as fear overtook him. "I saw her, in a dream. She followed golden specks of light into another world, and just... disappeared!"

"Who left you? Deneb? Did you see where she went?" Stan hurriedly reached for his glasses, just in time to capture the dismay on Altair's face.

"Vega. I had a dream about Vega," he admitted. "I ran to her room but she's not there. She's gone."

Realizing for the first time how much he cared for the girl, and the danger of such feelings, Stan replied, "I know this may sound a bit harsh, but when Vega travels it is typically because she wants to be somewhere else. I have no doubt that we can find her, but the question is, does she want to be found?"

Together they made their way to the open cellar door, just as the last drop of water trickled down the drain,

"Vega?" Altair called down the stairs into the darkness.

This book came to me in a series of dreams, which spawned research on the following sites.

http://survivalcell.blogspot.com/p/geomancy-of-st-peters-square-and.html

https://en.wikipedia.org/wiki/Hephaestus

https://www.ancient.eu/knossos/

https://www.ancient.eu/Minoan_Civilization/

https://en.wikipedia.org/wiki/Lamassu

http://www.interkriti.org/crete/pg/?pg=1512316

https://en.wikipedia.org/wiki/Axe_historique

http://www.interkriti.org/crete/pg/?pg=1512316

https://en.wikipedia.org/wiki/Greek_underworld

https://en.wikipedia.org/wiki/Tartarus

https://en.wikipedia.org/wiki/Chinese_guardian_lions

https://wicca.com/celtic/akasha/yule.htm

http://whitewicca.net/sabbats-2/litha.php

https://en.wikipedia.org/wiki/Heracleon

https://en.wikipedia.org/wiki/St._Peter%27s_Square

https://en.wikipedia.org/wiki/Olous

https://gnosticwarrior.com/the-serpent-goddess.html

https://en.wikipedia.org/wiki/Britomartis

http://www.fredriksborghotel.se/en/photogallery/ute-pa-fredriksborg

https://www.india-forums.com/forum_posts.asp?TID=4989336

https://en.wikipedia.org/wiki/Amphipolis

https://en.wikipedia.org/wiki/Lion_of_Amphipolis

https://en.wikipedia.org/wiki/Roxana

Opening page image from Vuillemin's "Tableau Uranographique et Cosmographique" from 1852

www.ingramcontent.com/pod-product-compliance
Lightning Source LLC
Chambersburg PA
CBHW020304200626
46814CB00006BA/2072